More praise for THE LETHAL PARTNER

"Jake Page's burly blind sleuth, T. Moore Bowdre, returns to unravel his fourth murder mystery in *The Lethal Partner*, a fast-paced whodunit set in Santa Fe's posh and predatory art world."

—*Santa Fe New Mexican*

"Its use of seven previously unknown Georgia O'Keeffe paintings to keep the pot bubbling and its unromantic thousand-yard stare at Santa Fe, New Mexico, home of much nonsense, is a welcome antidote to too many winter season glossy magazines enticing one to ski Taos."

—*The Boston Globe*

"Jack Page uses language deftly within a cinematic structure that is colorfully adorned with endearing irreverence."

—*Bloomsbury Review*

By Jake Page
Published by Ballantine Books:

Del Rey® science fiction
OPERATION SHATTERHAND

Mo Bowdre mysteries
THE STOLEN GODS
THE DEADLY CANYON
THE KNOTTED STRINGS
THE LETHAL PARTNER

THE LETHAL PARTNER

Jake Page

BALLANTINE BOOKS • NEW YORK

 Published in the United States by Ballantine Books, a division of Random House, Inc., New York, and simultaneously in Canada by Random House of Canada Limited, Toronto.

http://www.randomhouse.com

Library of Congress Catalog Card Number: 96-97058

ISBN: 0-345-38785-6

Manufactured in the United States of America

First Hardcover Edition: January 1996
First Mass Market Edition: February 1997

10 9 8 7 6 5 4 3 2

There's no limit
to how complicated things can get
on account of
one thing leading to another.
—E. B. White

author's note

This book is dedicated to my wife, Susanne, as have been the others in this series, and for the very good reason that they don't happen—or come out right—without her. For this one I am also indebted—and not for the first time nor, I would guess, the last—to Paul Bohannan. Among many others who have also abetted this effort are Tess Monahan of the New Mexico Attorney General's Office, Ruth Francis of Book Star, Kerry Green and her family, the editors of *Destination Discovery* with a helpful magazine assignment along the way, Rollie McKenna, and David Leeming. The standard caveats about imaginary characters and events and all that apply here, except of course for real historical (a.k.a. well-known dead) folk who are, as I understand it, fair game.

convergence

A silky Gulf breeze rattled the leaves overhead, and Elijah Potts sniffed deeply, inhaling the omnipresent scent of the sea, the perfumed exhalations of the island's piercingly red and hot pink bougainvilleas, and the perfume of the woman across from him. They sat at a wooden table in the outdoor dining area of Blue Heaven, a locally popular restaurant in Bahama Village, the gradually gentrifying black neighborhood of Key West, an island hospitable to loose ends.

With a satisfied smile, Potts folded a piece of fax paper into thirds, then in half, slipped it into the pocket of his faded red cotton shirt, and looked into the lavender eyes of the woman. He thought again, as he had many times in the past few years, how guarded were those lavender eyes, once transparently sparkling with the elation of the happy warrior, the two of them—she and he—taking on the world, come what may. Vagabonds among the settled mind-sets, nomads of the intellect, freelancers, freebooters. A little piracy, perhaps, on the bounding main of ideas.

His own eyes, he supposed, now had the same guarded look, the same opacity, as those of this woman sitting before him with the first streaks of silver-gray in her black hair. Peering in a mirror, he knew, is no way to judge the look in one's own eyes.

Most of the lunch crowd was now gone from the shaded sun-dappled yard, leaving the place to the two of them, the chickens, and a gay couple a few tables away in sandals, shorts, and matching rainbow T-shirts. The two men hunched over what Potts guessed were sketches of improvements they were hatching for the house they just bought on what he had overheard was Petronia Street. Newlyweds, perhaps.

A dully feathered hen bopped among the leaves scattered in the dirt, imitated spastically by a collection of eight fuzzy chicks. Under the watchful eye of a rooster bedecked in more colors than an oil slick, the chicken family approached Potts's table, and he flicked a few crumbs off into their path. The hen startled, raising her wings, and then settled down to business.

Potts looked up and watched the leaves overhead dancing in the breeze, thinking that the wind would be invisible if it weren't for leaves. Thinking that now, once again, he had to trade the semitropical breezes of Key West for the tail end of the spring winds—howling with dust and desert pollen—that battered New Mexico. Timing, he thought, is everything when you're a migratory bird.

His book was done, ruminations on the dark goddess of the Hispanic West, a ball-breaker but finally complete, packaged up, 339 manuscript pages of pure gold, to be carried to his editor in New York. He would enjoy an elegant publisher's lunch, a few visits to the galleries and museums, and then off he would fly to New Mexico. His annual three months in Key West were over, his Florida wardrobe now hanging neatly in the auxiliary closet of the house where this woman with the guarded lavender eyes lived year-round.

His wife. A perfect understanding.

They had learned with some pain over time that three months of each other's steady company was as much as either should be asked to bear. And she could bear even less happily the alien pollen of New Mexico, its arid, barren reaches, the very simplicity and violence of the land that terrified her, but delighted him as an antidote to the perfumed lushness of the sybaritic Keys. Or was it the other way around . . . the Keys the antidote? Well, never mind, Potts thought. Migrants have two homes, equally important. And now it was time for him to take wing to his other home, to the gallery on Canyon Road, to the elegant commerce of Santa Fe, the world of Art and Myth.

"I always hate to leave Key West," Potts said.

"Really," his wife answered.

"Of course. I miss it terribly," he said.

"For the first week or so."

"Or longer even." He smiled. "I guess it's time, isn't it?" He waited for her to stand up. He sniffed the air again. "Aahhhh," he said.

"And everything is . . . in train," she said.

Potts patted the fax in his breast pocket and smiled. "Oh, yes. On schedule. It'll be damned exciting, won't it?"

"To say the least."

"Well . . . I guess I'm off." He went around the table and kissed his wife on the cheek.

"Have a safe journey, Elijah." She smiled a bit distractedly. "And give my regards to Anita."

He looked again at the lavender eyes, now almost completely opaque, as if he had already gone.

"How very gracious of you," he said, stepped around the high, aromatic hedge onto the sidewalk and blinked once in the glare.

The man's brain erupted in a string of silent expletives, words so trite as to have lost any moorings they had in the copulatory and excretory functions of the body. Coursing through the man's brain cells, the stream of blunt-nosed clichés had the effect of a mantra, or perhaps a steam valve on a tawdry old iron radiator. He was momentarily relieved. But as he looked down again at the array of IDs fanned out in his hand, the bile in his soul was resurgent.

"A *spic*!" he said out loud. "A fucking spic? Hey! Hey, asshole . . ." But the man who had handed him the cards and had snatched the fifty dollar bill from his hand was gone, vanished somewhere in the teeming barrio.

Ramón Tofoya? Ramón *Tofoya*?

How the hell had that greasy sonofabitch gotten Ramón Tofoya out of Damon Townsend?

The man in the car, now holding a California driver's license and three other documents identifying him as Ramón Tofoya, looked up at his reflection in the rearview mirror. Light brown hair, the astounding new light brown mustache, hazel eyes, prison pallor to the skin. He sure didn't look like any Ramón Fucking Tofoya.

The man reflected on the months he had spent going

over names—what else was there to do while he put up with the abuse of his fellow man, scumbags all, ignorant scuzzballs?—and thought about what he would become once this gray interval in his life was over. He had kept his mind on the future, carefully reminding himself of his own limitations even as he rose in his own estimation relative to the lowlifes with whom he had been packed like some goddamn interchangeable cardboard carton in the federal warehouse outside San Diego for three years, two months, two weeks, and three days—finally set free not because of good behavior or any of the other half-baked excuses the penal system comes up with to justify letting hardened criminals back on the streets, but because even the frigging fascists in charge could see that the pen was inhumanely overcrowded. Better conditions in the damn zoo.

And so, in his meditations on misery, he had clutched at the future, the day he would walk free and loose again in the sun, get himself a new ID the way he'd seen guys do it on *60 Minutes*. What was his name—the old guy with the shit-eating grin? Morley Safer. Paid fifty clams and got himself a new ID right on the TV. From some spic on the street. Runs up like he's going to smear your window and offer to clean it for five bucks or whatever a squeegee man charges—and instead offers to sell you a new life, and by God, that's what he had wanted: a new life, a new idea, a new M.O., a new name. Damon Townsend—that was cool, classy. A man you could trust to do you right.

And now, instead, because of some wooden-skulled spic too dumb to use God's own tongue, the English language, he was Ramón Tofoya.

Ra*món* Tofoya.

Sounded like some kind of health food, for chrissakes. So he was a Chicano with hazel eyes and light brown hair.

Which is one reason why the man now named Ramón Tofoya headed east, weighing the dangers of being on familiar ground where some clown from his earlier life might spot him and put two and two together against the knowledge that in New Mexico the Hispanics were so mixed up that they came in all sizes, shapes, colors. The likelihood was that there, in New Mexico, in Santa Fe, he wouldn't have to explain why a guy named Tofoya looked like—well, he thought again—maybe Kevin Costner.

Ramón Tofoya, the new man, looked once more at his reflection in the mirror, and once more noticed the similarity to the Civil War officer out there in the Badlands, making a new life, screwing around with Indians and that wolf. Pausing impatiently at a stoplight, he surveyed the street, full of overweight, swarthy wetback women and furtive wetback men, and thought: Well, I may be one of 'em by name, but I don't have to hang out with 'em.

Ramón Tofoya, the new man, the free man, had emerged from the pen angry but calm, and determined to get even. It was a generalized sort of revenge that he had in mind. Against fate, the odds, a lousy deal of the cards of life—whatever. And now, thinking back on the old film they showed while the cons whooped with derision, the one with Burt Lancaster dicking around with his birds in Alcatraz, and thinking again of the sudden burst of inspiration the film had bestowed on him, Ramón Tofoya regained his icy calm, headed east now into the mid-morning sun of a brand-new day.

U.S. Route 8 stretched ahead, a shimmering ribbon of hope. Seven, maybe eight hours through the godforsaken desert to Phoenix. Then maybe he would go north, through the mountains, green and grand, sweeping vistas of canyons, take his time, enjoy the landscape.

Ramón Tofoya put out of his mind the proviso that lurked there like an unscratched chigger bite: if—*if*—the wreck of an old Mustang he had lifted didn't crap out. So what if it does? he said to himself. I'll stick out my thumb. I'm free to do that.

Free.

For an hour, ever since the American Airlines 727 Stretch left O'Hare Airport, the man in the window seat had busied himself with a lot of finicky tapping on the cramped keyboard of a laptop computer, pausing every so often to stare at the seat-belt sign where his muse evidently dwelled, while his pale fingers fluttered in midair, ready to record the next inspiration. Glancing across the empty middle seat a few times, Norah Vargas had noticed too many numbers popping up on the liquid crystal screen for this to be a novel in the making, or a short story. Probably some sort of quarterly report to a sales manager, or something equally dreary.

Norah reflected a bit wanly on how uninteresting most people were. Where was the flair in everybody's life? The sauce? Norah was the sort of person who was happy to put a little flair in other people's lives, however fleeting. What, after all, was the harm in that?

Norah turned her face to the man and smiled, holding it in place until he felt the silent intrusion and looked over at her. He was wearing a standard-issue business suit and tie, the jacket of which he had folded with military precision and placed lovingly in the overhead bin before he sat down. Insurance, Norah guessed.

"No rest for the weary traveler," Norah said in an accent that bore a hint of the Carolinas. The man smiled briefly, and Norah saw his eyes flick down over her chest and back to her face. Norah's figure, she was well aware, left nothing much to be desired—except maybe for guys who were into mammary gigantism. Her face, too, which she had studied with utter wonderment over the years, was the kind that made men dream: ebony black hair, ebony black eyes, a full, hungry mouth harboring teeth of a dazzling whiteness.

"Keeps you busy," the man said. He had a pleasant enough face—thin, nice cheekbones, dark eyes that seemed a little haunted. About forty, maybe. An ostentatiously wide gold wedding band.

"What line of work is it that keeps you so enrapt? If you don't mind me asking."

"Oh no, not at all. It's printing. We print most of the yellow pages in this country."

Norah clucked her fascination and learned that the man was a marketing type of some sort, worked with publishers of local yellow pages directories to teach them how to encourage local listees to take out bigger and bigger ads, thus making more pages, thus in turn making more printing in Chicago where the printing plant was located in a building the size of a hangar or two, an edifice the man evidently regarded with the awe normally reserved for the Sistine Chapel. The desire to broaden this nice man's horizons flamed high and bright in Norah Vargas's bosom, and before long, having exhausted the magic of printing, he laughed and said, "But what do you do?"

"I buy things," she said.

The man smiled, a bit deprecatingly.

"Like companies," Norah added. "Whatever Mrs. Barth wants."

The man's eyebrows rose a half-inch.

"You know, Mrs. G. Weatherhall Barth?" Norah asked. "She lives in Chicago. Surprised you never heard of her. She's a John Deere heir, you know, tractors. But she has the most amazing interests, and she hired me out of Wharton—the business school?—to help with her acquisitions. She's very direct about things. For example, she loves nice lingerie, so one day she sent me off to San Francisco to buy Victoria's Secret. That was fun. She bought a half-interest in the Colorado Rockies a few years ago—the baseball team? She wanted to learn about the business, so the league she's starting would be, well, professionally managed. It's a woman's baseball league, like the movie. Geena Davis, Madonna. Like that, but real. Starting up next year, if Mrs. Barth has anything to say. Six teams. I'm meeting some Albuquerque investors who want to be one of the six."

"Baseball? Like, um, hardball?"

"You bet. Mrs. Barth read somewhere that Hank Aaron said there was no reason why a woman couldn't play big-league second base, and Mrs. Barth, well, she wondered why they couldn't play any position, so she sent me to Denver to buy into the Rockies, learn the ropes. That was fun, but it's more like a hobby for her. She's really interested in communications, the information superhighway. It's like she wants to own every roadside attraction, every gas station on the highway. You won't tell anyone, will you, but I'm also on my way to talk to the people at Intel."

"Intel? The computer chip . . . ?" He smiled and looked at his laptop. "Like in here?"

"The very one. The biggest manufacturer in the world."

"But that's billions. . ."

Norah smiled beatifically. "Hey, it's just zeros. Mrs. Barth always says that addition and subtraction work the same for big numbers as for little numbers."

And so Norah Vargas revved herself up. Currently employed, in actual fact, as a hostess of one of Santa Fe's more expensive restaurants—but a hostess with her eye on better things, far better things—she spiced up the life of the Manager of Marketing Concepts for Ruskin Doneghal of Chicago, Printers Since 1887, until the aging 727 gunned it through the spring winds, thumping down onto the long, pilot-friendly runway of the Albuquerque airport and taxied up to the gate.

"I hope you have a profitable visit," Norah said as she stepped into the plane's narrow aisle and reached into the overhead bin for her bag.

"Thanks. And good luck with Intel," the man whispered conspiratorially.

one

"I do purely hate this, Connie."

T. Moore Bowdre stood erect as a post in the old mill house he had converted into a studio, his fists planted petulantly on his hips. They were big fists, covered now with a fine white powder that also dusted the blond hairs on his thick forearms. A surgical mask hung around his neck, and he seemed to be glaring at her through his sunglasses though she knew, of course, that he couldn't see her.

"You know I hate this from the depths of my soul."

"Yes, I know," Connie said, looking for the first time at the block of marble on the wooden table.

"I am a private man," Bowdre continued, his voice rising in pitch. "Self-sufficient. I ask little from these people. These . . . these *little* people."

The black-haired woman with broad shoulders and a round copper face looked at the marble block, about two feet square and now roughly hewn, headed for some new incarnation. She knew that T. Moore Bowdre used the word *little* not so much as a description of height or volume but as a disdainful epithet for hardscrabble, bedrock fools. She sighed, understanding in her genes the human need for spoken ritual, for each person on the planet to iterate and reiterate essential truths. Her tribe, the Hopi, were masters of such expression, after all.

Each year, at this time, the ritual was the same. T. Moore Bowdre raised his voice against the fundamental injustice—the very emblem of tyranny, he usually called it—represented by the act of signing his tax return.

"I am humiliated by this," Bowdre said, winding up like a pitcher on the mound. "Absolutely humiliated. I have no way of expressing the degradation I feel, signing this. It runs counter to my basic worldview, goddamn it."

"Mo, I understand," Connie said. "Here. Here is where you sign."

"I know where to sign," Mo said testily. "I'm just not ready to sign. This always comes as a terrible surprise."

"Okay. And now you're going to say . . . ?"

"I believe," Mo said, "I believe deep in my heart that our greatest responsibility in this little short life we got here on the planet is to keep money out—*out*—of the hands of irresponsible people. And every damn year, I gotta sign my name on this little form and . . ."

"It's terrible, Mo, I know it," Connie said.

". . . and break my heartfelt ideals, and send money to these little people . . ."

"We don't owe them anything," Connie said.

". . . in Washington, D.C., who got nothing better to do than dream up something they call policy. You know what *policy* is, Connie? Policy? Policy is a robot's version of human values, the tomb of community life." He paused, his arm halted in mid-gesture above his head.

"Did you say we don't owe 'em anything? Nothing? How did that work out?"

"Never mind, Mo. It's all legal," Connie said, and gently touched the ballpoint pen against the big man's right wrist.

"You made quarterly payments," he said.

"Something like that."

"Somehow that's not so immoral. It's just that you shouldn't have to think about those people in April, right when the world is about to turn fecund and sweet." He took the pen in a thick hand covered with marble dust, poked at the form with his other hand, and scrawled his name illegibly across the bottom of the dreaded paper in jagged letters nearly an inch in height.

"How's that?" he asked. "Are you satisfied now?"

"It's close enough," Connie said. "Now you can go back to work."

The big man snorted. "Work? How can I work with those faceless bureaucrats, all the little people, like elves, dancing around in my studio now with their idiotic schemes?"

Connie reached up and bussed him on his whiskered cheek. "You'll think of a way," she said, and walked out of the old mill house, smiling to herself. Halfway across the greening lawn between the mill house and the one-story adobe building where they lived, Connie heard a familiar noise behind her, the snare-drum burst of sound, not unlike the bark of a dog, that the big sculptor employed as laughter.

"Hah—hah—hah."

Connie paused on the lawn, feeling the welcome sun

on her face, streaming down from above the Sangre de Cristo Mountains that sheltered the old city of Santa Fe from the north and east. Abruptly, the walled yard filled with shadow as a cloud swept over the sun's face, and the temperature on Connie's skin dropped about ten degrees. Before long the breeze would change into a snapping wind; by the afternoon, it could even snow. The vagaries of spring matched—or did they bring about?—her restlessness, the soul's annual itch.

It was the moon's work. Back at home, on the Hopi mesas so far to the west, it was still the time of *kiyamiyaw*, the Windbreak Moon, the mischievous, wayward moon—a time of promise, but a time when the most careful plans could go awry, a fragile time before the seeds of corn could be planted in the moist places under the windblown sand. In so unpredictable a time, even the kachina spirits restricted their appearances to the warm, protected space of the underground kivas, singing through the cold nights in the firelight. . . .

Home.

Overhead, the cloud had sailed past and the sun again warmed her face. This too was home, here with the big man in the enclosed yard on the old, gallery-filled lane, Canyon Road, the quaint little boulevard of dreams in what the white people, the *bahanas*, liked to say was the oldest capital city in the nation. The inhabitants now of this old town desperately reminded themselves of older times, clung to old stories about themselves just as the Hopis did, while things changed around them.

It had taken her nearly a year to straighten out the sculptor's finances after she had moved in with him, how long ago? Was it five years already? Two IRS audits. Solemn guarantees acceded to by the sculptor while he glowered volcanically from behind his dark glasses at the scrawny accountant across the desk, saving face.

It was more than just orderliness that had appealed to this Hopi woman with the long-gone, unremembered Anglo father when she took her first university course in accounting. The numbers themselves charmed her, each representing a tale of action, just as certain Hopi words had several meanings, some present, some bespeaking whole stories that anchored her and her people in the world. Making these numbers work had struck Connie much like a song, a liturgy of actual events that came out right, a formal reiteration.

And now, in the waning of the Windbreak Moon, she could take down her figurative sign that said CPA. The annual crush was finished—for the time being, at least. Each year, in spite of the previous year's resolve to duck the task, she found herself giving in and helping a dozen local writers and artists with their income taxes. These were personalities—dreamers all—who seemed bent on making matters even more complicated for themselves than the freelance life required, half of them filing extensions after a flurry of failed attempts to get their records together. They would be back, of course, in a couple of months, clutching little piles of inept records, desperate again.

But she was free now to think about things like corn. Before long, her uncles would set out into the canyons to pray to mother eagles, and the kachinas would soon dance in the sunlit plazas. Such different harbingers of spring, she thought, in the two worlds she inhabited these days. She knew how little of the world's work occurred in this second week of April as people scrambled around to meet the Internal Revenue Service's iron deadline, an annual ceremony when the white world otherwise ceased to function. Just like at home at the time of the winter solstice, when everybody paused for a few days to help the Sun change course and set out for his summer house. The irony was not lost on Connie Barnes that the white man's most important prayers took the form of double-entry bookkeeping.

Sounds of metal on rock leapt through the air, the man whose eyes could not see quarrying some interior vision from fine-grained stone, a man who, beyond his bluster, his posturing, seemed bent on fulfilling the most peculiar dream that she could imagine.

A blind man making real what he alone could see, a maker of worlds.

She stepped across the remaining few feet to the patio door of her house and went inside, her eyes adjusting to the abrupt shift from bright sun to cool shadow.

Elijah Potts strolled happily in the blustery day down Canyon Road toward the Southwest Creations Gallery, shivering slightly as a cloud obscured the sun. Dressed in faded blue jeans, a collarless blue seersucker shirt under a peat-colored tweed Norfolk jacket with its tweed belt ends dangling, he had the casual, rumpled look of a man suddenly transported to this narrow lane in Santa Fe from Luxor, or Marrakesh, a man at home anywhere in the world. His hair, running to gray these last few years, fell jauntily over an unlined brow, and the corners of his mouth, even when in repose, turned up slightly in a perpetually youthful smile. From deep brown eyes that were tilted in a slight and merry slant, he looked fondly on the familiar adobe facades that crowded close to the narrow street like eager children. He beamed in the impetuous wind, and increased his stride, contemplating his good fortune, the way in which his life had been so often—and in the nick of time—blessed by visits from Lady Luck.

Anita Montague herself, trusted manager of the gallery, had been one of that capricious lady's blessings—dear Anita, with her confident manner, a disguise for her yearnings to be a big fish in the pond. And now she would, in fact, have her chance in the slipstream of his own celebrity, though what she would do with it once it came, how she would handle it—that was anyone's guess. It had always eluded her, passed her by.

As a young woman, Anita had risen quickly in the ranks of editorial researchers in the film department of the National Geographic Society, was on a first-name basis with some of the country's leading documentary filmmakers, had even—she confided to Potts once—been singled out for praise by the Society's president, Gil Grovesnor. But further ascent had been blocked by a glass ceiling in the person of her boss, ironically a woman, and one of impeccable social status in the nation's capital, whose hold, therefore, on the job of chief of editorial research, was impregnable. So Anita had sidestepped into public broadcasting, landing a job as an assistant producer of *Bill Moyers' Journal*, a spot that suited her intellectual interests more aptly than chasing down facts about the sex life of coelenterates and the hunting rituals of Ituri pygmies.

She had gloried in calling Mr. Moyers by his given name, and in not only meeting Joseph Campbell, but successfully pitching to Moyers a productive line of questioning in his long series of interviews with the great mythologist. But again her progress had been blocked—a lack of true recognition, she had felt, so she had ventured from the verge of the great pond of PBS to Albuquerque, taking a job as one of three producers of a weekly public TV show that showcased, with ponderous gravity, the artists and artistic traditions of New Mexico.

It was in this position that Potts had met her, during a show about the Hispanic tradition on the Black Madonna in which she had asked him some surprisingly trenchant questions about the distinction between folk art and fine art. This very trenchancy, born no doubt from hobnobbing with the likes of Bill Moyers's discussants, soon got her in trouble. New Mexico is a place given to uncritical celebration rather than the setting of invidious standards, particularly when it comes to art. Anita's questions were taken as abrasive and politically incorrect, not as the useful probing of a free-ranging intellect. So she was soon fired in a messy political squabble at the station that reached the local newspapers and brought forth the usual array of indignant, polarized gibberish in the letters to the editor.

Recognizing in Anita a person of unusual discrimination, Potts had bedded her twice before realizing that her slightly frantic writhing was something other than pure passion. Lying between her muscled thighs and tracing a circle on her flat stomach with his finger, he had said, "You go both ways." She had nodded with a brave smile. "And you really prefer . . ." And she had nodded. "We'll be good friends," Potts had said. "You should be free."

Later, Potts had offered her a job as manager of his gallery in Santa Fe, Southwest Creations, and she had agreed to a typical Santa Fe low salary only after he agreed to give her a ten percent interest, admiring her negotiating skill. The gallery had been doing fine ever since. For Anita had an excellent eye for what art would sell and, with Potts's encouragement, had come to separate that from her strongly held and accurate views of what art was truly of lasting value.

As he approached the gallery now, the wind gusted and the wooden sign over the door swung squeakily in the breeze. SOUTHWEST CREATIONS had been incised above a hand-carved silhouette of the hunchbacked flute-player Kokapelli, who anciently and in uncounted rock carvings bespoke the region's earthy fertility. Potts liked to think of the figure as the Anasazi Kilroy. In the gallery's front window, seated in gloomy solitude, was a shaman, its finely carved face full of wrinkles peering out from a highly polished, deltoid piece of rosewood about three feet tall and three foot wide at the base. It was, Potts knew, the work of an Oregonian transplant by the name of Helga Windrow, whose earnest, genderless figures—vaguely Indian—had begun to catch on.

Since none of the galleries along Canyon Road opened before ten o'clock, the street was empty but for a lone figure ambling indecisively up the hill toward Potts. He wore a straw cowboy hat and what seemed brand-new denim work clothes. A drooping mustache gave him a particularly lugubrious expression as he eyed the gallery fronts like an émigré lost in a strange city. The man stepped into the street and nodded curtly as Potts passed him.

"Good morning," Potts said, and turned down a narrow alley to the side entrance of the gallery. He paused as a cloud swept by overhead and the alley was filled with the pale glow of the sun. Through the wooden door, Potts could hear Anita talking, presumably on the telephone, an instrument she used as comfortably and skillfully among the gallery's clientele as a sculptor uses his fingers to mold clay. The door, as expected, was unlocked, and he stepped into the large room with its walls painted a slightly grayish white, a color carefully contrived to show to their best advantage the nearly monochromatic landscape paintings the gallery was featuring this month—all various subtle shades of brown. As expected, Anita was perched, one hip on the old mahogany desk in the back, talking into an antique telephone receiver.

Placing bold Southwestern art among the sophistication of European-style antiques—as opposed to the locally favored, rawboned territorial furniture—had been Anita's idea, and a good one. Her face lit up when Potts entered the room.

". . . yes, oh yes," she said, "and he just walked in the gallery. His very self. You'll be here tonight? Oh, good, wonderful." She hung up the phone. "Welcome, Elijah. Welcome back. Your fans are clamoring."

Elijah walked over and gave her a kiss on the cheek. In her late thirties, she was a taut-skinned and well-muscled woman, given to jogging and workouts in a gym to see to it that she stayed that way and didn't wind up plump. Hers was the kind of figure and complexion that Potts did not find all that appealing. She was a bit like an apple: ripe and just a bit waxy. Potts appreciated the affection bordering on adulation with which she beheld him. There were rumors, of course, that they were lovers as well as business partners, rumors that neither of them made any particular effort to dispel and which the lesbian community found amusing.

"That's a nice dress," Potts said. "Purple becomes you." It was long-sleeved, a deep violet that showed to perfection the strands of turquoise *heishe* beads festooned around her neck.

"That was Connie Barnes on the phone. . . ."

"Ah, the implacable Hopi goddess of numerical truth. Is she coming?"

"Yes, of course, and she says she'll try and bring Mo Bowdre along. But she says he isn't into painting and painters."

"I shouldn't think so. What could a painting mean to a blind man?"

"But," Anita went on, "Connie says he's kind of piqued by your topic."

"The great Georgia O'Keeffe," Potts said. "And what she *didn't* paint."

Anita smiled conspiratorially and breathed deeply. "You're going to announce it tonight, aren't you?"

Potts pushed his gray forelock away from his brow and grinned. "We'll see. It might be a propitious time." Outside, raindrops streaked the large window and a woman in a Mexican-style serape hustled past, clutching what improbably looked like a Tyrolean hat to her head against the wind that had just gusted up in the sudden gray.

"It's good to be back," he said.

"Exciting," Anita said, her back to him as she fiddled with the stems of some early hothouse irises in a silver vase.

"Very," Potts said.

The young woman from the State Medical Investigation office in Albuquerque hoisted herself up and leaned on the edge of the Dumpster's metal side, which had been painted a cheerful blue like the others in the gravel lot. The woman looked tired even though her day had barely begun. She squinted in the midmorning sun.

To her left, in the Dumpster with her, a flamboyant mountain of opaque white plastic milk bottles rose up, and more were scattered around on the ground, carefully strung together in bulging, twisted loops that reminded Sergeant Anthony Ramirez of the Santa Fe Police Department of milky white, segmented grubs like you might find under logs in the forest, maybe the early stages of some giant centipede species from Hell. Ramirez shuddered inwardly. He hated centipedes and their related tribes—spiders, and such—with a fear born in childhood if not infancy.

Also in the Dumpster, to the medical investigator's right, and out of sight, thank God, was the corpse of a young woman, grotesquely misshapen and partly decomposed, lying supine among the plastic bottles. Evidently an Anglo, maybe mid-twenties, apparently a shotgun blast to the head—so much Ramirez had been able to discern after he had stepped up onto the open end of the Dumpster.

It had been discovered at 8:45 that morning, about fifteen minutes after the first recycling center volunteers showed up for work. According to the uniforms who had responded first to the 911 call, the head volunteer, or whatever she was—a Ms. Weigle who wrote children's books, Patricia Weigle of Garcia Street—had smelled a "sickening" odor, and assumed it came from the Dumpster behind the restaurant beyond the wooden slat fence of the recycling center. Other arriving volunteers had doubted that anything a restaurant would throw away could smell like that, and one of them, a Vietnam vet, had known exactly what it was, so they tracked it by nose to the Dumpster reserved for plastic milk bottles. The vet proceeded to scrabble around in the Dumpster until he came across a human foot with the toenails painted red, protruding from a cluster of milk bottles. Patricia Weigle called 911 while two other recycling volunteers threw up on the gravel.

The first unit arrived within five minutes, and by the time Ramirez reached the yard, it had been cordoned off with yellow tape and several Santa Fe citizens were lined up in their vehicles wondering what the hell had happened and what were they going to do with several weeks worth of old newspapers, carefully sorted green and white wine bottles, crushed aluminum cans, tin cans, corrugated cardboard boxes (carefully flattened), and cardboard juice containers. Damned if they would take this stuff to the landfill—it was against their principles, and say, hadn't they discovered a body out there a couple of weeks ago, some woman buried in a shallow grave near the landfill, tossed away like so much garbage? And now, here, another woman, pitched into the recycling lot? What was this? A serial killer? Huh?

The big cop, Gutierrez, with a face as expressive as a slab of basalt, was now waving off the environmentally conscious citizens having taken over from Ms. Weigle, whose tendency, given her adrenaline rush, had been to explain everything in graphic detail to every stalled eco-citizen, idling their engines in the street, tying up an entire block and filling the area with exhaust fumes. Gutierrez, representing the intransigence if not the majesty of the Law, was more terse, and more effective in shunting the disgruntled drivers off.

"Well, Sergeant," the M.I. said when Ramirez approached. "Nothing much you didn't already know. She's an Anglo, mid- to late-twenties, cause of death a shotgun wound to the head. She's been here two days at least. I can't understand why somebody didn't notice this before today."

"They only open the recycling center a couple of times a week. Wednesdays and Saturdays," Ramirez said. "Maybe people on the street thought it came from that place over there."

"What place?"

"Over there," Ramirez said, gesturing with his head. "That restaurant."

"And they didn't call the public health people? Oh well, we're outta here. Take her back to Albuquerque. I'll let you know what we find. Tomorrow, probably.

She'll be tough to ID, no identifying marks, not much of the face left. You'll have to pray for dental records."

She ducked down behind the blue side of the Dumpster. "Talk to you later, huh?" Ramirez called out, and to himself said, "Mierda." No one like this had been reported missing locally, so far as he knew. And this was the second homicide in two weeks, the first being the one near the landfill. Both found where you take your garbage, but there the pattern ended. The landfill woman, still unidentified, had been strangled. And it was a lot easier to dig a shallow grave behind some piñon trees near the landfill than it was to hoist a body over the fence around the recycling yard.

That this one was dead when someone hauled her into the yard was clear: there wasn't enough blood among the white plastic bottles in the Dumpster for the blast to have taken place there—and no other tissue sprayed around, like brains. The first cops on the scene had spotted this, and had found the trail, dried blood in the gravel leading to the rear of the yard, more on the other side of the fence. She'd been hauled to the dusty lot behind the restaurant, already dead with most of her blonde head blown away, and somehow hoisted over the fence and buried in a Dumpster full of plastic milk bottles. The dead know no ignominy, Ramirez assumed, but to wind up in a clutter of plastic containers of two-percent milk seemed worse even than a shallow grave in a dump.

And, of course, unlike the landfill murder, this guy didn't care if she was found. Knew she would be found. It was a statement, like *in your face, motherfuckers.*

He could see the headlines now: THE SANTA FE

TRASHER, or some damned fool label like that. If the earnest recycling public could make such a connection, the press could, too—and would, Ramirez knew, unless he made sure the department emphasized the differences in whatever it released later today.

People had an understandable but perhaps exaggerated fear of serial killers, seeing lone stalkers everywhere, especially since movie and TV producers had found them so salable and started beaming serial-killer textbooks into every dysfunctional household across the land. It was a sad commentary on the American public, Ramirez reflected gloomily, that the old adage—*monkey see, monkey do*—applied to such deeds. The FBI had stats showing the sudden rise in chainsaw murders after each of the movies, and presumably there were weirdos who had launched themselves on interesting careers with that Brit, Anthony Hopkins in his iron mask, as their role model.

But in the cold accounting of a policeman, some things were even worse than serial killers.

There was nothing else for him to do here in the recycling yard. He walked toward his vehicle, hoping—even letting the words of a prayer form in his mind—that this killing wasn't what he thought it might be.

"Pigeons?" Connie Barnes said. "No. We don't have a problem with pigeons."

The man standing outside the screen door slumped, seeming disappointed. He turned his head to the left, then to the right. "I seen a lot of 'em on this street. I thought you might need . . ." His voice trailed off.

Connie had been startled to see this man with a straw

cowboy hat peering in the living room window that faced out onto Canyon Road. It was a small window, low to the ground, and the man was stooped over, his face pressed ominously against the screen.

"Anyone home?" he had said when he saw Connie through the window. "Oh, ma'am? I'm with Humane Control and we're making a special introductory offer to the folks here on Canyon Road. Can I have a moment of your time?"

"Humane what?" Connie had asked and, for reasons she could not explain, opened the big wooden door that nobody used anymore. But she left the screen door latched. The man stepped over to the door, where, silhouetted in the morning light, he explained that Humane Control was an organization with a mission, to help the people of Santa Fe rid their homes and businesses of roosting pigeons, an increasing urban problem what with diseases and all, pigeon poop can give you pneumonia, clog up your air ducts, but nobody likes to think of one's fellow creatures, even pigeons, dying in painful convulsions from some awful poison, so his firm had devised a humane way of taking care of the problem. Traps, ma'am . . . harmless, painless, guaranteed . . . But the man had looked stricken when Connie told him she had no pigeon problem.

Rallying, he said, "They *are* out there, ma'am, I seen them on the street, and there's no telling when they'll take a fancy to your place here, too. They're like termites, ma'am, cockroaches. Once they're in the neighborhood—"

"Well, no thanks," Connie said, realizing that until she shut the door, the man would go on talking, and realizing also that something about this man made her apprehensive, the way she sometimes felt among Navajos. "Not today."

"Well, okay, ma'am," the man said, fishing in his back pocket. "But maybe you'd take my card here, give me a call when they do start roosting here." He held out a white card with black type on it and smiled. "Remember, ma'am, guaranteed painless. No fuss or feathers. We just catch 'em and take 'em away."

Connie unlatched the screen, took the card, said thank you, and closed the big wooden door. She crossed the room, trying to remember what it was she had had in mind to do, and looked absently at the man's business card. It said:

RAMÓN TOFOYA, TECHNICAL ENGINEER
HUMANE CONTROL, INC.

with a post office box number in Santa Fe and a local telephone number. Pigeons, she said to herself, dropping the man's card on the low table in front of the big red sofa. What will they think of next? Humane pigeon control. What a way to make a living. She wondered what they did with them once they were trapped and carted off. Something real humane, she thought.

By noon a thick cloud cover had sunk over most of northern New Mexico, and the Sangre de Cristo Mountains that rise north of Santa Fe were obscured by angry gray tendrils clinging leadenly to the snow-covered upper slopes despite the wind. In a sudden and titanic gust, riding on a new weather front rocketing in from the southwest and blitzing up the great gash in the earth that is the Rio Grande rift valley, the wind had slammed into the lower slopes and the city nestled there, and settled into a steady, nerve-wracking assault. The air was mustard-yellow with fine particles of dust, propelled at a steady twenty miles an hour with gusts up to forty into every cranny and orifice in their path, covering the shiny tile floors of even the finest homes in Santa Fe with a microscopically thin, talcumlike film resistant to dry mop or vacuum.

Realtors and other boosters in New Mexico never explain to new pilgrims about the spring winds—especially that they can blow even into May—and the realtors actually benefit from the turnover, people from California and the East coming out in other months and saying "Wow, honey, let's do it," and move only to find that they go nuts in the wind. New Mexicans will say that such people can't take the dry climate, or it's too provincial, or the landscape is too big and impersonal, et cetera, but they don't mention the winds. Yet it is the winds, the dirty little secret in the Land of Enchantment, that play a major and overlooked role in weeding out wimps, delicate flowers, and other tenderfeet.

In the capricious onslaught, trees twist and thrash, cottonwoods losing brittle limbs in this, their season of violent purification. Lesser desert plants simply bow, cowering, obeisant—a universe of plant cells awash with hormones that signal up, *up*, UP against a force of relentless, gritty horizontality. Only those that keep their tender parts to themselves until May do well in this place. The world, for plants, goes mad.

The spring winds, unholy spirit of the warming earth, tend to arise in the afternoon beginning in March. They arrive in time to tear away the tattered patterns of winter and redistribute the carcasses of tumbleweeds. The wind—exhilarating, edgy, perfidious, abrasive—howls like a tormented child having a fit before being bundled finally off to bed by exhausted parents.

The idiotic winds turn people impatient, irritable, and those New Mexicans with the wherewithal to do so typically plan to be somewhere else in March and early April. Most simply sit and wait them out, hunkered down, licking the grit from between their lips and gums, hearing things in the wailing, seeing more ominous portents like greenhouse warming or the wrath of the Creator in each annual variation in the length of the windy season.

Horses and cattle swing their rumps passively south for the duration, keeping their heads low, eyes shut, their tails clamped down tight against the stinging invasion of what some New Mexicans are pleased to call Arizona topsoil.

Winds like that, if they go on too long, can make horses—and people—act crazy.

two

"Damn!" Mo Bowdre barked. This hadn't happened for years.

The block of marble had inexplicably, infuriatingly, split, a corner falling off on the table. Mo threw his heavy mallet made from lignum vitae wood across the room and heard it clatter off the wall onto the floor.

"Damn!" he said again. It had been years since he'd made such a dumb, careless mistake. By now he knew stone like a trainer knows horses and . . . Panic struck as the words *losing his touch* flitted into his mind.

Touch. That's all he had. And if that was going . . . But why would someone all of a sudden lose his touch, his feel for something? It wasn't that he had arthritis or that carpal tunnel syndrome that afflicted people who performed repetitive movements all the time. He'd just blown it. Blown a piece of marble.

In his heart of hearts where few people were allowed to enter, Mo Bowdre tended to look out upon this wayward world with the foreboding of a hypochondriac, ever aware of how fragile was his hold on things. He knew this was mostly a result of losing his vision in that stupid mine accident years before, the need now to grasp the world with all his other senses, to insist, by means of smell, touch, hearing, that both he and the rest of the world were real. . . . Sometimes the merest failure in the fragile web he had spun seemed catastrophic, and a mistake like this made him fear he had lost what little control he had over his remaining links to reality.

It all took such constant concentration.

Losing concentration? That was it. But why?

He jumped, startled by the big wooden door slamming behind him. The wind was up again. Damn wind, slamming doors and all, dropping the temperature. He hadn't noticed the wind, even though he could hear it now through the closed door, a baritone rush up and down the scales.

Hey. Why hadn't he noticed the wind before, when it had started? Because he was working, concentrating. And if he was concentrating that hard, how come he'd cracked the damn marble? Maybe, he thought, taking hope, maybe he wasn't losing his touch, or his concentration. Maybe it was just some trick the wind played on the nervous system. You got all these brain cells just peppering away, thinking they're doing fine, firing—bam, bam, bam—just like a finely tuned carburetor, but the wind has got the timing off in some subtle way. That must be it.

"See, son," he said aloud in his best campfire cowboy accent, "the wind outchere plays tricksh on a man."

He shivered. He was cold and also hungry. He reached out and lifted a black cowboy hat off the shelf, pinching the crown between dusty fingers, and stuffed it on his head. He kept his hand clamped on it as he opened the door into the wind and, in measured steps, marched across the lawn and into the house.

"Connie," he said in a loud voice. "I got me a theory." There was no answer, and he called her name again. "Are you here?"

"Mo, I'm in the kitchen."

He lumbered across the living room and into the kitchen. "What are you doing in here?" he asked.

She laughed. "I'm cooking. Isn't that what the kitchen is for? I'm making something for dinner tonight. I haven't had any time to cook for a week. All those taxes keep you real busy."

"Well, I know that. So you shouldn't be working now, you should be on vacation."

"I like to cook," she said, and he heard the sound of chopping, smelled carrots. "What's your theory?"

"Of cooking?" Mo said.

"No, you said you had a theory."

"Oh, yeah, that. Well, it's nothing. I just knocked a chunk off that marble, damned stupid. I figured it's the wind playing games with my aging brain cells, but that's probably all bullshit. Anyway, *I* am going on vacation. Not gonna touch another piece of rock, another piece of clay, till the wind stops. So when you're finished chopping up those carrots, let's go have lunch somewhere."

A half hour later they were in Mo's pickup, an enormous Ford a few years away from being registerable as a classic, its heavy-duty suspension creaking as it crept down Canyon Road.

"I wonder how many brain surgeons make mistakes

this time of year," Mo said, his head turned toward the passenger window.

"Is that part of your theory?" Connie asked, glancing over.

Mo nodded.

"I thought you said it was all—"

"Hah—hah. Well, so was continental drift until they proved it. Anyway, I'm on vacation, like I said."

"Free."

"On the loose."

"So you'll come to Anita's tonight?"

"Don't see why not. Old Elijah, what's he talking about? What Georgia O'Keeffe *didn't* paint? Only Potts could spin something out of that. Talk about living by your wits, that boy must be a direct descendant of Spider Woman."

Connie smiled, hanging a left on Camino del Monte Sol, knowing Mo meant no disrespect to the preeminent Hopi goddess who had spun the world into being out of nothing. She turned on the radio, and heard a news announcer on the local light rock station breathlessly reporting that a young woman's body had been found in the Dumpster at the recycling center. Police would have nothing further to report until some unspecified later time as to the woman's identity, cause of death . . .

Connie sighed.

"More work for Tony Ramirez," Mo said. "What the hell is going on in this town?"

At 12:03, Ramón Tofoya decided to hell with it. It just didn't work. Wasn't going to work. Nothing but rejection, must have talked to twenty different householders and not one of the snotty bastards wanted his services. Twenty doors closed on him. "No thanks." Slam.

It had begun to dawn on him through the morning that this was perhaps for a very good reason. He himself had not seen any pigeons along Canyon Road or any of the chichi residential streets off Canyon Road where he had made his pitch. But he'd studied up on pigeons in the prison library and he thought he knew enough about them to persuade these city people that they had a problem anyway. "Once they're in the neighborhood, ma'am . . ." His spiel, he thought, was irresistible, well-informed.

But the fucking snoots didn't go for it, and an increasingly despondent Ramón Tofoya faced the possibility that the whole idea—that he'd spent so much time studying up on, so much time thinking about, preparing—was a dud. Adding to his despair was hunger, and he had already concluded by looking at menus outside the spiffy little cafés that there was no way he could afford to eat anything for sale on Canyon Road. Just this cup of coffee was going to run him a couple of bucks.

He sat at a tiny round table near a window in one of the overpriced cafés, feeling profoundly sorry for himself. No one was outside in the courtyard alongside the road, thanks to the wind. All those closing doors. He had given the waitress a friendly smile when he told her all he wanted was a cup of coffee, and she had made a face like she had just smelled something bad. Damn snot.

And then, at 12:04, as the waitress approached with his coffee, he saw it. Sitting on the peaked roof of an old house that was now a gallery, preening itself like some goofy, windblown potentate, sun glinting off its neck like a brightly lit oil slick, was a pigeon.

Ramón's heart leapt. *"Columba livia!"* he said out loud.

"What?" the waitress said, stepping back from the table. "Columbus is alive? What are you talking about?" She looked over her shoulder to the door into the bar.

"Up there," Ramón said, pointing through the window. "A pigeon. On that roof. See? That's a pigeon!"

The waitress glanced up at the pigeon across the street and, her eyes now wide, reached over and put the coffee down on the table. "There," she said. She took the check from her pocket and put it on the table. "Enjoy your coffee."

Ignoring the polite and tentatively raised hands of a few customers in the café, the waitress strode back into the darkened bar, where the owner stood inspecting the bottles on the wall.

"Jimmy, we got one out there. A nut. Sitting there raving about Columbus being alive or something and then getting all goo-goo-eyed about a pigeon. A pigeon! Some of the people who show up here give me the willies."

"Here? In this place?"

"Here in this town."

Police Sergeant Anthony Ramirez was not a man from whose lips profanity often and easily bubbled forth, but for the second time that day he said, "Mierda!" He dropped the telephone receiver back into its cradle. A preliminary search, made at lightning speed by an FBI computer network which he could barely imagine, turned up no dental records matching the remaining dentition of the young woman whose body had been discovered in the Dumpster. It was not hopeless, of course. Something might turn up from further searches, but Ramirez knew the odds were against it. And nothing in the FBI's great brain matched the corpse's fingerprints, which meant nothing. Most people went through life without being fingerprinted.

The great slagheap of data on the information superhighway was not going to help, Ramirez felt, and so it was now a matter of poking around in the old-fashioned byways and alleys with the old-fashioned techniques. And chief among these techniques, Ramirez thought with resignation, was waiting for some young woman to be reported missing by the people who knew her, worked with her, maybe loved her, maybe thought she was . . . well, why speculate? Two unidentified young Anglo women dead in Santa Fe in two weeks, and except for some of the grisly details about how they died and what was done to them next, nobody knew anything. There was no place to go to start digging. Without an ID, the authorities' hands were effectively tied.

Ramirez reviewed in his mind the few gossamer threads of information he had. Neither of the women bore the signs of a life degraded by drugs, alcoholism, prostitution—any of that. Judging from the clothes and jewelry they wore, neither was especially poor, down-and-out, and neither appeared to be especially fancy. No one had reported anyone missing who might be the corpse found near the landfill—so maybe she was a tourist. And maybe this new one found today was another tourist. So eventually, when they didn't turn up back in Minnesota or wherever, the word would go out. Possible. Ramirez shrugged.

Maybe this new one was not a tourist but a local woman whose absence over two days—two weekdays—would not be noticed by anyone. Like her employer. Which meant she didn't work a normal work week, which meant she could be any of half the young women in town, employed by restaurants, galleries, all the places that were open in Santa Fe on weekends. Or some kind of freelancer or artist—people with no weekly schedule. The possibilities were innumerable; the means of narrowing them down to something useful pathetically few.

Ramirez's friend Mo Bowdre liked to quote some guy, Sam something, who said that in life the odds are six-to-five against. In solving this kind of death, the odds were immeasurably worse, and for a moment Ramirez allowed himself to dwell with something akin to self-pity on the melancholy calculus of law enforcement.

Ten years earlier, when Ramirez had been a new recruit in the SFPD, Santa Fe still clung to the reality of being a small town, not an urban place with real urban problems. The City of Holy Faith—three cultures all living in harmony, a place of low buildings, informality, art, passion, style—a place unlike the rest of America. In such a setting, the work of the police, too, was simpler. But now—growth, big real estate deals, a widening chasm between haves and have-nots, all these rich people from New York and California coming here, bringing their urban coastal problems with them.

Why, Ramirez wondered not for the first time, do rich

people bring so much trouble along with them wherever they go? How was it that the more rich people you have around, the more problems you get? Maybe it was true that the richer some people get, the poorer other people get, and after a while the poor get pissed off, do bad things. Greed breeding envy. So what else is new?

Too many people, Ramirez thought. Maybe that's it. Maybe there's some critical mass, some number of people beyond which a viable human community loses its way.

A one-time student of archaeology before entering the police academy, Ramirez had often dwelled on this magic figure while he stood in some of the old Indian ruins, the long-abandoned cliff dwellings that brood over the Southwest, silent reminders about the outcome of all human plans.

When his phone buzzed, Ramirez grabbed it, shaking off his gloomy requiem for humanity: "Ramirez . . . Sí, Maria . . . Good, very good. Tell them I'm on my way."

A waitress at that new restaurant, Mediterranean Light, had not reported for work that morning to get ready for the Saturday lunch crowd. The manager had called her home number, had spoken to her housemate, who also worked at the restaurant—nothing. And he had heard the news on local radio about the woman in the Dumpster. Maybe, the manager had thought . . .

Ramirez hung up the phone and plucked his blue blazer off the back of his chair with a tingle of what he knew was premature elation.

Norah Vargas, wearing a simple gray silk dress, with her black hair pulled up on her head rather like a Gibson

Girl, turned on a dazzling smile as a man entered the restaurant. Noting that he appeared to be alone, she took up one of the oversized thick vellum menus. She held her smile as it dawned on her that she had seen this man somewhere before, but lost the smile when she remembered where. This was the printing marketeer from Chicago: Mr. Yellow Pages. What was a printing salesman doing in a place like this?

She smiled again and bravely said, "Table for one for lunch?"

The man nodded, said yes, but he didn't have a reservation.

"No problem," Norah said, hastily turning toward the main dining room, hoping he hadn't recognized her. She led him through the tables to a small one by a window, set the menu down and, with her head averted, asked if this was satisfactory. She felt sweat erupt everywhere on her body in spite of the air-conditioning and guessed that she had turned red as well.

"Mrs. Barth getting into the restaurant business, too, I see," the man said, sitting down. "How did it go at Intel?"

Norah fled back to her station, gesturing violently at the substitute waitress to attend to the guy and thinking to herself: damn, damn, damn. She looked up to see the manager approaching, looking grim. He was a small man, about the same height as Norah, who was five-three. Intense and fussy about details, he was the general partner in the limited partnership that had launched Mediterranean Light four months ago, and he took his responsibilities so seriously that one of the chefs liked to say he could make a pot of coffee nervous. His name was Louis T. Campbell but was known to the public and his clientele as Luis, pronounced Loo-*wees*, which seemed more Mediterranean.

He approached, chewing on his bottom lip, and Norah noticed the restaurant door open again. A huge man, backlit by the sun outside, filled the frame, led by a dark-haired woman with a round face.

"Luis, the man at table twenty-one. Do you know him?"

The little man swiveled his head around like an owl. "No. I've seen him in here before. Out-of-town guy. I think he's some kind of art collector, art dealer. Like who isn't? Now, listen, Norah—"

"He told me he was a printing salesman," Norah interrupted. "He was on the plane with me the other day."

Luis shrugged. "So? People make up stuff on airplanes. Who's to know?" Norah felt her face redden again, but Luis the manager apparently didn't notice. "Norah," he said in a voice almost a whisper, "there is a policeman in my office. Sergeant Ramirez. He wants to talk to you about Carolyn. This could be very serious. There was a woman found dead this morning and . . . look, you go and talk to him, and I'll take over for you here."

Norah turned to go and recognized the big man with the dark-haired woman. Mo Bowdre, the wildlife sculptor, and his Hopi girlfriend. She heard him say to Luis, "Name's Bowdre. Called for a table for two?" Then she heard him say, "Did I hear you say Tony Ramirez's here? I thought this place was too refined to have guests like that. Hah—hah—hah."

Luis's office was upstairs, off a balcony from which the manager could look down at the main room of the restaurant and fretfully take soundings of customer satisfaction. The old wooden door was open and Norah saw a dark-haired man—clean-shaven, Hispanic, in a dark blue blazer—sitting erect on a territorial-style chair beside Luis's desk. He stood up as she entered and said, "Miz Vargas. I am Sergeant Ramirez. Please sit down, uh, anywhere, let's see." He turned the wooden chair around so that it faced a sofa against the wall. "There," Ramirez said, pointing to the sofa, and sat down.

Norah settled down on the soft sofa, crossed her legs, and listened with a sense of being in a dream as the policeman explained that a young woman's body had been discovered that morning in a Dumpster at the recycling yard, dead probably two days, unidentified, and went on to explain that the manager here at the restaurant had called to report that a waitress, Carolyn Marcy, had failed to report to the restaurant this morning after her two days off. So it had to be checked out, though there was nothing to say that the two women were the same, only the most superficial similarities, and he didn't want to make anyone unduly apprehensive, especially the Marcy woman's friend and roommate.

"Oh, my God," Norah said. "I hope . . ." The policeman—Ramirez?—looked at her calmly.

"Please tell me about Carolyn Marcy," he said.

"Well, uh, well, first of all she wasn't my roommate, really. We share a place, a little house, it's been made into two apartments, separate. Separate entrances and all." She mentioned the address and the policeman wrote it down in a notebook. She told him the landlord's name, and he wrote that down.

"We work here but we aren't what you'd call *friends*. I mean, I don't really know her that well. I knew she needed a place to live when she came to work here about, oh, three months ago, and this place next to me was . . ." Norah shrugged. "I didn't see that much of her, from day to day—except here. She had a different lifestyle than me."

Sergeant Ramirez's eyebrows danced briefly. "Can you describe that for me? I have her photograph from the restaurant's personnel file, by the way. Blonde, Anglo, pretty, five-four, hundred and fifteen pounds. Did she have any identifying marks, by the way, you know, birth-marks, that sort of thing?"

"Nothing that showed," Norah said, and smiled wanly. "I mean, I didn't, she wasn't like a roommate."

"Of course," Ramirez said. "It says she was from Illinois."

"Some town there, I don't remember."

"Champaign. University town. Came to Santa Fe three months ago, this was her first job here. Tell me about this lifestyle that differed from yours."

Norah sensed a kind of relentless quality below this policeman's velvety voice.

"She's kind of wild."

"Wild?"

"Usually on her days off, she doesn't spend any time at the house. That I know of. Like she was gone yes-terday, the day before, all three nights."

"Oh, a boyfriend," Ramirez said.

"Not exactly."

Ramirez looked at her with his eyebrows raised.

"Sergeant, my people are from Rio Arriba County, near Ensenada."

"Oh," Ramirez said. "That Vargas. Sí. An important old lineage." He smiled.

"So perhaps you will understand," Norah said, "when I tell you that some of us are not as enamored of La Raza as, well, others."

"Some of the newcomers," Ramirez said. "Their version of La Raza?" Mentally he shook his head over the complexity of things. There were, especially here in New Mexico, so many different ways people had of expressing their Hispanic destiny. La Raza, the cosmic race—so many versions.

"Yes, that's it," Norah said.

"To a policeman, a lowlife is a lowlife. It is unfortunate. And that is what you are saying?"

Norah uncrossed her legs carefully and shifted on the sofa. "Carolyn hangs out places where, well, where she picks up guys like that, you know the types. Wear their anger like tattoos. I thought it was crazy, crazy for anyone, and an Anglo woman? But . . ." She shrugged.

"Not your responsibility."

"No."

The policeman was silent. Norah could hear the slight hum of the air-conditioning system.

"So she didn't come home last night."

"Not that I know of. Lots of times she just came straight to work from wherever she . . ."

Ramirez nodded. "But not this morning."

"No."

"Do you know any of the places where she goes?"

"No, we didn't, I didn't . . ."

"And the last time you saw her?"

"Wednesday night. Here. At work."

"Your days off?"

"Monday and Tuesday."

Ramirez stood up, put his notebook in his jacket pocket. "Thank you, Miz Vargas. You've been helpful to me. We may get back in touch."

"Sergeant, do you think . . . ?"

The policeman suddenly looked sad, distracted. "It's too early to say." He held out a business card. "Please, if you think of anything else, any identifying thing. And, of course, if you see Miz Marcy, and I hope you do, tell her to call me immediately."

The interview was over. Norah Vargas stood up, smoothed her gray silk dress over her hips, nodded, and stepped out on the balcony. She thought she heard the policeman sigh.

"Now, that," Mo Dowdre said, forking his last bite of fish stew into his mouth, "is as good as it gets." He chewed happily, swallowed, and said, "Hate to see it end."

It had taken considerable time to order lunch. Connie had read the menu out loud and announced with lightning decisiveness that she would have tabouli, explaining again that it was a cold salady mix of tomatoes, fresh mint, and bulgur wheat with lemon and garlic and olive oil. "Rabbit food," Mo had snorted mildly. "But mind you," he added graciously, "there's nothing wrong with that."

He had asked Connie to read him the details of the lamb kebab and the fish stew again. Roasted garlics on the skewer along with all the rest intrigued him, but so did the idea of an entire grouper steak made into a stew with white wine and all the other stuff they used in all this Mediterranean food—garlic, pepper, paprika, olive oil, capers, lemon. So in the end, noting that as he remembered it Mediterranean people tended to be relatively small in stature, he had ordered both, along with an order of garlic bread, and they had topped it off with a bottle of cold white wine, the last sip of which Mo savored now before swallowing it.

"How was the tabouli?" he asked. "Sounds like some kind of puppet master, circus guy, you know? In the center ring, the Great Tabouli and his Twelve Talking Dogs."

Connie laughed in spite of herself and said, "It was great, Mo. Coming here was a great idea."

"It was your idea," Mo said.

"Right. A great idea. You want some espresso?"

"Another good idea. Say, I wonder what Tony Ramirez is doing here. Suppose it has something to do with that woman they found? I wonder what the connection could be with this place. You'd have to say it's taking the recycling craze to an extreme."

"Mo! That's terrible."

"You're right. It just slipped out. Sorry."

"Tony left about a half hour ago. He came down those stairs from up there—up where it looks like they have some offices. He looked unhappy."

"He's always a little glum. Thinks too much about the human condition. I guess it goes with the job."

"He looked *real* unhappy," Connie said.

"Maybe we should take him out to dinner, invite him over, cheer him up."

"You just want to know what he's working on. Anyway, we're going to that talk, Elijah Potts tonight. Remember?"

"Oh, yeah. I don't suppose Tony'd want to sit through an hour of Elijah carrying on in artspeak about Georgia O'Keeffe, would he? You know, Connie, it's a great burden being an artist in this town. You gotta support the art community, all your brothers and sisters in creativity, not to mention all the resident experts and gurus. Solidarity. But the way some of 'em talk, so fancy and all, it's hard on an old country boy. You remember when Elijah started talking about that eagle I made, telling that little reporter about the release of archey-typal Jungian symbology, or some damn thing. Hell, I don't know anything about that. Felt dumb as a box of rocks. But it was good for sales."

"Maybe Elijah will surprise you," Connie said, and Mo cocked his head, wondering what was up.

Ramón Tofoya spent two hours getting his distraught nerves together before taking the next logical—and perhaps pivotal—step in his new career after seeing a pigeon preening on the roof of the gallery on Canyon Road. If this didn't work out, the frigging deal was off, a no-hoper, and he would have to bag the whole scam, think of something else, and right now he couldn't think of anything else. And without something else, he was up the creek again, dead meat.

After the two-dollar-and-forty-fucking-cent coffee that tasted like some kind of Turkish perfume, his stomach had growled in protest and he had decided he'd better put something American in it to get up his strength. So he'd walked back to his car, driven around the city until he found a Wendy's, where he bought a double cheeseburger and a salad bar plate and, when no one was looking, cheated by taking an added plateful from the baked potato and cheese bar. Feeling better, he had driven around for another half hour in the wind, dust blowing around and people's shit flying through the air, and finally found a parking space.

He got out of the car, stared longingly at the dark green Mercedes in the space ahead of him, and wondered when, among other things, the goddamned wind was going to let up, Christ, it was like living in some aerospace experiment, one of those wind tunnels he'd read about in some old magazine in the pen.

Five minutes later he stood in front of the door of Southwest Creations and stared blankly at the raisin-faced shaman in the window. He took two deep breaths and entered a long room with light gray walls and chichi tables around, bunch of brown paintings on the wall, and some more wooden stuff strewn around that looked like it was made by the person who'd done the shaman in the window. Toward the back of the room was an elegant, polished desk, and a nice-looking woman—smooth, what looked to be good tits under the purple dress—stood up with a tentative smile.

"Yes?" she said.

"I'd like to see the manager, ma'am."

"I'm the manager. What can I do for you?"

Ramón took a few steps toward the desk, and held out his card. "I'm a technical engineer with Humane Control, ma'am. I noticed you got pigeons here. On the roof. Looks to me like a real infestation."

"Of pigeons?"

"Yes, ma'am." Ramon's heart pounded. The woman was smiling. He began to explain the problem of pigeons, pointing out that a two-story house with a peaked roof like this one was just the kind of place they could invade, and he noticed happily that she continued to smile. Not a big smile, but clearly not anything like derision. She was actually interested. God*damn*! In response to a question, she told him that the second floor was now used only for storage.

"Well, ma'am, you don't want to be storing anything that's of any value in a place where there's pigeon droppings. All kinds of ammonia and other noxious gases, over time they'll take the finish off a fine piece of furniture like varnish remover. Not to mention the dangerous bacterial organisms, get in your lungs if you go up there. I don't want to scare you none, but they been saying—the people at NIH, you know, National Institutes of Health—they been saying that maybe that strep thing, the flesh-eating strep, it may be from pigeon droppings. So our service . . ."

And he had rattled on about his company's humane removal policies, and the woman had said she would talk to her partner, and would he call back again tomorrow, maybe in the late afternoon, but it sounded like a very good idea.

"You need the work, don't you?" the woman said.

"Well, ma'am, we're just starting out and—"

"Do you do anything else?"

"Like what?" Ramón said, coiling up inside like a rattlesnake.

"Well, I don't want to suggest anything beneath your, ah, qualifications, but we're having a talk here tonight, a kind of lecture, and the man who was going to set out the chairs for me is sick. Do you . . . ?"

"Ma'am, I'd be glad to help you out. Where are they? I'll do it right this minute, if that's okay."

The woman smiled again. "Ten dollars okay? They're right back here, in the back room."

The inner fucking sanctum, Ramón thought. I can get a bead on this whole place. "Sure, ma'am, and while I'm here I could run up and look at that storage area, tell you what you got to deal with up there. Most people," he babbled on, "have a real affection for birds, and so do we, so we just think they should live where they belong and not . . ."

three

Mo Bowdre sat in one of the forty-odd padded folding chairs that had been set up in rows in Southwest Creations Gallery and, as was his habit, listened in on the conversations around him—which in most cases the conversers imagined were private.

To his right a woman's voice he didn't recognize said: "I can't imagine what there is new to say about Georgia. Good heavens, Annie, the woman and her work have been picked over by everyone."

"You wait," came the reply from Annie, whom Mo recognized as a potter from nearby Tesuque who was currently into green glazes. "Elijah Potts has the most amazing way of turning things around in his mind—like a crystal, you know—and he always finds a new facet, something no one had imagined. You wait."

To Mo Bowdre's left and about two rows back, he heard another unfamiliar woman's voice: "He has the most astonishing—well, per*ception* of the female. I mean, did you read his book on Mary? Mariology? The irrepressible goddess reemergent—"

"Yes, I read it. You gave it to me, remember? He's gay, isn't he? So he'd understand—"

"Oh, no. Gay? Not by a long shot, let me tell you."

"Maybe he goes both ways. How else can you—"

"Jonathan, there's more to the female than just fucking, for heaven's sake."

"Tell me."

"Sometimes you make me sick, Jonathan."

"Hey, just kidding."

"Some things you don't joke about."

"I know, I know. Sorry."

Mo Bowdre jiggled with a nearly silent chuckle.

"What?" Connie asked, sitting to his left.

"Maybe Tony Ramirez ought to be here after all," Mo said. "You can learn a hell of a lot of new stuff about the human condition just sitting here. Hah—hah."

Anita Montague issued forth from the door in the rear, stepped around the white screen that stood on an easel and beamed out at the audience. She approached the lectern, adjusted the mike, and said: "Welcome. Welcome. It's so nice to see you all here again. I always take the resumption of our monthly series as the official end of winter and the beginning of our mutual growth period for the year. This season, as you know, our theme is 'Art from the Interior: the Work and the Soul.'

"We're going to be hearing from some of our own local artists, including Hernando Antonio Mendez, whose work you all know, redefining the Hispanic life force. And we'll be meeting a new face on the scene, Marnie Beshadie, a montage artist who's—well, she's brilliant. She was orphaned as a baby, grew to adulthood in Amarillo, and only recently came to know of her Jicarilla Apache heritage. Her art reflects her encounters with her self along the borders of two cultures, and I'm sure we'll all be enlightened and heartened by her presentation. But tonight . . ."

Anita turned her head toward the rear of the gallery.

"Tonight," she continued, "we'll hear from our longtime friend, neighbor, and mentor in the arts, in myth, in meaning and personal growth, who needs no introduction . . . we've read his books, we look forward to his new book, which I understand is *in press*, a definitive rumination on the Black Madonna of the American Southwest. . . . Elijah? There you are."

Elijah Potts appeared in the door, pushing back his forelock of prematurely graying hair, smiling boyishly, and walked toward the lectern. He waved shyly.

Mo Bowdre leaned over and, in a whisper, asked, "What's he wearing?"

Connie leaned into the big man's ear. "A blue cotton vest, looks like faded indigo, an off-white shirt, you know, without any collar . . ."

"Like Thomas Jefferson," Mo said. "A little rumpled?"

"And some kind of fancy khaki pants."

"Like a British officer?" Mo asked, still whispering, while polite applause rippled around him.

"How would I know?" Connie asked.

"I have heard it confirmed yet again—right here tonight from one of the impeachable sources in this here audience—that Elijah Potts buys all his duds from the J. Peterman catalogue, you know, that guy from Kentucky who talks about hotels in Cairo and the bathrobes they provide. Sells stuff to modern-day Humphrey Bogarts."

"Mo, ssshh."

"And Lauren Bacalls. It's called the presentation of self. Real important."

"Mo!"

Elijah Potts stood at the lectern, smiling out at the audience, his mischievous eyes dancing from face to face. He stood with one hand in the pocket of his tan cavalry twill trousers, the other resting on the lectern. Then, still smiling like a proud father, he spoke.

"I'm just back from Key West," he said. "It is a wonderful place, with its own magic. But a man cannot live on magic alone." (Audience laughter.) "And, for my taste, it's not dusty enough." (More laughter.) "I'm really happy as always to be back here in Santa Fe under this grand sky, and to be talking here with you. Over the past couple of years, since we started this series, I have come to think of you—of this group—we who consult here in a semiformal way and let these monthly sessions inform our daily lives, our communication with each other, to make—in a sense—an art form out of our lives and relationships . . . I have come to think of you"—he gestured with his free hand—"as a kind of extended family. A community of people who have come here recently or long ago and have combined into a congress of mutual interest. A quest that we all share. In this mobile world in which we live, this is rare, and I for one am grateful, and I thank you for being here."

He paused, while people in the audience smiled at each other.

"It's because of these feelings of kinship I have for you here in this group that I don't feel as awkward as I might have in changing the topic of my talk tonight. To something—an announcement—that is very exciting, monumental. And it seems quite miraculous—to me.

"My plan last fall was to open this series with some thoughts about Georgia O'Keeffe, and what she *didn't* paint. I wanted to think about that with you as an avenue of insight into the soul of this artist whom no one—no critic or academic commentator—has been able to categorize successfully. What category could contain Georgia O'Keeffe? Realist? Abstract expressionist? Feminist? I could go on and on. And on. A cascade of words could not presume to pigeonhole the vision of Georgia O'Keeffe. And of course words are just that, pigeonholes. Art, at its best, is beyond words.

"We can look at O'Keeffe's paintings of flowers, the interior of flowers, and like many of the shocked and amazed critics of the time, see a thinly disguised expression of Freudian fascination with the female sex organ. What was it one her sisters said? Something about having a vulva in the dining room?" (Laughter.)

"Thank heavens we have progressed a bit since then in our sense and sensibility. There were others at the time who looked at O'Keeffe's paintings of cattle skulls—the white, dead bone so prominently in the foreground with the eternal expanse of the New Mexican landscape in the distant background—people could look at those and see, however unimaginatively, a woman trying to confront the notion of death. Period. Noticing that there was no *middle* ground in these paintings—nothing in between the near presence of death and the distant presence of eternity—some could spin fantastic pop-psychology notions of a woman who had found that life was without meaning. On and on they went.

"Of course, we know that O'Keeffe herself thought all this theorizing was absolute bullshit." (Laughter.)

"I have heard some of my colleagues go to remarkable lengths to make O'Keeffe's symbols accord with the ancient, even prehistoric, archetypal symbols of Goddess. The cow skull? The dead bull, of course. The annual sacrifice of the male just like in Ishtar's Babylonia, in Minoan Crete.

"Those stark crosses from the *moradas* of the Hispanic world in which she sojourned? Clearly, the superimposition of patriarchical Christianity over the pagan curves of the Earth Goddess. A feminine protest.

"Yes? Does that sound good? Or perhaps a bit simpleminded? A bit farfetched? In fact, you have to be pretty careful about us mythologists." (Prolonged laughter.)

"Of course, she painted what was in her soul. And that is what we are interested in in this series. She released to the world only those paintings that she thought truly achieved the expression of what was in her soul—a soul and a sensorium that were inseparable. She saw. She saw and she felt—and she painted. What we have is the particular legacy of a particular soul at a particular time in the universe, and that, friends, is the power of Georgia O'Keeffe.

"It is not that she was perhaps the first woman ever to

do art with commercial success. She is one of a relative handful who have *ever* accomplished the heights of artistic expression—to paint directly from the upwellings of the soul. You could easily make the case—and that was going to be part of my lecture—that she didn't draw on archetypal images so much as *create* them. New ones."

Potts paused to let this notion sink in—the notion that the basic images, the basic myths shared in common by all human beings through time—are not fixed, not unchanging, but can grow like an evolving garden. The audience, coming to this understanding, gasped.

"But O'Keeffe," Potts went on, "rejected much of her own work, threw it away. Whole series of paintings she evidently decided didn't make it and she chucked them. There's a story about one fellow up in Abiquiu who went to the town dump, found one of her rejects, and trotted on down to the bank and used it to secure a twelve-thousand-dollar loan to build a house.

"I had wanted to imagine for a while what she didn't paint, what didn't emerge from her soul as important. Then I began to think that a key to O'Keeffe was not what we can imagine she didn't paint. That would be a list a computer could make. Instead, a key might be in what she did paint and then *threw away*. And of course that is something we can't know. We can only speculate. If only, I thought last fall, we could see what she rejected.

"But thinking intensely about her art and her life, I recalled one of her friends saying that by the 1940s she had utterly stopped thinking about the child she never had." Potts paused, looking at the audience, and pushed his forelock back from his forehead. "And this struck me as nonsense. Can you imagine it? I simply cannot imagine any woman, any childless woman, who wouldn't from time to time imagine what might have been . . . what might have emerged. . . ."

Potts looked down at the lectern for a moment, then resumed. "It was at that time in her life, also, that she came across the famous pelvis, the great bone with its circular opening through which she looked at—and painted—her beloved mountain, Pedernal. How many versions of the pelvis and the mountain are there? I've seen at least a dozen, and there are surely more. And I thought about pelvises. I thought about what a young woman taking an art school anatomy course early this century might have had implanted in her mind about pelvises, and I checked back. Even in those prudish times, it was common to point out the difference between the male and female pelvis, the female's being larger to allow the passage of a baby's head through it.

"So, for this colloquy, when I was thinking about it early last fall, I was going to throw out the speculation that Georgia O'Keeffe made a painting—or more likely several—looking through that pelvis at a representation of the baby she never had. And then threw them away."

Potts stopped, and smiled at his audience. He shrugged.

"It was simply a speculation, a discussion point, perhaps a useful game. A way that we might talk together about a *what-if* and maybe get closer to our own souls. We've done that here before."

People in the audience nodded.

"Instead, I want to show you something." Potts turned

and took two steps toward the back of the room, then returned to the lectern.

"At about the time last year that I was thinking about these things, I signed a contract to buy a small house in Canones—you know, that little village back in the mountains about ten miles past Abiquiu. I took possession in November, and around Christmastime I drove up to look around again. It needed a lot of work, and I wanted to be thinking about it while I was in Key West. A couple of friends of mine came with me, and we started poking around, looking in the old outbuildings. And we found something."

He turned and darted back around the easel and went through the door, returning a moment later carrying an unframed canvas, some sixteen by twenty inches, with its back to the audience. Gingerly, he turned the painting face out, placed it on the easel, and stood back.

The sound from the audience was more like a geyser than a synchronous gasp.

"Jesus Christ!" someone said.

"Please come up and have a closer look," Elijah Potts's voice said, and Mo Bowdre heard a lot of chairs being pushed back. "This is one," Potts said, with a dramatic pause, "of *seven*. All variations on the same theme."

"Don't tell me," Mo said to Connie. "Let me guess. No, tell me."

"It's a Georgia O'Keeffe painting. It's like those pictures of the pelvis and the mountain she did, except that on this one, through the hole in the pelvis, there's this blue and red swirl."

"A swirl?" Mo said. "What, like a galaxy?"

"More like a baby."

"Well, I'll be goddamned. And there's seven more?"

"No, six more. Seven in all. Different levels of abstraction, you know, of the baby."

"How do you know that?" Mo asked.

"I was there when he found them. In the shed in Canones."

Mo clamped his jaw shut and folded his beefy forearms across his chest. With his lower teeth he reached up and pulled at his blond mustache, and the chin of his blond beard jutted out like a tank on maneuvers.

"Me and Anita, here at the gallery," Connie said. "We went out there with Elijah. Anita wanted me to learn how to use a mountain bike. But we got busy poking around the place. It was Anita who found them, actually."

Mo chewed his mustache. He could sense that no one remained in the chairs nearby, and he could hear the multitudinous buzz of voices up by the painting. "And you knew all about this?"

"Uh-huh."

"Since last year?"

"Yes."

"And you didn't say even a teeny-weeny word about it to anyone—not even me."

"Uh, no. Not to anybody."

Mo reached out and put a big paw on Connie's arm. "The secret life of Connie Barnes, Hopi Eagle clan, certified public accountant, and Indian art appraiser. Hah—hah. How much are these things worth?"

"Millions. If they're real."

"Are they?"

"I don't know. Georgia O'Keeffe wasn't an Indian. But I'm sure Elijah has had them authenticated. There's been a few O'Keeffe fakes already, remember? I'm sure he's been more than careful."

"And I guess we'll hear about that next. Hah—hah. I'm real glad."

"About . . ."

"Your secret. I worry sometimes. I ask so much of you, I think sometimes maybe you don't have anything of your own. So tell me, woman, what else do you do when I ain't lookin'?"

Potts had elected to walk. The wind had died down for the night, and he needed the air, the time to review the day's work. He walked at a leisurely pace—there was no hurry, it wasn't eleven yet—past the now dark facade of the Roundhouse, seat of the state government, turned left on Dan Gaspar, and took the familiar course through the maze of side streets.

He reflected on the glow of his triumphant show-and-tell at the gallery. After the group had come forward to inspect the painting, the oohs and ahs bubbling up from the usually sophisticated veneer, he had explained more about his remarkable find. He told of his astonishment, his doubts—all the greater since here by some extraordinary happenstance were almost exactly the paintings he had imagined the artist creating. There was something almost mystical about it, and, he had said, it would have been far easier to say that he had simply found them. To confess that he had, in a sense, *predicted* them, might well sound strange to cynics, and might even make the paintings' authenticity seem *less* likely. But it was so extraordinary a thing that he, Potts, had known from the outset that he would have to be utterly up-front, explain every detail, even those that seemed dubious. He did, he said, have a record on his PC—the notes he had made to himself last year about his upcoming lecture—but of course, he pointed out, a cynic could say that nothing was simpler than rigging a date in a computer. He had shrugged and smiled.

In any case, this was too important a moment in the history of American art, among other things, for anyone associated with it to be anything but totally forthcoming. He went on to explain, sparsely, the nature of the authentication process he had subjected the paintings to, saying that when he held his press conference the next day, he would have time to provide more detail, and all the documentation, of course.

Of course, the announcement was momentous to the max, he had said, and the impact would certainly have been greater if he had simply called a press conference first and announced it to the world at large. But he felt a particular loyalty to this group who had shared so much with him over the past couple of years. "I wanted you to be the first to know," he had said simply. "I suppose some public relations hotshot would say that was stupid, sentimental, but . . ." He had shrugged again and smiled, looking into the distance, and the group had all understood the unspoken: money, fame, none of that meant as much as the art form embodied in true and honest human relationships.

At 11:05, Potts let himself through the gate of the chain-link fence that surrounded a one-story stucco box of a house, brown stucco like its neighbors, small windows with metal mullions painted Virgin Mary blue, one of a row of 1950s-vintage houses in an Hispanic neighborhood that was not, he reflected, long for this world. Not far off, this side of Cerrillos Road, young artist types, what would earlier have been called hippies, had begun moving into the superannuated old warehouses, fixing them up into slightly less bedraggled pads, and these had soon given way to more accomplished artists and craftspeople, with more money (or talent). The perimeters of the old neighborhood were becoming gentrified, and, in the nature of things, the center would have to give.

Soon an old house like this would be worth less as a structure than the quarter acre it commanded, and it would be razed and replaced by a house worth at least a quarter of a million dollars. Where, he wondered, will all these people go? And where would the blacks on Key West go? Potts sympathized with their frustration and anger over the juggernaut—a kind of invisible force field, or a restless spirit, that entered a neighborhood and couldn't be fended off by any magic known to mankind: economics. Potts also knew that he, with his gallery and all the rest, was precisely part of the problem here in Santa Fe, one of the very lodestars that brought new people, new values, and big bucks into this old and tired City of the Holy Faith. Once a vivacious and ever-rejuvenating courtesan, someone had said about Santa Fe, it had become now a slightly tired old whore.

God, how he loved this city, this splendid old whore.

From the pocket of his Peterman twill pants he took a key ring and inserted one of its several keys into the lock on the front door—a shiny, new, and more formidable lock located two inches above the frail old one. A crisp new lock with sharp edges that jerked a more powerful bolt from its lodging place; not the friendly worn-down slot the key slid into with a minimally metallic purr. Another sign of changing times, he sighed.

He entered directly into a living room, sparsely furnished, with a few excellent pots from the Rio Grande pueblos blending harmoniously with the pious santos on the white walls. A single table lamp illuminated the room with an orange glow, and light glinted from the thick, passionate brush strokes of a Namingha painting on the wall, a small but superior early work that Potts had bestowed on the house from his own small but admirable collection. In the painting, a large figure with a beaked mask arose from a sunstruck mesa, commanding, even providing in some strange way, the sky. Before the painting, in a white terry-cloth robe that ended just above mid-thigh, with her long, rich black hair hanging wet around her shoulders, the woman stood barefoot, extending toward him a blown glass tumbler filled with ice and golden-brown liquid. Her black eyes danced.

"How did it go?" Norah Vargas asked.

"Great," Potts said.

"Here. Have some of this and take off your clothes."

"Don't mind if I do," Potts said.

God, how he loved this city. He looked down at the

top of Norah Vargas's raven-haired head as she unbuckled the belt of his tweed jacket.

"You'll tell me *all* about it after," she murmured.

Connie Barnes sat on the edge of the bed, brushing her long black hair in deliberate, powerful strokes like a calisthenic. It was one of the most satisfying rituals of her day, letting her mind idle.

She was, at this moment, recalling some old black-and-white photographs of her people back in the 1870s or thereabouts. It's funny, she thought. Since then we've all become so *modest*. In the old pictures, children could be seen running around naked among the old stone houses, and even some of the women wore nothing but a skirt woven out of cotton, just like the men. She wondered why the olden-time Hopis, who had not particularly welcomed most of the ideas of missionaries and the other white people, had taken so thoroughly to their ideas of proper dress, covering the body.

By now this kind of modesty was ingrained in Hopi people, and she guessed other Indian people, too. What a funny trick. It had been only a couple of years ago—after three years living here with Mo—that she had begun to feel comfortable being openly, flagrantly, naked. And Mo, of course, couldn't even see her. It had taken her three years to realize that, when it came to nakedness, the lights were always out for Mo. So who cared?

She had. But gradually she had taken to the idea and found the practice—the feeling of the air everywhere on her—delicious and a bit, well, mischievous. Even now.

"I love it," Mo said, lying on his back on the other side

of the bed, "when you don't put on those voluminous goddamn nightgowns. Spend half the night fightin' my way through all that cloth. Never did understand how you put up with that, all that stuff bunching up around your hips."

Connie continued stroking her hair, idly inspecting the big man's body. So familiar, so unutterably strange.

"How do you know what I'm wearing?"

"You remember how W. C. Fields used to say, when he had a hangover, that his head hurt from the crashing of dandruff on his velvet Chesterfield collar?"

"Mo, I never heard of W. C. Fields."

"Just as well. Terrible person. Anyway, tonight I can't hear the awful grating, the metallic screech, of all that damn silk you used to wrap yourself in every night before we went to bed. It was like a fingernail on the chalkboard."

"It put you off."

"Not for long, as I recall."

Connie put the brush down on the bed table and switched off the lamp. "Don't you have any questions?"

"About what?" Mo asked, alarmed.

"About Elijah. Those paintings."

"Oh, that." Mo sighed in the dark. "Well, it does raise the whiskers of a man's curiosity. But it'll keep. As a matter of fact, I would've thought that before you turned off that light there, my current interest was kind of clear."

Connie laughed, a soft, high-pitched sound. "That's a real interesting name for it."

"For what?"

"Hi, there, current interest."

four

Carolyn Marcy—resident of 12B Lovatos Street in Santa Fe, employed as a waitress at the Mediterranean Light restaurant on Guadalupe Street since January 14—had been an undergraduate student at the University of Illinois in Urbana for three and a half years. She had taken a few years off between high school and college, enrolling as a freshman at age twenty-one. She was from a small town in southern Illinois, Olney, and was the sole child of Dr. James and Mary Ellen Marcy. She had lived off campus in a group house in nearby Champaign, been an average student, relatively unambitious but bright enough to get by, majored in art history, and played two years on the women's soccer team. She had left at the end of the previous semester, halfway through her final year, "for personal reasons," declaring her intention to return a year hence and finish her major. The only medical records in the university files showed that she had, in her freshman year, done some minor damage to the anterior cruciate of her right knee in soccer practice.

"No, Sergeant, there are no dental records." The woman on the other end of the phone laughed. "College age kids just don't go to the dentist, as a rule. Unless something gets broken. Now, the ice hockey team . . ."

Ramirez quickly thanked her for her help and hung up.

Olney, Illinois. Ramirez pulled a three-year-old Rand McNally road atlas out of his desk drawer, thumbed to Illinois, and found Olney—a dot on the map. He leafed into the index and found that Olney possessed 9,026 souls, one of which had once been Carolyn Marcy. He wondered if she was still counted as a resident. Back to the state map: from the network of frail lines around the area of Olney, he suspected he was looking at farm country, but nothing by way of an image came to mind. He had never been east of San Antonio or north of Denver. But a town of nine thousand was big enough to have its own police department.

He had wanted to make these calls yesterday afternoon soon after his interviews at the restaurant, but first he had spent an hour assigning the few men he could manage to get at his disposal to see what, if anything, they could turn up at the bars and auto shops where a lot of those guys Carolyn Marcy was evidently attracted to hung out. Then he had been summoned by his lieutenant to a departmental meeting—another discussion of procedure and *intercultural* relations. The general idea was that these relations were falling apart in Santa Fe, and the chief had some thoughts about making some minor changes in procedure that would be less inflammatory.

Ramirez, who considered himself inherently courteous, was nevertheless known as very prickly about no-goods, and during the meeting he spent most of the time wondering to himself why people who make a practice of breaking all the laws they can think of then get so uppity when someone calls them on it. There is no hypocrite like the criminal hypocrite, Ramirez had concluded, and not for the first time. And he kept to himself the suspicion that had started nagging him since he was confronted with the woman in the Dumpster.

By the time the meeting ended, the people at the University of Illinois had gone home for the day.

Now, he noted, looking at his watch, it was nine-thirty in Illinois. He picked up the phone, punched the buttons for southern Illinois information, and within two minutes had introduced himself to Chief Eggerton ("that's Bobby Jay Eggerton") of the Olney Police Department, whose voice reminded Ramirez of the time he had heard a guy on the sidewalk making some kind of awful music using a muffled drumstick and a crosscut saw. Chief Eggerton knew the Marcy girl, of course—"pretty thing, but kind of stuck up"—but was unaware that she had left the university and wound up in Santa Fe. "Ain't that some kind of art colony?" he asked. "I think she was studying art or something up at Urbana."

Ramirez patiently explained his interest—the Marcy girl not reporting for work, matching in a general way the body they had found—and asked the chief if there was any way he might be able to obtain any dental records for the Marcy woman. Perhaps this could be done without alerting any next of kin, no sense in getting anyone upset unduly when . . . Ramirez trailed off and listened to the chief, who was taking long, deep breaths apparently through his nose. Ramirez guessed the man had a deviated septum.

"Chief?"

The man emitted a snort. "Well, now, that's not gonna be so goddamned easy. Only one dentist here in Olney. Name is James Marcy. Carolyn's dad."

"Mierda," Ramirez said.

"Huh?"

"Clearing my throat."

"Oh. Well, this is a pisser, let me tell you." The chief sighed. "I'll get back to you."

Ramirez gave him the number in his office and hung up. No matter how it turned out, that poor bastard James Marcy was going to have a lousy day. He wondered if Dr. Marcy, the dentist, would keep it to himself until it was clear whether their daughter was merely AWOL from work, or dead. Or would his wife Mary Ellen get to share the day, maybe two days, of terror?

What was it Chief Bobby Jay had said? She was "kind of stuck up"? That didn't sound right, didn't sound like a girl who'd get her kicks from putting out for the low-rider crowd.

Ramirez turned to the pile of paper in his in-box. Routine junk, the blood of the department. He was hungry. Again, second day in a row, he had skipped breakfast.

The phone on his desk buzzed and he picked it up: "Ramirez . . . No, we won't have anything to say about that until . . . Yes, at the regularly scheduled . . . Well, that's very interesting, but it's not a conclusion we have reached . . . No, we're not even actively looking into it . . . It's only about eight-thirty in the morning. Are you trying to be the early worm?. . . Right, bird. Early bird . . . Always a pleasure, Miz Burgess."

* * *

Samantha Burgess placed the phone receiver in its cradle with exaggerated care and looked up to the heavens, or at least as far in that direction as the dead-white acoustic tile that formed the low ceiling above her claustrophobic little cubicle in the reporters' bullpen at the Santa Fe *New Mexican*.

She shook her head. Early worm? How did a guy butcher clichés like that? Ramirez, the homicide detective, was smooth, highly professional, and a worthy quarry for the *New Mexican*'s investigative reporter. He knew how to use the press and how to stiff the press, played a great game. How was it a guy like that got his clichés so mixed up? A regular Dan Quayle.

Samantha had a lot on her plate this morning—or, she reflected, maybe too many chefs passing the plates, as Ramirez might say. First, the woman in the Dumpster, then the story she'd heard about Potts and his O'Keeffes. She'd had the thought the night before, sitting on the Hide-A-Bed sofa before opening it up for the night, that the woman in the Dumpster had a couple of salient things in common with the woman in the landfill besides the fact that they were both murder victims. Both had been treated as garbage, and both were Anglo. So, her mind fueled by suspicion, a bit of tequila, and hope for a real story, she had thought maybe it's ethnic. It was no secret that some of the Hispanic population in Santa Fe resented what was going on at a dizzying rate in the city. Maybe the gangs, recently sprouted, were up to more than tagging. Ramirez seemed to be saying that he didn't think that was a factor.

Sure.

Then the phone had rung and a friend told her about hearing Elijah Potts make his announcement at the Southwest Gallery. Seven new O'Keeffes, oils—all on the theme of a baby? A formal announcement to the press tomorrow.

Which was today. So how come there hadn't been some official word, some announcement of a press conference? Then it struck her. Why would *she* have been notified? Art wasn't her beat. She glanced across the bullpen—array of empty, messy desks, each with low movable walls on two sides—a sop to noise prevention—and each with a PC staring with a dead eye at an empty chair. It was, after all, pretty early. Across the room, the new art editor's chair was empty like the others. Samantha rose, made her way through the maze and peered over his desk. He kept his calendar pinned to the wall.

POTTS, it said. 11 AM.

Samantha smelled fraud. Fake. O'Keeffe was eminently fakeable. In fact, Samantha had arrived in Santa Fe only a few months after the last great O'Keeffe fraud case had been tried in state court and people had still been buzzing about it. At the time she was barely managing to support herself by writing freelance—mostly puff pieces about local artists for one of those magazines they put in the hotels. The fraud case—*New Mexico* v. *Wittgenstein*—involved a middle-aged woman named Herta Wittgenstein from Austria who was selling phony O'Keeffe sculptures to greedy yuppies and got caught—and around the same time she was caught for practicing medicine without a license. She served twenty months in prison out of a possible four and a half years.

"Investigating my desk?" a voice said behind her. She turned to see a pinched frown become a fake smile on the face of the new art editor. He was a slender man, wiry, with a face that looked younger than she knew he was, and a controlled bush of curly, light brown hair. A Californian newly arrived, he had adapted like a chameleon to his new ecosystem and was now a study in blue denim and turquoise.

"Oh, hi, David, I was just checking on the time of that press conference at Southwest Creations."

"It's an announcement of some sort," David said pointedly, "to the art world."

"Do you know about what?"

David shrugged. "No, something they're trying to hype. They used the word *historic* twice in the come-on. Why?"

"I thought I'd go," Samantha said.

"Whatever for? I thought you were confined to dead things—dead bodies, deadbeats in government." He smiled again, from the upper lip down.

Bastard, Samantha thought, saying, "I've always been an art buff."

It was, Mo Bowdre admitted to himself, a virtuoso performance, and he had been prepared to be bored, annoyed, and skeptical. But he had sat, erect as a post, in the same chair he had inhabited the night before, all his available senses scanning the scene like a set of radar screens slowly turning in the night sky, listening for the telltale insect sound of falsehood, half-truth—a con. The quaver in the voice, or words going by a little too fast in the explanation of something complicated, or the unconscious over-accenting of the hypnotic words of authenticity.

He had no particular reason to mistrust this man, Elijah Potts, who had always seemed congenial and self-contained and serious since he had arrived on the Santa Fe scene—what was it?—a decade ago. Talked a lot of bullshit about art and myth and all that, but who the hell didn't? But the sudden emergence of several million dollars of liquid assets in the form of seven heretofore unknown paintings by Georgia O'Keeffe, the absolute frigging icon of the Southwestern art world—their appearance by some marvelous accident in the hands of precisely someone who would know how to make the most of it—well, he himself would have been as dumb, Mo thought, as Texas dust not to be suspicious. Like everyone else in the room—that is, the Press.

Evidently the room was packed, all the little chairs filled up, and he had heard people whisper that the art man from *Time* magazine was there, as well as a guy who said he was representing *Newsweek*. Two of the four TV networks were on hand, along with CNN. Mo could feel the heat of the lights. He had been allowed in—it was otherwise confined to the press—because, Connie had told him, she was part of the story, having been present when the paintings were first found in the shed in Canones.

"And you're going to testify about that?" Mo had asked her earlier that morning at breakfast when she announced her intention to take him with her to the gallery that morning.

"It's not a trial, you know," she had answered. "Elijah just wants to get the whole story out at once."

"How do you feel about that?"

"About what?"

"About being put on public display, bearing witness to all this."

"I was a witness to when they were found. I don't mind saying that. Anyway, I wrote it all down for him already."

Mo's shaggy blond eyebrows had danced over his sunglasses, and he had lapsed into silence, addressing instead the last of three pieces of bacon on his plate.

Now, sitting in the gallery among the predators of the press, it occurred to him that, so far as he knew, no one had yet tried to palm a fake T. Moore Bowdre sculpture off on a greedy and unwitting public. He turned aside the thought as nothing but envy and unearned vainglory—and then thought how sad it was that everyone, including him, had come here with eyes already veiled by presumption of fraud. But then again, why not? It was a slippery and often felonious world, the commerce of Art—this world he had stumbled into mostly by accident.

Yet by noon most of the members of the press were convinced that these paintings were authentic. Rejected by the artist—yes—but authentically her work nonetheless. Engagingly, slowly, Potts told the story in chronological order, beginning with his imaginings of what paintings O'Keeffe might have painted and not kept, then finding them in the shed of the house in Canones he had bought. He was joined that day in December by Anita Montague and Connie Barnes, the CPA and Indian art appraiser, and the paintings had come to light when, in the course of exploring the new place, they noticed a collapsing false adobe wall in the shed. They dug around, pulling away some more of the rain-eroded adobe bricks, and came across the cache in a metal trunk. Anita Montague had been first to spot them, and had pulled back, having also spotted a festooning of spiderwebs and fearing black widows.

At this, Connie whispered, Anita smiled and stuck out her tongue.

Then Potts stepped over to the wall, and Mo heard a curtain screeching and swishing across the room. While the crowd could be heard murmuring and swearing, Connie told him that all seven paintings were mounted on easels.

"You can imagine, perhaps, the shock of recognition we felt. . . . Here, certainly, were works in the style of O'Keeffe, the pelvises she painted beginning in the Forties, but with a difference which I am sure you have all noticed. Clearly, in one degree or another of abstraction, we have here a child, an undeveloped child—seen through the pelvis and, in this one over here, having faded almost invisibly into her beloved mountain, Pedernal. There. You see how it has now become almost indistinguishable from a mere highlight on the mountain itself. Like a sublimation, or perhaps"—he paused—"a silent interment."

Potts waited a moment, and then said, "And of course you can imagine the suspicion that flooded over us. Fakes, of course. But O'Keeffe threw away a lot of her work that didn't suit her, and it was reasonable, even likely, that when she got caught up by those cow pelvises, she made some paintings that didn't work. So maybe, we thought, she threw these out, someone found them, and cleverly added this representation of a baby, a fetus, whatever. And somehow they ended up in this secret niche in Canones. And, oh—for you out-of-towners, Canones is a small village about ten miles west of Abiquiu, the town where O'Keeffe lived and worked almost till the end of her life. Canones is almost literally in the shadow of her mountain, Pedernal.

"Now, you will forgive me, I hope, if I provide a little lesson in science. There are numerous ways to tell if a painting has been retouched or altered after it was originally painted. One is X rays; another is ultraviolet rays. Basically, in ultraviolet you take a mercury vapor lamp and shine it in the dark at the painting or object. With a special lens on the camera, you photograph the object, and only ultraviolet radiation reaches the film."

Potts held up a large black-and-white photograph of an elaborate metal box with legs. "This is an eleventh-century Chinese vessel, apparently in perfect shape." He held up another print. "This is from an X ray of the vessel, and you can see that the lower right-hand corner of the vessel has been resoldered, and rather clumsily. It had been damaged and then, at some point, restored."

Potts held up yet a third photograph. "The sloppy soldering was then covered over by a new patina. The patina had in it an organic compound to make it bind with the metal and solder, and that compound fluoresces in ultraviolet light. You see? These light swirls here, whereas the rest of the vessel is utterly black."

Potts put the photographs aside and said, "We subjected these seven paintings to the same X-ray and ultraviolet treatment. There was no fluorescence, no sign of restoration or alteration of the originals. In the press kits you will receive after this meeting, you'll find a similar set of photographs of one of these paintings. It is accompanied by an affidavit from Microbeam, a lab in Chicago, where they performed this test, and others I'll characterize as briefly as possible."

He went on to explain that X-ray analysis, which can show the details of what lies below a painting's surface as well as what lies below the skin, found the same elaborate underpainting of the canvas—several colors under a layer of white—that O'Keeffe commonly used. Infrared analysis had confirmed this. Chemical analysis, he went on, had shown that the pigments used on the seven paintings were identical to those O'Keeffe was known to have used in this period.

"In short," Potts said, "and there's a great deal more detail on all this in your press kits, for all that the techniques of science can show, these are not fakes. But that doesn't prove conclusively that they are authentic. There's more to art than even modern science can analyze.

"Let's think for a moment about what a forger confronts. He—or, of course, she—has in front of her the work of another artist. An authentic painting. A painting tends to grow from the first brush strokes to the last, and in ways that may not always be completely predictable by the artist. In that sense, the painting has something of a life of its own. On the other hand, the forger is starting with a firm idea in his mind of what this other artist's paintings look like as finished products. He or she has to work backward from that idea—not forward, not inventively, not spontaneously. And to a practiced eye, there may be little signs of hesitation, of too great care. There are also other subtle matters of style, brushwork, composition, color—in all, the verve of a great artist—that a forger may not be able to quite perfectly match. These are judgments that usually only the original artist or a true expert can make. And we have one with us here today. I'd like to have Mr. Nelson Adams Lockman speak to these matters. He is, as I'm sure you know, curator of twentieth-century American painting at the Chicago Institute of Fine Arts. Mr. Lockman?"

Mo heard people turn in their chairs as the man called Lockman walked from the back of the room to the front. "What's he look like?" Mo whispered.

"Business suit," Connie whispered. "Gray. Pinstripe. Real white skin. Hair's blond, blonder than yours. Maybe forty, forty-five."

People shuffled their feet, an impatient and restless classroom.

"He's got a nice smile," Connie whispered.

"I think I'll stand over here, Elijah. Ladies and gentlemen, I'll be brief. I know you have questions for Elijah bursting in your very hearts. As you may know, the Chicago Institute of Fine Arts owns a significant collection of O'Keeffes, thirteen in all, including one called *Pelvis and Blue* from the same period as these would appear to be. That is, between 1943 and 1946. Ours was done in 1944. Stylistically—for example, the practically invisible brush strokes O'Keeffe mastered, producing a finish that seems almost photographic—there is no noticeable difference between these paintings here and the ones in our possession.

"These paintings, you can see, were painted beyond the canvas, around the edge of the frames on which the canvas is meticulously stretched, particularly meticulous at the corners, in O'Keeffe's manner. In every detail that I have scrutinized, and that is every detail on these canvases, there is nothing technical or stylistic to suggest that they were not painted by O'Keeffe."

The crowd murmured.

"But," Lockman said, "there was something about them that bothered me, a kind of gut reaction after I had looked at them the first time. This uneasy feeling stayed with me throughout my detailed examination. It finally struck me that these paintings simply didn't *work*. They were missing some slight degree of passion, or spirit, or—what was your word, Elijah?—verve that O'Keeffe infused her paintings with. This one, in particular," he said. "You see how she came in close on the pelvis, like a close-up photograph. Too close, in fact. There's not enough pelvis, too much sky. There's a lack of her amazingly subtle compositional balance. Of all of them, this one works the least.

"I was about to inform Elijah here that he had uncovered some preternaturally skillful forgeries of O'Keeffe paintings—unbelievably skillful—when it dawned on me. They weren't fakes. They were rejects. And when Elijah told me where exactly they had been found, it made perfect sense. The woman threw away uncounted works, and she wasn't always careful about how she disposed of them.

"So it is my conclusion, which is spelled out formally in the next issue of *Ars Longa*, the Chicago Institute's journal, that these are in fact authentic paintings by Georgia O'Keeffe, produced in the mid-Forties."

There was a single loud gasp from the crowd and a voice sang out: "What are they worth?"

"That would be hard to say," Lockman replied quickly.

"Why?" the voice insisted.

"Because it is a matter under present negotiation."

"You mean, the Institute—"

"That's really all I can say about that."

Voices erupted. "How about a ballpark figure?"—"Are we talking six figures? Seven?"—"Mr. Lockman, what if you're wrong? There's been a lot of . . ."—"Mr. Potts, who'd ya buy the house from?"

"Elijah?" Lockman said, and the voices subsided.

"From a local bank, as a matter of fact," Potts said. "The previous owner died, unfortunately, in great poverty and with a mortgage. So the bank took possession and auctioned it off. The owner before *him* is something of a shadowy figure. A fellow named Ricardo Gallegos whose name turns up in county records in the late Forties. Apparently a resident of Abiquiu, and maybe the same R. Gallegos who lived in Las Trampas for a few years before that. I heard he won the house in Canones in a poker game in the late Forties, and then disappeared. The house was vacant for about ten years after that."

"So this guy Gallegos . . . ?"

"Who knows?" Potts said. "One can easily speculate. But that's about all. Maybe it's a mystery that will never be solved. But the paintings exist. Are there any further questions about them?"

By twelve-fifteen the press had left Anita Montague's gallery and word of the new O'Keeffes bustled around the world on wire and modem in plenty of time to make the evening news programs. Locally, word of the O'Keeffes had already spread through the town's art crowd like a wildfire borne on Santa Ana winds through Malibu's posh backyards. A few Santa Feans began to show up at the gallery, only to find a sign on the door: CLOSED UNTIL APRIL 20.

Ramón Tofoya approached the gallery at about this time, for an appointment with Anita Montague that she had totally forgotten. His hopes to land his first assignment as humane pigeon eradicator were dashed by the sign on the door, and the f-stop of his mind narrowed down instantly to a familiar paranoia and loathing. Standing on the cement step before the door, he unleashed his mantra out loud, finishing up the standard catalogue of bodily functions with a flip of the bird at the gallery door, and stalked off, much to the amusement of a handful of onlookers.

Waiters at Coyote Cafe, Santacafe, and the other spiffy restaurants heard nothing else emanating from their tables but talk of Potts, Montague, and the O'Keeffes—some of it celebratory, some of it suspicious, all of it eventually veering off into old-fashioned gold-standard gossip about the two principals and their presumed sexual preferences and exploits.

At Mediterranean Light that lunch hour, without going beyond her normal duties of squiring diners to their tables and making them comfortable, Norah Vargas overheard at least three women who had separately concluded that Georgia may have been a lesbian, but everyone knows she carried on as well with the dark young men in Abiquiu until . . . well, yes, until young Juan Hamilton came along and took care of her in her dotage. Yes, I surely remember the name Gallegos coming up. Who was it now, who told me about that?

Norah merely smiled. And smiled more broadly when, at another table, she caught a snippet of informed opinion that Elijah Potts was, of course, gay.

Speculation at the tables about price was rampant, ranging from the low six figures by those purists who took it seriously that, after all, these paintings were rejected by the artist herself, to more than a million apiece by the more commercially astute.

By one o'clock that afternoon Samantha Burgess of the *New Mexican* had eaten a hamburger and drunk a Dr Pepper so fast it gave her stomach pains, and she was on her way in her aging Toyota to Canones, followed later by three out-of-town reporters in rental cars, each of whom took wrong turns in Espanola and spent more than an hour exploring the wrong Hispanic towns of northern New Mexico.

By three o'clock that afternoon Mo Bowdre realized that he was hearing an eerie silence. The wind had not come up, and he recalled his bargain with himself. Having made arrangements to meet his friend Tony Ramirez of the SFPD for dinner at a restaurant called Maria's on West Cordova Road, he shuffled off to his studio made of stone. But once there, he discovered that he didn't feel like working. He persuaded himself that just because the wind hadn't come up today didn't mean the spring winds were over for the year, so he punched the button on his small but efficient CD player and listened to the first bars of Brahms's Symphony No. 3 and began sharpening his tools, the most calming ritual known to mankind.

Once, years before, Sergeant Anthony Ramirez had been visiting a friend with an overgrazed backyard and two horses in it that decided to cavort and dance while he was looking at them across the wire fence. They kicked up great clouds of dust, and Ramirez had gotten something in his left eye. Whatever it was, it caused an immediate and violent allergic reaction. His eye swelled shut, he sneezed in grand paroxysms, and before long he had a deep-seated itch in the palms of both hands as well. His host, who was a doctor named Daitz, gave him four Benadryls and the last Chlor-Trimeton in the house, and soon enough the allergic reaction subsided but for the itching palms, which persisted for twenty-four hours, an insatiable, demanding sensation that allowed him no peace to concentrate for long on other things, even after he got over the antihistamine haze.

Now, when he hung up the phone after agreeing to meet Mo Bowdre for dinner, he realized that he couldn't remember where they had said they would meet. It would come to him, but he was distracted—possessed even—like the time his palms had itched so infuriatingly. But now the insistent itch buzzed from somewhere in his brain. It needed scratching—though Ramirez knew full well that would not make it go away. It would recur until it went away on its own, victim of facts. But not having much in the way of facts—only his itch—Ramirez left the office and drove out of the police station's chain-link-fenced parking lot and out into the traffic on Cerrillos Road, taking a side street over to Aqua Fría.

Ten minutes later he was standing just inside a gaping garage door that faced out onto an empty cement parking area surrounded with weeds and, beyond them, a low Cyclone fence. A few dingy residences lay beyond the fence, their yards cluttered with toys, old tools and machinery, and fossil cars. He let his eyes adjust to the shade in the garage, taking in what appeared to be a 1970 Chevy Impala, sitting up six inches off the garage floor on four jacks. It looked like it was made of maroon glass. The lid of the trunk gaped open before him, an empty maw. Emanating from somewhere up front, orange sparks danced in an arc to the floor, and a pair of expensive multicolored running shoes protruded out to the side from under the front end. On the oil-stained cement floor was an array of red-and-white marine batteries—six in all, cables, shiny metal cylinders, and two gleaming metal pumps. The running shoes belonged to Manuel Trujillo, and Manuel, Ramirez knew, manufactured the pumps and the cylinders himself, not trusting to anyone else the heart of the hydraulic system that turned simple

American-made vehicles of usually great age into shiny and bristling, custom-made extensions of the Hispanic male ego. With Manuel's hydraulics installed, this car would be capable of rising, dropping to within an inch of the pavement, hopping, pancaking down the road at four miles an hour in the mechanical minuet of the low rider.

"Hey, Manuel," Ramirez said.

The orange sparks stopped arcing out of the car's underbelly.

"I thought that was you," Manuel's high, gravelly voice said. "I could hear your cylinder, the one I already told you about. Got this characteristic sound of shit on shit. Man, you guys made a mistake when you decided to do your own maintenance over there."

"Manuel . . . ?"

"Like what mechanic, man, is going to bust his ass on salary? I tole you, piecework is it. Guy sets a price, does the job. You don't like the job the guy did, you go somewhere else. The guy knows that. Bust his ass for you. How come all you government people don't know nothing about human beings? It must be hard being a homicide detective, not knowing nothing about human beings, you know what I mean?"

"Manuel."

"Business, huh?"

"Yeah, sort of."

Legs and an associated body emerged from under the Impala, which Ramirez noticed had gold wire wheels with what looked like a gold propeller in the center of each hubcap. Thin whitewall tires.

"These are Daytons," Manuel said, following the

policeman's eyes to the gaudy wheels. "Top of the line rims, man. Eighteen hunnerd seventy-five for four. Best rims you can get. In L.A. they call 'em Killer Daytons. That's because the blacks'll kill you for 'em."

"Whose ride?" Ramirez asked as Manuel Trujillo stood up. He was five-foot-two, with graying hair in a short ponytail and two diamond earrings in his left lobe. He wiped his hands on a scarlet T-shirt that advertised Trujillo's World Champion Auto Service and Hydraulics.

"Kid. He put in a three-thousand-dollar patio at my place so I'm putting in his hydraulics. It's a good deal. Top of the line. Side-by-side, front and back—hey. See them coils over there on the floor? Hunnerd twenty-five dollars a pair—just the coils. So what's your problem?" Manuel's eyes were perpetually squinted, as if he were having trouble focusing, and he held his head tilted back above a startlingly thick chest. "Dead people again, I guess, huh?" he added, with a sound between a chuckle and throat-clearing.

"Two. Those Anglo women. You heard. So is this . . . ?"

Manuel laughed, a sound that came from deep in his throat. "An uprising? The Black Hand? Come on, amigo."

"You hear anything like that?"

"You jumping to conclusions?" Manuel said.

"It's my job. I also listen."

Manuel turned and walked over to a bench littered with tools. He picked out a large pipe wrench and gesticulated with it in a thick hand.

"We had a community here," he said. "Poor, yeah, but

a community. What happened? I was planning on being a wise man, an elder, a referee, someone who could make some sense to all these people. They got testosterone running high as a river in spring, comin' out of their ears. You know? Yeah, you know. Sons can do no wrong, right? Even if they do wrong, they can't do any wrong. So?" He shrugged and waved the pipe wrench.

"So we had elders," he continued, "explain things like cause and effect. Get things settled down. Like I was gonna be one of those, you know, in my mind. That's what I do this low-rider stuff for. Get the kids onto something besides their . . . but some of these guys, the gangs. Bang on each *other*, for chrissakes. Like self-mutilation. It's like their eyes've gone dead." He shook the pipe wrench at Ramirez, and then slumped. "Well, Anthony, you know how old men want to think they help create the world."

"You're waving that wrench around like I'm the problem," Ramirez said. "But I'm not the problem. I'm just a cop."

Manuel squinted even more tightly.

"So I'll keep my ears open," the barrel-chested mechanic said. "But I don't think it's that—a La Raza thing. But then, you know, the guys come here, the ones I see, they're into their vehicles. It's the bangers who raise all the shit."

"And you'll hear about it, right? If that's what it is."

"I hope I don't," he said. He put his hand on the glassy hood of the Impala. "You know, this kid here? He's saving the money to get Vicente Leyba to paint his hood.

You know Vicente? The airbrush legend. Two thousand dollars, man. Kid wants to put a coupla clowns on it."

"Clowns," Ramirez said. "Like the circus?"

"Kid says a lot of people don't like low riders but everyone likes clowns."

five

Route 84 plunges westward between sandstone bastions through which the once wild Río Chama flows east and south through a few dams, and Samantha Burgess caught an occasional glimpse of the nearly ten-thousand-foot, flat-topped mountain, Pedernal, ahead of her, looming above the other lesser, rounded mountains of the Jemez range. It looked just as O'Keeffe had painted it so many times—a perfect blue mountain. The reclusive artist had laid claim to it late in life. What was it she said? Samantha blinked. "God said that if I painted it enough, I could have it." Something like that.

Such simple words, the young reporter thought. Such mysterious simple words, meaning what, exactly? Probably something like the dance of reflected light on the surface of a stream—a distraction designed to keep people's eyes off what might lie below in the shadows of the water. O'Keeffe was like that, Samantha thought, painting and repainting her shadowed world in bright colors, deliberately obscuring its meaning, like an ancient oracle. Samantha shuddered as she passed the ragtag town of Abiquiu, perched on the little hills to her left, and soon swung off the highway onto the road that crossed the dam of Abiquiu Lake.

To Samantha, there was something sinister in the old Spanish settlements from here north into Colorado, isolated villages looking inward, living in some incomprehensible past, morbidly keeping to themselves and the secretive rituals of the Penitentes—the ominous reenactments, for all Samantha knew, of the Passion, invented when the settlers were forsaken by the friars, and still carried out in the secrecy of the little churches called *moradas*. O'Keeffe had painted *moradas*—stark, reductionist buildings with a simple cross, almost colorless in the sun that obscured whatever it was that went on inside their nearly windowless walls.

The little town of Canones was sprinkled haphazardly in a rumpled valley, surrounded on three sides with mountain slopes and etched with dirt roads that meandered and veered without evident design among silent, low houses, tiny farm fields, and the forgotten junk of rural life. Here and there the seemingly aimless road dipped to cross a narrow sliver of water, Canones Creek, that wound with singular purpose northward into Abiquiu Lake some three miles away.

Samantha bounced past what she took to be the local *morada*, obscured by thickets of brush, followed the dirt road past an outcrop of rock, and found herself faced with a choice. The road split into a fork. She slowed to a stop, looked at the map open on the seat next to her, frowned, and took the left, soon arriving at a galvanized steel farm gate, beyond which was an aged brown horse standing as still as a sculpture, dozing in the afternoon sun alongside the matte-finish blue remains of a sway-backed panel truck, sagging to the side on wheelless axles.

Samantha backed up, took the other fork and, having driven slowly past a few ramshackle masonry houses that seemed to have been evacuated only minutes before, finally stopped five minutes later outside a small adobe house surrounded with a low wall. It was on a low bluff that Samantha guessed rose above Canones Creek, and about half a mile from the nearest dwelling. She saw a few patches on the wall of the house where the stucco had fallen away from the adobe brick beneath. In back, among a healthy growth of last year's weeds, she spotted a second adobe building with the stucco flaking off, smaller than the house. A corner of the roof had fallen in. Rising from the low wall in front along the road, an adobe archway sported a heavy gate with a floral motif carved into its well-oiled, thick-grained wood. Brand-new. This, she thought, had to be the place—Potts's home away from home, the source of his coup and one-time residence of poker player Ricardo Gallegos, who subsequently vanished like a puff of incense. . . .

Oh, yeah? And where there's incense, she thought to herself, there's some secret. She didn't expect to turn up any secrets here, from this house, she merely wanted to see it, experience it, be on the ground. Whatever secrets were here probably dwelled in the memories of some of the old villagers, hidden in the run-down houses behind her, probably pondering at her passage through town from behind curtained windows and hooded eyes, here in the veritable shadow of O'Keeffe's mountain, Pedernal, which she knew from the map was only a few miles due west of Canones beyond a couple of smaller mountains. The story—whatever it was—lay here, she was sure of it, and she would worm it out somehow.

She got out of her car and closed the door quietly, as the sun vanished behind the green mountainside that hemmed in the valley to the west. She shivered, and pushed open the new wooden gate, wondering if that was the only improvement that Potts had made so far and, if so, what that said about the man.

Stepping through the low weeds around the house, she peered in a murky window beside the (unrefurbished) front door. She saw an empty room with white stucco walls and a highly polished wood floor. Around the corner of the house, another windowpane revealed a room cluttered with dropcloths and tools, buckets and ladders, with an ancient black woodstove, its stovepipe rising at a rakish angle toward the ceiling, stopping short of the hole in the flaking plaster.

She turned another corner, and saw the other building, the outbuilding where Potts said he had—they had—found the paintings. Against the near wall, a motorcycle was parked, a Harley, old, with New Mexico plates. One corner of the building was collapsed, as she had seen from the road, and she noticed that the entire building seemed to sag to one side like a tired animal about to lie down.

The shed, if that's what it was, lay beyond an overgrown patio of red sandstone, and sitting empty among the old dead stalks of snakeweed growing between the stones was a brand-new outdoor lounge chair pointed toward the west. On a white table beside it were two tall glasses, beaded with moisture, topped by slices of lime and full of what had to be beer. Samantha's mouth filled reflexively with saliva before it struck her that there was no one in the backyard. Just the beers, the table, the chair, the weeds, and the silence, except the murmur of the creek that lay beyond some willow thickets. So whose beers?

Samantha ducked her head into her shoulders as her eyes darted around the vacant yard, and she turned around, keeping her shoulder against the stucco wall of the house. She thought she heard something—a scuffle of a foot against the rough dirt and weeds around the house? She slipped around the corner and down the side wall of the house, passing the window of the cluttered kitchen, to the next corner. She breathed silently through her mouth and, eyes fixed resolutely on the weedy ground before her feet, stepped around the corner toward the gate and her car in the road beyond it. She took a deep breath, squared her shoulders and stepped over to the front door. She knocked three times, paused and heard nothing. She knocked again. Nothing. An icicle of panic grew in her chest and she was ashamed of it. Even so, she bolted across the yard and into her car.

After U-turning back toward town, she looked in the rearview mirror and saw a man standing with his arms folded in the archway, white hair gleaming against the reddish-brown adobe. Some old guy, maybe a local doing some work around the place, having some of the ranchero's beer with a pal. She wished now she hadn't been so jumpy.

Passing a few houses in the ramshackle town, she stopped in front of one made of gray stucco, a long narrow affair with a ragged porch with a tin roof. Two little boys in plaid shirts and jeans were playing in the dirt in front of the stoop. Samantha rolled down her window and the boys looked up.

"Hi, guys. Your mama home?" she called with an ingratiating smile. The boys looked down at the dirt, stood up and went in the house. Samantha turned off the engine, waited a full minute, and only then got out of the car. She had heard that was how you approached a Navajo house, and thought, What the hell, maybe . . .

She pulled open a creaking screen door and tapped on the windowpane. Presently, the door opened and a small woman as wrinkled as a raisin looked up at her, no expression discernible on the road map of her face.

"Um, ma'am, I'm looking for some informa—for someone who knew Ricardo Gallegos. He used to live here."

The old woman stood still.

"Ricardo Gallegos?" Samantha repeated.

She thought she saw the old woman's lips move and leaned forward. "Ma'am?"

The lips moved again and Samantha thought she heard the word "Nada." And the old woman closed the door.

This was going to be murder, she thought, trying to do anything in this eerie goddamned place. By the time she had driven past the cool blue reach of Abiquiu Lake, she reexamined and put out of mind the old woman and the man leaning against the archway at Potts's place. If it was Potts's place. She looked at her watch. Still time to get back to the SFPD and see if anything had developed with those two homicides.

Marvin Steiner was still amazed by the exotic decor of his adobe house off Garcia Street in Santa Fe. He had taken early retirement from the ad agency in New York, the kids were long out of college, married, all that, he had plenty of money. So he migrated to this shining other world of quaint streets, the oldest capital city in North America—if you didn't include Mexico in North America, which Marvin didn't—a place of style, art, and quiet. Marvin sat on a wide sofa, looking up at the ceiling—huge, round crossbeams, ponderosa pines the guy had said, with those poles lying across them. *Latillas*. That's what they were called. Rustic elegance, colonial gentility, old world charm under the big sky, the open country, the new life for a new man in his brand-new hacienda.

His wife Myrna had sprinkled Indian pots and kachina dolls around the place, in the niches of the walls, on a wall high above that screened off the upstairs foyer-entrance to the second-story guest quarters. In one corner, lit by a cleverly concealed, narrow-beam spot-light, was a glistening wood sculpture, curvilinear and smooth, but with a face like leather carved in it—some kind of shaman. It all looked new, exotic, and friendly to Marvin Steiner, who had just returned from a day spent at the bank and with his broker, and he sat sipping his first cold martini from a long-stemmed glass, luxuriant as the icy silver slipped down his gullet and exploded, a sensuous paradox of heat and cold in his stomach.

His wife, a short woman with round hips, appeared

in a long, loose-fitting multicolored garment—mostly oranges and reds—bearing a tray of hors d'oeuvres and a glass of red wine. She stood beaming on the tiled step that led into the sunken living room, and turned sideways.

"Do you like it?" she asked, and there was a loud thump. Myrna looked up and Marvin leaned forward on the sofa. Some of his martini lapped over the side of the shallow glass.

"What the hell was that?" he barked.

"It must be the pigeon man," Myrna said, stepping down onto the tiles of the living room.

"Pigeon man? What the hell is a pigeon man?" Marvin, who hated surprises, especially since his minor but terrifying heart attack right outside his office on Third Avenue in the middle of all those goddamned people, now heard his voice rising.

"Marvin, calm down," Myrna said, swinging her round hips onto the sofa. She put a hand on his knee. "I'll explain. A man came by this afternoon from the Humane Animal Control people, I think that's what it's called. He said he'd give the house a free inspection for pigeons roosting, they're getting to be a problem here in Santa Fe, and he said if he found we had a problem here, he could take care of it for us. No poison, or anything like that. He traps them, takes them away. Humane."

"Then what does he do with 'em?"

"He didn't say, Marvin, but—"

"Probably sells 'em to some Chinese food distributor for Kung Pao chicken. So?"

There was another thump from above.

"So he found droppings up there, in that attic-like place. He came back to catch them. He brought some traps. They look something like lobster pots, but bigger."

Marvin Steiner took another sip of his martini and felt better.

"A hundred dollars," his wife said. "He'll get rid of them and come back once a month for three months to make sure no others show up. Now have some of these carrots." There was another thump.

Marvin said, "Sounds more like he's tackling the little motherfuckers, not trapping 'em." He took another sip of liquid silver. "I made three and a half thousand dollars today," he said casually. "Over-the-counter stuff. Let's go to that gallery tomorrow. You know, the one you liked? Whatever your heart desires."

The antique phone on the antique desk in Southwest Creations rang with a genteel tinkle, and Anita Montague, glancing at her watch, picked it up. It was four minutes before six and she had begun to think hungrily about the salmon in her refrigerator, soft pink meat wrapped in crisp white butcher paper. Spread it with mayonnaise, the way her friend in Seattle did, and . . .

"Southwest Creations," she said. "Good evening." It was, in fact, beginning to darken outside the big window in front. But what did these newspeople care about time? Well, one more call and then . . .

"Is this Anita Montague?" said a woman's voice with the vaguely imperious tone of someone whose questions receive prompt and unambiguous replies.

"Yes."

"My name is Fredericka Ball Mansfield," the voice said. "Perhaps you have heard of me." It was not a question.

"Why, yes," Anita said. "Of course."

"I am from the Hensley Museum of Baton Rouge . . ."

"Yes, of course."

" . . . and, as I am sure you know, I've been commissioned by the O'Keeffe Foundation and the Hensley to produce a complete volume including all of the artist's known work. Two thousand two hundred in all. Everything. Naturally, I—"

"Yes, you would like to see the seven that have just come to light?"

"Precisely," said Fredericka Ball Mansfield. Anita reckoned, from her tone and her voice, that she was about six feet tall, in her late fifties. "I'll need to talk to you and Mister—ah—Potts about their provenance, inspect them carefully. This is not a development, I must say, that makes a scholar confident. But the proof is in the pudding."

"Of course," Anita said. "Perhaps you know Mr. Lockman of the Chicago—"

"Oh, yes. I know all about him. When can I see them, Ms. Montague? I am here in Santa Fe. At La Fonda."

"Perhaps tomorrow morning? I'll check with Elijah. Mr. Potts. Can you call at, say, nine-thirty?"

"Certainly," the voice said, and the phone went dead. Battle-ax, Anita said to herself, scowling, and added a protruding wicked-witch chin and, to the Mansfield frame, about thirty-five pounds. Another gauntlet to be run, and an important one. Anita hung up and saw a figure in the gallery window, a man with a straw cowboy hat and an absurd mustache—oh, God. That man about pigeons. He tapped lightly on the glass, smiled under the mouse-colored handlebars and raised his eyebrows obsequiously. Anita strode to the front and opened the door.

"I'm sorry, Mister, Mister . . . Tofoya, yes. I'm afraid I forgot all about our appointment yesterday. I'm terribly sorry. And of course, today we're closed. Would you come by tomorrow? Perhaps in the late morning. Thank you so much." She shut the door as the humane pigeon exterminator bobbed his head in peasantlike assent.

At last, Anita thought, crossing over to the desk. A whole evening to herself. A turn on her mountain bike, maybe up Bishops Lodge Road to Tesuque and back, a wickedly long shower, and that salmon.

Luscious.

She looked around at the gallery walls, the bold but somehow subtle landscapes in innumerable, unnameable shades of brown. The man was clever. But second rate, at best. As were the androgynous wooden sculptures of her sometime lover, Helga Windrow, she had to admit. The basic monochromatic look of the art featured now for two weeks had begun to pall on Anita's eye. It had been interesting at first, but now . . . ? Well, soon it would all come down for the grand display of the O'Keeffes.

My God, she thought. A fortune. And I own ten percent of a fortune. Just my share, she calculated, and not for the first time, is surely worth half again this entire gallery and everything in it. Even with that early Namingha painting, the one of the kachina rising up out of a dawn sky that Elijah had bought years before.

Come to think of it, she hadn't seen that painting for a few months.

She thought again of her share of the O'Keeffes. Maybe, she grinned, not *quite* half again what the whole place was worth. But she would soon be out of the gallery business. She couldn't imagine that Elijah would hang on to it after the O'Keeffes were sold. Who needed it? Certainly she wouldn't.

She wondered again where the Namingha was. It hadn't been on exhibit for several months. Elijah seemed to be unusually ambivalent about it, saying it was for sale, then changing his mind. So it spent a good deal of time upstairs among several other paintings. And Anita hadn't noticed it up there since . . . She couldn't remember. Curious, she went into the back room and up the stairs into the storeroom, returning ten minutes later, shaking her head. It was nowhere to be found. Maybe Elijah had loaned it to someone without telling her. He had done that a few times. Secretive devil, Anita thought with another smile, her curiosity raised even further.

The thick carved door slammed behind Sergeant Anthony Ramirez. Several people in the small room looked up from their tables, annoyed, their hair and words suddenly torn by the brief gust of wind. Ramirez smiled and shrugged at no one in particular and craned his neck to look around the room. It was the bar of Maria's Restaurant, with a separate entrance from the street, an entrance into which Ramirez had just let a resurgence of the tiresome spring wind. It was crowded, the eight cloth-covered wooden tables close together in a bustling camaraderie. A waitress with a big tray athletically slid her hips between chairs amid the buzz of conversation in both English and Spanish, punctuated by laughter mid-wived by sangría and margaritas. From some invisible loudspeaker Mexican music played with a cheerful tinniness, its volume cleverly gauged to provide an unobtrusive backdrop.

At a table close under the shoulder of the bar, Ramirez recognized a pretty woman who worked as an investigator for the State Attorney General's Office—infractions of the state's environmental regulations—and waved. She smiled, wiggled the fingers of her left hand at him, and returned her attention to a couple sitting with her.

In the far corner Ramirez saw his friend and dinner partner for the evening, Mo Bowdre, sitting oddly by himself, wearing a black cowboy hat that always seemed a size too small perched on the back of his big blond head, his beefy hand surrounding a mug of golden brown beer that Ramirez knew would be Negra Modelo. Some things do not change.

Bowdre was a creature of habit—and no wonder. Repetitive activities would be simpler for a blind man. For several years he had frequented—or perhaps held court was a better way of putting it—at Tiny's Restaurant, farther toward the center of town, and Ramirez guessed that it was mostly because Mo had memorized the serpentine path that took him home from there. But then, this afternoon, Mo had suggested Maria's and, hearing surprise in Ramirez's voice on the phone, had explained that Emma had retired to Silver City. Emma had been the waitress at Tiny's, a white-haired wraith who emerged at opportune times in the gloom to ask if everyone was happy. "Without Emma there," Mo had said, "it's just another trough. Friend of mine says to try Maria's as a hangout."

"Hey," Ramirez said, approaching the table.

"I wondered if that was you, washed in like flotsam and jetsam." The big man's smile gleamed through his blond beard. "I ordered you one of Maria's forty different kinds of margarita. You guess which one, I'll pay for it."

"Great odds," Ramirez said, sitting down. "Anyway, who *were* Flotsam and Jetsam? Some guys from that kids' book about wonderland?"

"Hah—hah. I think it was twin sons of that TV cartoon caveman. So what's new?"

Ramirez, who had had the sensation all afternoon that his brain was somehow unhooked from the actual world lying out there beyond his senses, began to relax in the presence of his oversized friend.

"Same old same old," he said.

"Right, just a couple of routine homicides, two women dumped in dumps, right, in two weeks? Now, Tony, that has all the earmarks of a serial killer, a monster loose in the streets. People already calling him the Santa Fe Trasher. Heard it on the radio." Mo leaned back, took a swallow of beer, and wiped his beard with his forearm. "Got a thing for Anglo waitresses. Dispatches 'em, throws 'em away like trash. That should narrow it down to some personality type. See, this homicide stuff is easy."

"What? What about waitresses?"

"Well, wasn't one of them a waitress or something at that place Mediterranean Light?"

"Where'd you hear that?"

"I was there when you were poking around. Put two and two together. That's not the kind of place you eat lunch."

Ramirez sipped at the edge of the huge glass bowl on an opaque glass stem that contained his margarita. "We don't have an ID on the first one yet. So, yeah, the second one was a waitress at that restaurant for the last three months. College kid. Came from Illinois. We got a dental match late today. Her father, for chrissakes, he's the town's only dentist."

Mo lowered his head and Ramirez let out a sigh.

"Think of it, man," Ramirez said. "That first one, it's two weeks now and no one—nobody—has reported anyone like her missing. I mean, she wasn't some kind of drifter, or something, from her clothes and all. But *no one* has called. Can you imagine? Nobody, no family who gives enough of a shit to wonder where she is after two weeks? How many people are there like that, I wonder?" Ramirez shook his head. "And, yeah, we've checked around, see if any other waitresses are missing. No die."

"Dice," Mo corrected unconsciously.

"Not even one," Ramirez said quickly. "Anyway, two bodies doesn't make a series. Those serial freaks usually do it the same way, and they usually don't do them so close together. You know, they get a big release, a big high, then wait till a head of steam builds up again, do the same thing like a ritual. One of these women was strangled, the other was a shotgun. Also no sex stuff. Those sickos almost always got some screwed-up sexual wiring. Both these women were even fully dressed. So we don't know what the hell is going on," he said. "Yet."

"They're both Anglo," Mo said.

"So what? Anyway, I thought of that. You don't get a pattern out of two. But I hate that idea, man, I hate it. Racial stuff. You can't do anything about it. It's like this fucking wind. So, let's eat, huh? You want me to read you what's on this menu?"

"Sure. You heard about the new O'Keeffe paintings? Seven of 'em, never seen before."

"Fakes?"

"Tony, don't you have any joy, any innocence, any trust left in that there gloomy Iberian soul of yours?"

"I'm a cop. That's how it is."

"You gotta put some faith in something, amigo. You ever thought of gettin' *ree*-born? You know, hallelujah? Speakin' in tongues, all that good stuff? Do you a world of good. I know. Had a cousin once, down-in-the-mouth kind of guy, like you sometimes, got himself reborn in a great big tent outside of Carrizozo and now he prays on his knees two times a day and God knows how many times on Sunday. Owns half of some shopping mall in San Antonio. Happy as a road runner on a lizard farm."

"Okay," Ramirez said, "They got your beef fajitas here, and your chicken fajitas, and your vegetable fajitas . . ."

* * *

At exactly ten-thirty, Marvin Steiner turned onto his street off Garcia and walked through the yellow pool of light cast on the ground by a streetlamp.

"Come *on*, Osborne!" he said, tugging on the leash at the other end of which was a typically floppy and good-natured Labrador retriever, sniffing up the delights of his local universe. As a kid, Marvin had heard of the advertising agency called Batten, Barton, Durstine & Osborne (now long defunct) and he had laughed, thinking it sounded like an empty trunk falling down a staircase. So, of course, when Myrna had come home from the pound with this two-year-old dog to share their golden years in the City of Holy Faith, Marvin had named it Osborne. Marvin was not unaware, either, that Myrna had rigged the whole dog thing to get her husband out on a brisk evening stroll—a half hour every night—for his quirky damned heart. Now a relaxed man, Marvin went along with the ruse happily, and felt better for it.

Osborne leaped ahead, paused, moved on, paused again, as they approached the Steiner driveway, shadowed between two vaguely circular patches of light, compliments of the city. Osborne lifted his leg on a lilac bush and peed long and loudly, Marvin waiting benignly as the warm liquid streamed off into the ditch that ran through a corrugated steel pipe under Marvin's driveway.

"Okay, boy? Home."

But Osborne paused again, snuffling at the steel pipe, his tail waving frantically in the shadows.

"Come on," Marvin said. "Let's go." But Osborne had dug in, snuffling mightily.

"What're you doing, Osborne? Come *on*! Get your nose outta there. What is that you got there?"

Marvin leaned down and peered into the pipe from which Osborne's jaws—clamped and with teeth bared—were tugging something. Marvin caught a flash of gold, something shiny and red, and then saw what it was.

"Auugh!" he shouted. "Jesus! Osborne, Jesus, let go for Christ's sake! Oh Christ, oh, God. Myrna! Osborne, goddamn it, let go. Christ, you pissed on it, Osborne! Jesus, a fucking *hand*! Myrna! Myrna, call the damn police!" With a superhuman wrench, Marvin pulled his dog away from the pipe, dragging it up the driveway, shrieking his wife's name in a voice that rose nearly to falsetto.

Five minutes later two uniformed policemen pulled up in a squad car, flashing garish blue light into the quiet street, and they were joined immediately by yet another squad car. Within another five minutes the police had ascertained that a woman's body had indeed been stuffed in the steel pipe under Marvin Steiner's driveway and that from what they could see of it—the head, an arm with a raggedly chewed hand—it showed signs of having been mutilated with something that left marks exactly like a bicycle chain.

Ramirez smiled to himself as his vehicle drifted down Canyon Road, having dropped Mo Bowdre off at his house there.

"What the hell are *cueritos*?" Bowdre had asked when Ramirez got to Maria's homemade posole on the menu, a dish said to consist of pork, posole, and cueritos. "Something creepy like brains?"

"No, no, like little pieces of bacon."

"Oh, okay, I'll have that. A bowl."

In fact, Bowdre had gone on to have three bowls of posole in succession while he distracted Ramirez with egregiously embellished stories of his youth in Lincoln County when, with a couple of mischievous friends, he had tried his damnedest to make Lincoln County famous for something else besides New Mexico's two best known former residents: Billy the Kid and Smokey the Bear. Ramirez had been unaware that a real Smokey the Bear had been found as a cub with burns from a forest fire in the Lincoln National Forest, brought back to health, and stashed in the National Zoo in Washington, where he got so much mail from kids that the zoo hired him his own secretary. Not likely, Ramirez had thought. A bear with a secretary. Even in Washington.

"See, New Mexico doesn't confer much by way of fame on its sons and daughters," Mo had gone on. "You name one New Mexican today who's a household word—besides maybe Tony Hillerman."

"And that O'Keeffe woman."

"Well, yeah, but she's dead."

"Well, what about all these Hollywood people moving in here?"

"Hah—hah—hah. Those folks got a long way to go before they're New Mexicans. Takes more'n an adobe house. Say, that posole is all right. Maybe I'll have just one more. . . ."

Ramirez's radio crackled now with his name, wrenching

him back to the present. D.B. outside a residence on a side street off Garcia, two units at the scene. He swung left on Camino del Monte Sol with his lights flashing and spun through the narrow, walled streets, arriving in less than three minutes, adding his headlights to the blue ones blinking violently among the posh homes. A uniformed cop trotted up to his vehicle, gestured to the Steiners' driveway, under which the body lay in a pipe, and said that two of the cops had located an abandoned mountain bike—a blue Single Track Trek 990—behind some pyrocanthus bushes a block away. The bike was intact, chain and all. In the little zippered pouch behind the seat they had found a pair of pliers, a couple of small wrenches, a pressure gauge, and an owner's manual which the uniform held up in a gloved hand.

"There's a name here on the owner's manual, Sergeant." The uniform, a young Anglo named Jameson, squinted at the booklet in the flashing lights. "Says Anita Montague. I guess that's her in the pipe, huh?"

"Mierda."

"Huh?"

Ramirez looked at the uniform's face. Maybe twenty-three, twenty-four. Freckles, for God's sake. An earnest young recruit with his face screwed up into what he imagined was a professional expressionlessness.

"Officer Jameson, what I said is 'shit.' "

six

A vast gap there, right in front. Damn. His tongue probed it with idiotic fervor—this new geography. Where was the tooth? Just a ripply, silky soft place through the gap, like the membrane of a bat's wing, so soft. Oh, there it is, the hard cylinder under his tongue, there! His tooth! How disgusting, he thought, dimly aware that he was only dreaming about his teeth falling out even as he grieved at the horror of decay, gums receding into mushy little shriveled. . . . And he woke up.

He lurched up out of bed, swearing to himself, and made his way into the bathroom, reaching for the little plastic container of dental floss.

"Nothin' like a damn premonition to make a boy behave," Mo Bowdre said, pulling off a long strand of floss and applying it to the still solid ramparts of his excellent big teeth. Within minutes he was standing under the plangent spray of the shower, the dial on its chromium head turned to MASSAGE, its rhythmic assault drumming on his neck and reverberating into his very sinuses. He breathed deeply of the hot steam that billowed up around him and knew he had a few years left in spite of his dream. He raised his head and let the hot water beat on it, and heard Connie's voice.

"What?" he shouted, and heard her voice again. "Wait a minute, I got water in my ears. Can't hear you." He turned off the shower and banged his head, one side then the other, with the heel of a palm.

"It's Anita," Connie said.

Mo pushed open the glass and aluminum door to the shower.

"Anita?" he said. "Anita Montague? What, is she on the phone?"

"No, Mo. She's *dead*." Connie's normally alto voice was a croak.

"Jesus. Dead? What happened?"

"They found her in a drainage pipe. Under a driveway. Over near Garcia Street." Connie's words came out in bunches, riding on exhalations from deep in her diaphragm.

"When?"

"Last night."

Mo reached out for her and felt a towel being thrust into his hands.

In the visionless dark of Mo's world, he sensed a shadow passing over him, like a diver knowing a manta ray has slipped by overhead. It wasn't *seeing*, but the sensation of sight, like he'd heard about amputees feeling a long-lost member tingling as if it were still there.

"Maybe you better sit down," he said. He heard the toilet lid drop, heard her sit down. "Well, goddamn," he said, and toweled himself off.

Connie nudged his hand, and he took his dark glasses

from her and jammed them over his nose. Wrapping the huge towel around his waist, he sat on the edge of the tub and sniffed in the vanishing steam.

"How'd you . . . ?"

"Molly called. She heard it on the radio. A bulletin, you know. They called the police around ten-thirty last night. Some guy's dog found it. Her. She was out on her bike. It's awful. I mean . . . Anita." Connie emitted a sound—*Eeeeeee*—that Mo had long since learned was an ancient Hopi response to the arrival of trouble, tragedy, or outright evil in their midst, a sound oft-repeated over the centuries the Hopi had dwelled on their remote mesas to the west.

"Uh, well, how did she die?"

"They didn't say, Molly said. Not an accident. A homicide."

"In a drainpipe? Jesus Christ," Mo said. "That's three."

"Three? Three what?"

Mo stood up. "Three Anglo women, killed in about two weeks, and dumped. In a dump, in a Dumpster, and in a drainpipe. That's the sort of pattern Tony Ramirez is always looking for. He was sayin' there might be something racial about it. Some of these Hispanic people are pissed off about what's happening here in Santa Fe. Hell of a way to make a statement—equating white women with trash."

"Mo, this is a friend of ours."

"Well, damn it, I *know* that. I'm just . . . well, what the hell are we going to do?"

"Call Tony?"

"We don't have to. Anyway, sure as hell he's in his o-fishul mode, you know, all clipped and terse. We'll just turn on the police band. Had it installed a couple of months ago, remember?"

Twenty minutes later, sitting in the living room on a large red sofa that faced a huge array of sound equipment, Mo and Connie knew just about everything they could bear to hear about the death of Anita Montague. The businesslike lingo cops use in the privacy—or assumed privacy—of their own world, including their radio band, can strike the laity as coldhearted at best, and the black humor they resort to while gossiping can seem ghoulish.

Mo reached out and pressed a button. "They just talk like that," he said. "Otherwise they'd go nuts."

"I know," Connie said, and sighed.

The medical investigator had been summoned last night to the scene—the driveway of the Steiner residence on a side street off Garcia. Steiner, evidently, had been so excited that he began suffering pain in his chest and arrhythmia, and his wife demanded that the cops call an ambulance, which carted him off to the emergency room for surveillance and tests. She told the police herself what had happened—Steiner out with the dog, the dog finding the corpse, evidently chewing on its hand, Steiner running in dragging the dog, yelling for the missus to call 911, and that's all she knew. She didn't know if Mr. Steiner had seen anything strange, or anybody, when he was walking the dog.

The M.I. had arrived by about midnight, and pronounced the cause of death a broken neck. Time of death probably between eight-thirty and nine-thirty. Evidently, someone had struck out at her with a bicycle chain, presumably as she rode past on her own bicycle, whipping her off the bike and onto the ground—various welts and bruises attested to such a fall, as did some evidently new scrapes on the bike itself, which had been found in some bushes not far off. The chain had wrapped around her neck twice and up around the lower part of her face—the marks in her flesh, both contusions and graphite in fine geometric patterns, were conclusive. Her lower lip had been torn partly off. Blood from this and other abrasions had been found on the ground and in the drainpipe, and tests would surely show it to be hers. Then the perp had simply snapped her neck from behind and shoved her, feet first, into the drainpipe under the Steiners' driveway. Scrapes on her legs, hips, and arms had resulted, along with a couple of tears in her biking suit. Her helmet was nowhere to be seen. The cops were well aware that this was the third Anglo woman in a little more than two weeks to be killed and dumped, like trash. The other two had been women in their twenties—early to mid-twenties—but this one was older. Mid-thirties.

"That's ugly," Mo said, leaning back in the sofa. Connie sighed again. A long time ago, at a community dance in a gymnasium in Salida, Colorado, where Mo and a buddy from the mine had eventually wound up one Saturday night in a fruitless quest for the working man's Holy Grail, two guys in cowboy hats had electrified the place by commandeering the middle of the floor, standing back to back and swinging bicycle chains over their heads in a lethal hum. Everyone had moved back against the wall and watched the chains, immobilized, the way mice might stare at a snake. Mo's friend, a guy named Fred who wore rimless glasses over eyes that looked like ice on a lake and who had never been known to smile, watched along with the others and eventually turned to Mo, saying, "I think we can get in under those chains." Mo had dragged Fred out of the gym and into their car and headed back to the mine. The picture was still fresh in Mo's mind, the two drunks with chains whirring over their heads like chain saws.

"Maybe we should call Elijah," Connie said. "Maybe he'll need—"

"Did Anita have family?" Mo asked, shaking his head to free it from the gym in Salida.

"I don't know, Mo. Isn't that real sad? I don't know."

Whenever events conspired to remind Mo Bowdre of the enormous chasm that separates women from men in so much of their approach to the world, he was given to seeking the answers for it in what he had learned at the University of New Mexico years before as an undergraduate, studying for a bachelor's degree in wildlife biology. He had early on been stunned by the sheer beauty of evolution, the canny way that nature had it worked out to produce such a grand and changing array of living things over such a long, even unimaginable time. Evolution was, one of his professors had pointed out memorably, the longest running drama ever, played out on a constantly changing ecological stage. This vision of the world had struck him as comfortingly true, something a man could hang his hat on. It gave him an immediate sense of place in what suddenly struck him as the grand cathedral of life, and while he realized that his niche in the cathedral was no more important than any other, it was no less important either. All this made a great deal more sense to him than the easy assertions about how the world works that were common to people like his Baptist parents.

When, as a boy, Mo would come across what was obviously the fossil of a fish nine thousand feet up on a mountain, it was a hell of a lot easier to think the mountaintop had been at the bottom of a sea zillions of years ago than to imagine the sea had covered the ground, receded, and then all those dinosaurs got spawned, coming and going for a while until the ground had leapt up nine thousand feet—all this activity in the paltry few thousand years since God, his minister taught, had decided to get things going in one fell swoop. Nothing, Mo imagined even as a junior high school kid, could happen all *that* fast, and he was relieved to discover the ponderous stretches of geological time and the sensible dance of evolution once he got to the university. It seemed perfectly reasonable to him that God or Whoever might well have simply created the rule book and sat back to see how the game unfolded. After all, if He was all-seeing and all-powerful, he was probably all-patient . . . and He just *had* to have a sense of humor.

All this, of course, was one of the subjects it had been easier not to discuss with his parents as he grew apart from them and the simple, unconcerned world of his childhood in Ruidoso, New Mexico. In Ruidoso, daily life was far removed from the grand tides of history and thought—and even the cacophony of rowdy new musical forms pounding the airwaves. In Ruidoso in those days, practically no one paid much attention to such alien phenomena as rock 'n' roll, even when they saw those strange people—"look like they got a bad case of St. Vitus dance and sound like a bunch of goats got their tits caught in the wringer"—on *The Ed Sullivan Show.*

His father had thought it just fine that Mo would turn out to be a wildlife manager, work outdoors for twenty, thirty years the way a man should, and get a nice pension from the state Department of Fish and Game. He thought it even better when his firstborn son decided, instead, to try his hand at medical school, to which he had been awarded a full scholarship, in Austin, Texas. Neither parent could understand why Mo left medical school after two years: so what if the professors said he wouldn't ever make a surgeon—there were lots of kinds of doctors, and all of them got rich.

There was simply no way for Mo to describe to them his discomfort—an unease he could hardly explain to himself—that he felt in the presence of the medical world. His father had simply stared at the wall in frustrated incomprehension when Mo—with all the arrogance and inarticulateness of youth—had exploded: "Damn it, Dad, a human being ain't the same as a carburetor, and I ain't about to be a glorified mechanic."

They had been standing in the family hardware store, and his father simply turned away and began poking through the wooden drawers with brass fittings that covered most of the paneled wall behind the counter, taking inventory of what he could understand. In fact, Mo himself didn't understand what he had just said, either, but he had said it, and the membrane between him and his father had somehow from that moment become impermeable to all but the kind of small talk that passes between acquaintances.

Now, sitting in a chair propped against a wall in the back of Southwest Creations, Mo's mind meandered comfortably in an ancient Pleistocene landscape largely of his own invention, a time when small bands of hunters and gatherers roamed a precarious and dangerous world, skirting the walls of ice that reached from the north, sketching giant antelope and bison on the rock walls of caves, inventing magic, and making themselves into human beings. All the basic stuff had to have come about then, Mo was sure, all of human nature, even the reasons why women always seemed more able to deal with a death than men. Hell, men were good enough at the practical stuff, scooping up the mess and getting rid of it, all that, but women always seemed capable of doing the right thing right away for the grieving. Say the right thing. Or not say anything, just offer a soft bosom in comfort. Make food materialize. That sort of thing. It surely had to be something about death being more understandable if you were also able to make life right there before your eyes.

Mo had not been able to think of anything appropriate to say when they had arrived at Southwest Creations that morning, invited in by a greatly subdued Elijah Potts.

"Well, damn, Elijah," is all Mo had summoned up and blurted out as he grasped the man's damp hand. "This is just terrible."

"I know, I know," Elijah had murmured, and Mo heard him enveloped in Connie's embrace, heard a small sob that he guessed was from Elijah. They had stood just inside the door, as in a frieze, for a long minute, the world around them silent but for the gusting of the wind outside, clawing up Canyon Road and making the gallery's carved wooden sign begin to squeak.

"Well," Potts said, and cleared his throat. "This is good of . . . I'm awfully glad you called, came over here. Nothing prepares you for . . . well, the police called. Early. Asked me to identify the, uh, body. She has an aunt, you know, somewhere in Delaware, I think. Parents died years back. God, it's all so *senseless*. Here, I can make some coffee."

Mo heard Connie say that she would take care of that, that Potts should sit down.

"In the back room," Potts said. "Through the door. There's a kind of kitchen."

"I know." Mo heard Connie walk to the back of the gallery, and felt Potts touch him on the elbow.

"We can sit down back there," Potts said. "The police will be coming over in a while."

"Is that Sergeant Ramirez?"

"Uh, yes. He was at the morgue earlier. Said he'd need to . . . talk to me."

"He's a good man," Mo said.

"A friend of yours."

"Yeah." Guided by Potts's light touch at the elbow, Mo stopped, turned and fit himself into a wing chair. "Tony's a gentleman."

Potts sat down. "Hmh," he said. "That's a word you don't hear much anymore." He sighed.

The two men sat in an uncomfortable silence until Connie returned, setting two mugs down on the table between them. The phone rang and she said she would get it, crossing over to the antique desk.

"Hello," she said in an abrupt but sullen voice. Mo cocked his head. "Huh? Yeah, this iss tha gall'ry. Huh? No. Nobody here. It's closed." She hung up.

"Who was that?" Mo asked.

"A reporter."

"And who were *you*?"

"Just the Inn-yinn help," Connie said. "Playing dumb. It always works."

Mo snorted. Potts said, "Thanks, Connie. Thanks. You know, this atrocity—people didn't used to die like this. Senseless. Pointless. There was always a reason. I can't think of any great story, any of the old myths, where someone dies for no reason at all. A lot of it sounds pretty arbitrary to us today—the way some goddess like Artemis gets furious because a mortal saw her naked by accident, and he gets run down like a deer. But at least there was an understandable human reaction, some explanation. But Anita . . . just out riding her bike. How do you explain that? Jesus. Yesterday—Yesterday here she was, her world really beginning to flower, the gallery and all, and bam, she's gone."

Mo reflected on the bizarre requirements of the human mind. Everyone needs to reckon with death, and here was this man Potts trying to rationalize a random killing on the streets of Santa Fe by searching through the files of old Greek myths, trying to think of what arrogant pig-headed deity of today could have been offended. Silly abstract thought. The intellectual's Band-Aid. It's called denial, Mo thought. The first step in the grieving process they'd talked about way back in medical school: DABDA. First denial, then anger, then bargaining ("bring her back, God, and I'll be good"), then depression, then—with luck—acceptance. Men, Mo reckoned, probably spend more time in the denial end of things than women.

"Didn't they have monsters back then?" Mo asked. "Just plain bad monsters, with ten heads and slavering jaws and all, lurkin' around in the rocks?"

"Personifications of evil," Potts said.

"Welcome to the streets of America."

Again Potts sighed.

Someone knocked on the door, and the next few minutes Mo would recall more like an unseen play on a darkened stage, a kaleidoscope of disembodied voices.

POTTS: Now who's that?

CONNIE: I'll go.

POTTS: No, I'll get it . . . I'm sorry, sir, we're closed.

VOICE: Closed? But the manager, she told me—

POTTS: I'm sorry, we're closed.

VOICE: Look, I'm not . . . the *woman*, the manager, I talked to her last night, she said I should—

POTTS: Excuse me, sir—

VOICE: Tofoya. Ramón Tofoya. Humane Control.

The manager, she said I should come by. . .

POTTS: I am *very* sorry—

TOFOYA: . . . about the pigeons.

POTTS: Pigeons? What are you talking about?

TOFOYA: You got a pigeon problem—

POTTS: What's this *pigeon* shit . . . ?

TOFOYA: Exactly, you got pigeon shit upstairs and—

POTTS: Officer! Officer! Can you help me here?

TOFOYA: Huh?

POTTS: Officer, we've had a tragedy here and this man—

TOFOYA: Shit.

VOICE: Hey, you, hey, mon . . . come back here!

POTTS: It's okay, officer, just some pest. Let him go.

NEW VOICE: Who was that?

POTTS: Oh, Sergeant Ramirez. I don't know. Some nut. Carrying on about pigeons, or some damned thing. My God.

RAMIREZ: May I come in? Gutierrez, you wanta wait out here? Mr. Potts, I just need a moment of . . . Hey, Connie.

POTTS: She and Mo have been holding my hand here. Come in.

RAMIREZ: That's good. Friends. You need friends at times like this.

CONNIE: You want us to . . . ?

RAMIREZ: No, no. It's okay. Stay put. Who was that guy again?

POTTS: I don't know. Some gibberish about pigeons upstairs.

RAMIREZ: Huh. Funny. The guy looked sort of familiar. Anyway. I'm sorry to bother you again. There's a few things I need to ask you about.

POTTS: Of course. Over here?

RAMIREZ: Miz Montague, she was the manager here in the gallery.

POTTS: Yes. And a ten percent partner. I hold the rest.

RAMIREZ: Kin?

POTTS: No, no relation . . .

RAMIREZ: I was thinking about her next of kin, Mr. Potts.

POTTS: Oh. Yes. She had an aunt in Delaware. I'll get you the address.

CONNIE: It's here. In her address book. I'll write it down for you, Tony.

RAMIREZ: Funny you should think I was talking about—

POTTS: There are rumors, Sergeant, about . . . us. More than business associates. That sort of thing. All hogwash, but you know how Santa Fe is.

RAMIREZ: Yeah. Under every bed there's a pea.

POTTS: What?

RAMIREZ: Nothing. Do you know about her whereabouts yesterday?

POTTS: She was here in the morning. We were conferring about the O'Keeffes. You heard about that? A great deal to be done, thought through, as you can imagine. A major exhibit. And she was going to be here all afternoon. The gallery was closed but she . . . business calls, reporters wanting information, all that. I don't know when she left. Normally she's here until the gallery closes at seven.

CONNIE: I talked to her about seven, Tony. I called her to see how things were going, you know? All the excitement. She said she was going to go ride her bike, get her equilibrium back? Then she was going to cook this salmon for herself. She went on and on about this salmon, how she was gonna cook it.

RAMIREZ: That was about seven?

CONNIE: Right around there. Lots of mayonnaise.

RAMIREZ: Huh?

CONNIE: On the salmon.

RAMIREZ: Oh. What happens now? To the gallery, I mean.

POTTS: The gallery? Oh, ownership? Well, I have the option to buy her share. It's a bit more complicated than that.

RAMIREZ: Yeah, I guess. They always are. Uh-oh. Now who's that?

POTTS: I'll take care of it. . . . I'm sorry, the gallery is closed.

VOICE: I was told . . .

POTTS: Excuse me, ma'am, but the gallery is—

VOICE: . . . to stop in this morning to see the paintings.

POTTS: Ma'am—

VOICE: The alleged O'Keeffes. Now, who are you?

POTTS: Who are *you*?

VOICE: I am Fredericka Ball Mansfield, young man. I'm with the O'Keeffe Foundation and I am here to—

POTTS: Uh. Oh, Ms. Mansfield, I'm glad to meet you but—

MANSFIELD: And you're Elijah Potts, I suppose?

POTTS: Yes, and we, well, there's been a—

RAMIREZ: Pardon me, but I am Sergeant Ramirez with the Santa Fe Police Department. There has been a tragedy. If you don't mind perhaps you could come back later. Tomorrow, maybe?

MANSFIELD: Dear God. A tragedy? Something about the paintings?

RAMIREZ: About Miz Montague.

MANSFIELD: Oh, dear. Well, of course, please forgive me. Serious?

RAMIREZ: Well, ma'am, she's dead.

MANSFIELD: How awful. I'm so sorry. I'm, uh, staying at La Fonda.

POTTS: We'll call you. Thank you. Jesus, that's . . . she's . . . the paintings. Christ, what a damned mess!

RAMIREZ: Now who is she? Nothing to do with pigeons, right?

POTTS: She's with the Hensley Museum in Baton Rouge. An O'Keeffe expert. The O'Keeffe Foundation has her tracking the entire O'Keeffe *oeuvre* for a catalogue raisonné. This could be . . . God, what am I . . . ? Poor Anita. This is just awful.

RAMIREZ: Yes.

POTTS: Well, what's going to happen, Sergeant? Are you people going to be able to find the monster who did this? This is senseless. God. Damn . . . Who would do this? What kind of a world is this we've made?

Sitting with his back to the wall of the gallery in the overly snug wing chair, listening to the pageant, Mo thought to himself that at least, with all the confusion, Elijah Potts had made the transition from denial to anger. That was a start.

And he wondered how many times his friend Ramirez had watched this sorry old human pattern unfold.

And then he thought about pigeon control. *Humane* pigeon control? Never heard of such a thing in all his born days. What next? People for the Ethical Treatment of Stomach Parasites and Botflies?

Then he heard his friend Ramirez resume in an off-handed but apologetic tone.

"Just a detail, Mr. Potts. Routine. We have to—"

"Oh, yes, of course, Sergeant. Yesterday afternoon I went out to my house in Canones. An old place I bought out there, it needs a lot of work. Then I came back to Santa Fe, had dinner at Mediterranean Light, you know the place? And went home. I'd say I left the restaurant at about nine-thirty. Spent the evening at home. Reading. A book on the Salem witch trials."

"That would be your house here in town?"

"Yes," Potts said. He gave a street number on Camino del Monte Sol. "I rent there."

"Bueno," Ramirez said. "I'm sorry, but it's just routine, as I said. You don't know anyone who'd . . . ?"

"Anita? Good heavens, as far as I know, everyone loved her. She was a—well—a ray of sunshine, an enthusiast."

"Yes, I am sure. We'll do all we can to—"

"Yes."

Ramón Tofoya's knees felt like spaghetti, and twice as he walked down Canyon Road from the gallery in ever longer, faster strides, terrified to look back, he thought they would give out, squish, crumple, leaving him in a heap on the fucking sidewalk, and that big beaner cop like a Mexican Schwarzenegger would scoop him up like so much ice cream spilt on the ground, and that weasel-faced Chiclet plainclothes motherfucker would . . . hey! He *recognized* those guys! The big sonofabitch had watched him through the bars for a whole night, never said a goddamn word, and the weasel—he'd . . .

Two years plus in the can.

He snuck a look back over his shoulder now that he was some forty yards down the street and hadn't been collared. The big dumb guy with the neck like a sumo wrestler's thigh was standing outside the gallery, already bored. A frigging robot. The weasel-fucker, he guessed, was inside. So they hadn't recognized *him.*

He grabbed at his straw hat as a gust of wind tried to tear it off—what is *with* this wind?—and slowed down, suddenly enveloped in the icy realization that he was playing a dangerous, a really dangerous game. His knees weakened again. He felt as if his brain had been shaken loose from his skull, sloshing around in there, fucking water on the brain. What was this? This panic that jumped him like some frigging tiger—bam! No warning. Like last night.

He had talked that old bag, what was her name? Steiner. Talked her into letting him go up into the upstairs of their adobe temple, must be worth four hundred large, put the toothpaste and brown chalk mixture—looked just like bird shit and dried in an hour—around in that atticlike place in case the old bag didn't trust him, wanted to see for herself. So he got the job, put in the traps he'd cobbled together that morning out of chicken wire and some scrap he lifted from a construction-site Dumpster—perfect. Looked around up there for good stuff he'd get later when he came back to "check the traps," and then left.

All taken care of, ma'am. No problem. Back in a few days.

Line up a few places, maybe eight, ten, then on the great appointed day, clean 'em all out and head for Texas, maybe New Orleans. Grab himself a little Creole nookie, sway to the music in the Big Easy—yeah! A little zydeco.

The appointed day, he thought happily, and out loud he intoned, "Four . . . three . . . two . . . one . . . liftoff!" Everything'll be okay, he said to himself, A-okay. Just like those wonk-astronauts: mission fucking accomplished, honey, you're talking to a man of *wealth* and, yes, a bit of mystery. That's it, babe, shake it.

He could see it now, a new image: him in his three-hundred-dollar shades on some lounge chair in the sun, hand resting cool on some *hot*, *round* Creole fanny while he had another pull at his Cuban cigar.

Cool.

But then what were these goddamned panic attacks? Like last night?

Last night Ramón Tofoya had walked out of the Steiners' house, on the street in the gathering dark, just a smudge of yellow light in the western sky and a whole new career finally, truly begun. He even had a reference from poshville now—"Yes, you know Mrs. Steiner? She's very pleased with our service; you can call her." Things were definitely going his way.

It was past seven-thirty when he got in his cruddy Mustang, and even though it was a few serpentine blocks out of his way, he found himself drifting down Canyon Road toward Southwest Creations. It looked closed up, but from down the side alley a light glowed faintly. He let the car roll downhill a block, parked, and walked back to the gallery, slipping down the side alley, walking as quietly as the dirt road would let him. Might as well check it out at night, see how complicated it was going to be. On the appointed night he would have to get upstairs again. He'd had time to look around up there when he was fetching those chairs. There was a lot of stuff up there, dusty sculptures, racks of prints. Had to be worth something.

He had put the bird shit around, over by the vent that had the rotten screen over the slats. Some big fucking tree outside it. And then he'd noticed that big new-looking wooden panel in the wall with state-of-the-art security system—ITI, installed by American Security Systems—a piece of fucking cake. He knew about this kind of thing, hadn't just been picking his nose all that time in the can. He knew about security and human stupidity from the experts.

Had to be something in there, something worth megabucks. People didn't put worthless crap behind a top-of-the-line security system like that. All he needed to do on the appointed night, D-Day, liftoff, was . . .

So Ramón Tofoya had slipped through the shadows down the alley, checking things out. To his right a long, high wall of naked adobe bricks with some stucco slathered over the top. He slipped along the wall, his eye on the window from which light glowed in the back room of Southwest Creations. The windowsill was at eye level across the alley, and from his angle he could see obliquely inside. On the white interior wall was a big calendar that seemed to show three months at a time, and a shelf that held some big books—maybe ledgers of some sort.

He saw a graceful hand reach out and pull one of the ledgers down and out of sight. He took two more steps down the alley to get a better angle and leaned against the adobe bricks. It was that manager, the broad. She had her hair pulled up in a knot, and was wearing half glasses like some kind of schoolmarm—peering down, turning pages. Even with the glasses, she was a piece of ass. Ramón felt an odd sense of proprietorship. Comfortably in the shadows, he crossed his arms over his chest and watched her reading. She reached up toward the shelf and her fingers danced over a couple of the books on the shelf, pausing, then dancing again. Ramón hadn't felt fingers dancing on *him* for almost three years.

Down came another book, and she riffled through the pages, flipping back and forth, still looking for something. Then she found it. She leaned forward, concentrating, frowning. Picked up a pencil, put it in her mouth, chewed on the eraser—even white teeth—looked up, pulled the half glasses off, looked back down at the book. She reached out and lifted a phone receiver into view—one of those dinky little walk-around phones with a one-foot rod sticking up from it. Glancing down again, she pressed out some numbers. Ramón noticed that she had small hands, delicate. Then she put the phone to her ear, still frowning, almost pouting, her lips puckered together, listening. She opened her mouth like she was going to talk, closed it, and began talking, slowly, forming each word carefully. An answering machine, Tofoya reckoned.

She put down the phone, turned and moved out of sight, into the interior of the room. Tofoya looked around and saw a place low on the wall where an adobe brick had broken off, forming a handy foothold. He put his foot in it and hoisted himself up, gaining about a foot and a half, and looked in the window. She was down at the other end of the room, her back to him.

Holy shit. Holy shit. She was pulling her dress up over her head.

His eyes bored in on the pink bra strap across her back. She was folding the dress, putting it aside. Her hands reached around to the clasp of the bra strap and Tofoya held his breath. But she simply scratched under the strap for a moment, raised her shoulders and let them fall, like she was sighing. Put her head back like she was stretching her neck, then rolled her head back and forth.

Tofoya's hand slipped on the adobe wall and he grasped wildly, catching himself.

She was turning now, sideways, reaching out, and Tofoya was watching the magic curve from underarm to the soft plunge in lacy lingerie, his eyes yearning. She picked up this shiny black thing like a shirt, thrust her arms down into it, pulled it over her head, over her chest, tugging it down over her waist. Then she bent forward and Tofoya craned his neck, began to feel his foot slip, and watched her turn to face the window. She was in one of those plastic bike outfits, tight as a frogman suit, shrink-wrapped like a piece of fruit, and he looked at her face and fell off the wall, landing on one knee, biting back a yelp.

The smile. Like some kind of mask. Tofoya had panicked, ice on his neck, and ran out of the alley and down Canyon Road to his car. Behind the wheel, he noticed that his hands were shaking and the knee of his jeans was torn where he had fallen. Hit some goddamned rock. Bleeding.

That had been last night at the gallery. And now,

today, those fucking cops turning up there. He needed some rest. He needed to think.

The subtropical sun gleamed from Claudia Potts's legs, the half-moon of her haunches, and most of her back, all of which had been carefully impregnated with a half ounce or so of number sixteen sunscreen with aloe only fifteen minutes earlier by the man who now with the grace of an athlete wielded a long blue metal pole with a flat net at its end, scooping up the hot pink bougainvillea blossoms floating on the pool's dazzling surface. The man had a Redfordian shock of unruly blond hair and sun-whitened hairs on his forearms, his legs, even his toes, along with a perfect, deep tan that one day down the line he might regret, but not now. At his age, regret was not part of the worldview.

A nearly imperceptible breeze made its way among the leaves overhead and eddied down within the eight-foot wooden fence that surrounded the pool and deck. The pink flowers rafted obediently into the net. Claudia's back-door Eden was redolent with the perfume of the sea, of bromeliads, passion flowers, and various non-botanical pheromones. She sighed in the shade of her hat, a large, floppy-rimmed affair of off-white hemp imported from Thailand, thinking that in a minute or so it would have grown altogether too hot to be outdoors.

"Know what these flowers remind me of, sort of?" the man said.

Claudia Potts laughed, a throaty sound. "Don't tell me. Let me guess."

Through orange-tinted Polaroid lenses she watched the

ropy muscles in the man's back move as he swayed fluidly back and forth with his pole. In a week or two, she thought, it would be altogether too hot to lie in the sun at all. Key West summers. She sighed again, and the piercing shrill of the portable phone cut the air.

"Jimmy, would you be a dear and hand me that?" she said.

"Sure." He put down the pole, stepped over to a wrought-iron table and picked up the plastic receiver, which looked like a toy in his hand. He stepped over to Claudia's chaise longue, smiled as she lifted up onto her elbows, and handed her the phone with a beep of the PHONE button.

"Hello? Yes. Yes. Fine. Sure, I saw it on CNN. Last night. Yes, and on *Good Morning America.* Yes, this morning, about a minute and a half. Well, that's pretty good for a show that usually has airhead celebs on to talk about their memoirs. Yes, they showed two of them. Joan Lunden was all ooohs and ahs. So it's all . . . *What*? *Anita*? Last night? How?"

Claudia Potts wriggled up into a sitting position, legs crossed like a guru, absentmindedly folding her arm across her breasts.

"On the street? What, like a mugger? Oh, I see . . . two others? God, what has happened to the sleepy little City of Holy Faith? Christ." She listened, alternately nodding and shaking her head. "How awful," she said. "What an awful . . . well, of *course* I mean it. It's horrible. Oh, for God's sake . . . Yes, of course I'll be here. Jesus."

With a frown, she poked the OFF button on the receiver's belly and leaned down to set it on the wooden deck. She conjured Anita Montague up in her mind, never an image she liked to dwell on, and all the more difficult since she had met her but once, two, three years ago on her last visit to Elijah's other realm. Small, solid, full-figured, the athletic type with skin drawn tight over her wrists, strong forearms, no bones showing—probably lifted weights—and a gamine smile, almost cocky. Muscle-bound little *proprietor*, was the way Claudia sometimes referred to her mentally, with a patrician scorn for people in retail sales. Never had liked her, the bitch, and hated the idea of Elijah clamped between those solid thighs in the back room of the gallery, or God knew where, but . . . a deal was a deal and . . . but, Christ, a *drain*pipe. She shuddered. A bicycle chain.

The blond man, Jimmy, sat down behind her, straddling the chaise, and she felt his big hands on her shoulders, felt them slide around under her arms, felt them lifting her breasts.

"Trouble?" he said.

"Nothing to do about it," Claudia said.

"Oh."

Poor Elijah, she thought, and reached a hand around behind her. "So maybe we'd better do something about that."

"This?"

"That," she said, marveling again at the beauty and vigor of youth.

seven

By noon that day the wind had gusted up again, tossing gum wrappers and other junk around the city in irritable eddies, and Santa Fe's third murder in two weeks of single Anglo women, their bodies all treated like trash in one way or another, had made the national newscasts, bulletins interrupting even some of the talk shows where people, under the cloak of first-name anonymity, can happily say things in public they wouldn't dream of telling their mothers.

"Big deal," Howard Stern in New York said when they cut back to him. "Three in two weeks is bush league. Some kinda amateurs," he snorted. No one in his national listening audience was offended, having long since become inured to being pegged as bush league by the gotham grunge-guru. Even Rush Limbaugh would get around to it that day, asking what else would you expect from such a hotbed of godless liberalism and goo-goo-eyed multicultural claptrap as Santa Fe.

The news, of course, had spread like a prairie fire through Santa Fe, eclipsing any gossip or even further thought about the newfound O'Keeffe paintings, even among the art crowd here in what had recently emerged as the third largest art market (dollarwise) on the planet. The hypothetical Trasher had taken on the dimension of a real and lethal demon, lurking anywhere, and the flames of speculation were building up to the critical point of igniting panic. The chief of the Santa Fe police and his counterpart in the State Police Department went on radio to give the standard advice for avoiding such predatory acts, none of which made any of their female listeners any more confident. Where were you supposed to park at the supermarket but in the parking lot? In their statements, both officials had peremptorily dismissed the suggestion of a serial killer prowling the streets, and no one believed them. Just because there were three different M.O.'s didn't necessarily mean anything. You'd expect creativity in Santa Fe, after all. In offices, restaurants, and boutiques, people whispered darkly about the preeminent fact in all this, for God's sake, plain as your face: all three women were Anglos.

Sergeant Anthony Ramirez took a break at noon, just long enough to buy a Coke and doughnut made of low-grade cement generously glazed with polyurethane in the fast-food joint across Cerrillos Road from the police station. The food was better even from the machines in the station house, but he wanted to sit for a few quiet moments out of the melee and think.

The chief had announced that morning that he would personally take command of the investigation—which, Ramirez knew, was bullshit. He and his immediate superior, Lieutenant Ortiz, would still be handling it while the chief made public noises and useless suggestions, as always; but it burned his ass anyway. Mainly, he hated what he was hearing about—all the speculation, all the signs of an incipient panic. He decided he had better call on the Low-Rider King again.

At the next table two middle-aged men in Western-cut shirts and straw cowboy hats that looked new or at least unused in any cattle drive leaned forward while a third said, "Look, I say it's a serial killer. I made a study of these people. Main thing is they all got sex hang-ups. Really screwed-up wiring, cannibals and shit. But none of these women have been raped or mutilated that way or nothin', right?"

The other two men nodded—eagerly, Ramirez thought.

"So I figure this guy's some kind of *per*verted vigilante and all these three women was dykes. None of 'em had husbands, right? I figure the guy is on some weird vendetta against lesbians. Maybe he was young, caught his mother doin' it with some broad, fucked up his head. Maybe he was *raised* by lesbians, got abused by 'em. I mean, who knows what goes on with those people, faggots getting married in *churches*, for Christ's sake. Anyway, the guy would be disgusted by dykes, just want to kill 'em. I mean who'd want to screw a dyke? See? That's gotta be it, huh?"

Ramirez dropped what was left of his leaden doughnut on the paper plate and stood up. Maybe it was the doughnut giving him this stomachache.

"Hey, Val," said one of the men as Ramirez headed for the trash receptacle with his Coke cup, his paper plate, and his half-eaten doughnut. "Maybe it's a she, you know . . ."

No, Ramirez thought, as he dumped it in the bin, it wasn't the doughnut.

He walked back to the table, facing the men, and put three tickets down among their coffee cups.

"What's this?" asked the man called Val, looking up with hostility.

"Three tickets to the Police Benevolent Association Car Rally. Next month. Only ten dollars apiece. Keeps kids off the streets."

"We don't want 'em," Val said and looked down.

"Oh, sí. Yes, you do," Ramirez said and opened his blue blazer so Val and his friends could see what was obviously a police-issue revolver on his hip, just in case they were even dumber than he imagined. "That pickup out there, it's yours, isn't it? And it's parked real funny. All sorts of flagrant violations you got out there, eighty, maybe eighty-five bucks. This car rally? Only thirty bucks for the three of you. You'll feel good. A bunch of Samaritans. You can tell your wives."

Mo Bowdre lay supine on the big red sofa in his living room, the toes of his old, scarred, but lustrously polished Tony Lama cowboy boots pointed skyward. He had his big hands behind his head, and his hat had crept down almost to his nose. He had eaten two tuna fish salad sandwiches made with celery and capers—now wanting capers in everything and anything since lunch the other day in Mediterranean Light—on Jewish rye bread. He had also drunk two bottles of Corona beer, and was determining if he wanted the banana Connie had offered.

"Sure, why not?" he said. "Got potassium in it. Maybe it'll de-cramp my brain. I don't know when I'll ever work again, what with this damn wind still blowin' my fragile little muse to hell. Old Frazier wants me to do that mountain lion series I was thinking about, but—well, it's just not there now. Crept off on little cat paws, or whatever that Chicago poet said. It was about fog, I think. Cat's *feet*. That's it, crept off on little cat feet. Hah—hah—hah. You can tell the muse has decamped, I'm just babbling."

"Here's the banana," Connie said.

Mo peeled it and took a bite.

"You know," he said, "Elijah seemed genuinely devastated."

"Why wouldn't he be? They were partners, friends."

"But nothing else?"

"She was gay, Mo."

"Hmh," Mo said.

"What are you thinking?" Connie asked with a dubious tone in her voice, somewhere between mild alarm and annoyance.

"Nothin'," Mo said, taking another bite of banana.

"Good, because it's none of your business."

Mo flapped his right hand back and forth loosely on his big wrist. "Whoo-eee. The Earth Mother speaks. What isn't our business?"

"Mo . . ."

"Okay, see, these killings. They could be random, unrelated, probably are. Hell of a lot of bad people out there, like those Greek monsters waiting in the mountains. Doesn't have to be one guy, a serial killer, either. Different M.O.'s, and that's usually key. Probably isn't, but it might be one guy. It does seem awful coincidental, three in quick succession, all Anglo. Then there's Tony's idea it might be racial, a bunch of dispossessed Hispanic guys making a statement about increased property taxes, Anglo imperialism in general. So maybe it's some kind of racial vendetta. A gang thing, maybe."

"Mo, it's not our business."

"Well, why not? Anita was our friend. Yours anyway."

"Well . . ."

"And you were with her when those paintings turned up at Elijah's place in Canones."

"The paintings? What . . . ?"

"I'm sure I'm not the first person in town to wonder what old Elijah would gain by having one less business partner now that these paintings have come to light."

"Mo, I'd really rather you didn't do this. Leave it to Tony. It's none of your business."

"You're right. That's why it's so damn interesting." He finished the banana and laid the peel carefully on the coffee table. "Will you listen to that wind? Like to tear the damn roof off. Now, don't you worry. I'm just bored. Sculptor's cramp. You know."

Connie knew that three times in as many years, Mo had gotten involved in criminal cases—helping figure things out with Tony, and sometimes that crazy FBI agent Collins who was going to graduate school somewhere or something—and it was dangerous. A few years back, when Mo would get bored, he'd do something unpredictable, sure. Once he'd simply shown up with airplane tickets for a week in Australia and they had left from the Albuquerque airport three hours later.

But the last few years, he'd begun to take up being what one of their friends called "the redneck Nero Wolfe," and it was dangerous. He still had an ugly round scar from the bullet a creepy little smuggler had shot through his love handle almost two years ago now down in Hidalgo County by the border. Sometimes Connie wished they'd get married so she could lay down the law more effectively, the way Hopi wives had been doing since before memory. She looked over and noticed that the big man was asleep. She laughed to herself. What made her imagine that this coyote of a white man—this bahana trickster—could ever be so easily tamed?

She stood up, leaned over and kissed him lightly on the tip of his nose, and he murmured contentedly in his sleep. He would sleep for a couple of hours, time for her to go back to the gallery and help Elijah make all the sorry arrangements, arrangements that struck her as so businesslike, so *hygienic*. Death, Connie reflected, was something white people weren't very good at. She wondered why.

Outside, the sky had gone gray again, the Windbreak Moon playing its games. Maybe more rain. More wind. Even snow. She would probably need a jacket. Turning toward the coat closet near the rarely used front door that exited onto Canyon Road, she noticed the business card lying on the table. The pigeon man. Same as had come to the gallery today. A creep. Something blown in on the wind from somewhere else, a stupid interruption, like being bothered by a housefly that won't go away—you keep brushing it away from your face.

"This is art, man. Art."

"I never saw one of these," Ramirez said. "What is it?"

Manuel Trujillo looked up at him through squinted eyes, and his chest swelled by another inch.

"This," Manuel said, "is one of four 1939 Chevy delivery sedans left in the world. I bought it from a guy in Lordsburg for twennyfive hunnert. It's worth sixty thou today, at least."

This came as a shock to Sergeant Anthony Ramirez, who paid little attention to the automotive world and understood it less. To him the small, almost quaintly small, vehicle looked just like any other antique, its boxy shape looking hopelessly unaerodynamic, the more so because its edges rested only an inch off the concrete floor. But its charcoal-green rear end gleamed a deep emerald-black bespeaking polish, care, and many applications of money.

"Come here," Manuel said, scooting round to the front. "Look at this." On the narrow hood someone had contrived to paint—airbrush, no doubt—a grinning skeleton with a gold pharaoh headdress emerging like a vampire out of a gaudy sarcophagus. The sarcophagus sat in a desert that stretched back to a horizon dominated by a purple and peach sunset, a flagrantly phallic obelisk, and a muscle-bound guy with the head of a hawk.

"I don't mean just this," Manuel said, gesturing at the gleaming painting on the hood. "The whole thing. The rims, the hydraulics, the paint, the interior—all of it. This is *thousands*, amigo, tens and tens of thousands of dollars. Took months, months. Now that's art, isn't it? Just as much as some statue of Coronado on his horse, made out of bronze in some big kiln, sittin' out in the park. I mean, if that guy Crisco wraps up mountains and bridges with tarpaulins, or that other guy blows up shit in the desert, or that broad sits onstage playing a cello in the nude while guys cover her body with Hershey chocolate—if all that is art, then so is this, man." Manuel rocked back on his heels and breathed heavily. "Hell of a lot more soul in this, amigo, than some dainty little fuckin' watercolor, believe me."

"Well, sure, I suppose so," Ramirez said. "How do you know it's worth sixty thousand?"

"Japanese guy offered me that for it last week. Japs are getting into low riders. I've sold about twelve of 'em to guys in Tokyo. They want 'em all done, finished. They don't wanta do any of the work. Just put 'em on the boat, okay? Cash, amigo, cash. They just peel off the bills. You wait, next they'll be in Singapore. Monkey see, monkey do, right?"

"You going to sell it to the guy?" Ramirez asked.

"For sixty?" Manuel laughed his phlegmy laugh. "These days I'm thinking maybe it's worth seventy-five. What the hell."

Manuel hitched his jeans up under a solid-looking round potbelly. "So what have I heard, huh? About those girls—and, jeez, you got another one, huh? Last night? Another gringa." He shook his head, crossed his thick short forearms over his chest. He cleared his throat, reached an arm up and scratched the ear from which hung two diamond earrings, then crossed his arms again.

"Well, Antonio, I'll tell you what I heard. A bunch of guys went through here about two weeks ago, from Texas, talking big, you know? Like they were going to stay. But then they left, *brusco*, all of a sudden, poof!"

"When was that?"

" 'Bout two weeks ago, like I said. Around the time that girl got killed, turned up out at the lan'fill. Some people think—well, that's what some people think."

"How many?"

"How many what?"

"How many of these guys, these Texas guys?"

"Three. People like that, they come and go. They're like those bacteria, you know, floating around, make people sick, then turn up somewhere else. You never know."

"Descriptions?"

"Not so you could pick 'em out from all the rest of those bums. At least nothin' I heard."

"What about the others? The second one, she was a waitress. At that swanky restaurant, Mediterranean Light. They say she used to like to hang with Hispanic guys."

"Yeah. I heard about that."

"You did?" Ramirez said. "When did you hear about her?"

"Last night, amigo, last night and this morning. When I'm asking about this shit. For you. Doing the Santa Fe Police Department a favor, right?" Manuel laughed again, then shook his head. Ramirez noticed that all the time Manuel had been talking, he had gazed unswervingly ahead at the ghoulish mural on the hood of the Chevy delivery sedan made in Detroit in 1939. Probably around the time Manuel Trujillo had come gleaming and sticky and crying into this world from the safety of his mother's womb. Now Manuel sighed, and squinted up at Ramirez.

"Some of the guys, I guess some of them gave her whatever she wanted. You know? I mean, when they stick it right in front of you, whadda you gonna do? But what I hear, nobody, I mean none of them . . ."

"Blew her head off with a shotgun," Ramirez said.

"Yeah."

"And the Montague woman, last night."

Manuel shook his head again. "No. Nothin'. Nobody. . ." Manuel looked tired, smaller, like he had shrunk. Ramirez put a hand out, rested it on the little man's shoulder.

"Thanks, amigo. Thanks."

Manuel grunted, looking again at the Chevy delivery sedan. "But what do I know, huh? An old man. A fuckin' elder. Maybe I don't talk to the right people anymore."

"Yeah, maybe, but maybe you'll sell this ride for seventy-five."

"Yeah, maybe. Good luck to you, too."

Ramirez walked out of the garage into the wind, biting at a ragged place on the nail of his little finger. He could feel that doughnut, the half he had eaten, sitting in his gut, defying the acids of his stomach to erode it into something useful.

Hearsay. Worse than hearsay. Nothing was more unreliable than guys telling the Heroic Adventures of Peter the Great. Everyone wants to be a legendary cocksman. Ramirez had been there. Who the hell hadn't?

Hey, Ma, hey, look at me! Look what I can do!

Mierda. God save us.

The hospital, he thought. He'd have to go to the hospital and see if that guy Steiner's heart palpitations had died down enough for him to answer some questions, not that he would have seen anything on the street a half hour or more after the Montague woman got stuffed in the drainpipe. But you had to cross all the bases.

"These people are great, just great, Sergeant. I mean highly professional."

Anthony Ramirez had introduced himself to Marvin Steiner five minutes earlier, after the duty nurse said the patient was fine, they'd check him out of the hospital tomorrow. Steiner, a large florid man with a long strand of thinning black hair pulled over a balding dome, had seemed delighted to have company in his hospital room, to have someone he could talk to about himself and his condition. Ramirez judged that the man, like so many others with chronic low-grade heart problems, really felt most comfortable in hospitals, surrounded with all the TLC and machinery of salvation. And like so many others, he liked to talk about his condition in detail to anyone passing by, as if talking about it objectively made it tame. Ramirez had already heard about Steiner's heart attack in the middle of a New York street, and how he'd soon taken early retirement and come to Santa Fe, how the evening walk in the seven-thousand-foot elevation was strengthening his cardiovascular system, and now how professional all the staff was here, as if it was surprising that anyone outside of New York City—but especially in a remote province like New Mexico—could have attained proficiency in so demanding a field as medicine.

Steiner returned to his focal point—his heart—saying how it did still tend to flutter in the face of surprises, had even had a minor flutter last evening while he was sitting down to have his nightly martini.

"They've told me that's a no-no," Steiner said with a wink, "but some things you just can't change. I mean, life without a martini? One sin. Just one. We all need one minor sin, right, Sergeant?"

Ramirez nodded. "You had a surprise?"

"Damn right. I mean how many times do you find a corpse in your driveway?"

"You said you'd had an earlier surprise?"

"Oh. Yeah. Well, it was nothing. A big thump in the house while I'm having my martini—you don't expect big thumps in the house after your kids are grown, and ours have all flown the coop, one's in medical school in fact. . . ."

"A thump."

"Yeah, yeah. This thump. I jumped, heart jumped, I can tell, you know, and well, it was just some guy upstairs my wife had hired. Get this, Sergeant. Some kind of pigeon control guy, putting traps in the upstairs to catch pigeons. They're unsanitary. I never saw the guy. Left when we were having dinner. Then we watched the TV for a while, a movie it was. I used to be in advertising so I know what's going on, but I hate the way they break up movies on TV with those ads, you know, more and more toward the end when you're hooked—well, anyway, then I took Osborne for our walk . . . and . . ." Steiner's florid face went slightly pale.

"I don't want to disturb you, Mr. Steiner. Bring up bad memories. I just want to know if you saw anything strange, any strangers in the neighborhood while you were walking your dog. It's a Labrador retriever, you said earlier. Nice dogs. They never bite people, like some breeds. So, while you and, um—Osborne, was it?—were out walking, did you . . . ?"

"Nothing, Sergeant. Nothing. Nobody." Steiner seemed disappointed.

Ramirez stood up, patted Steiner on the leg and thanked him. "You've been very helpful, Mr. Steiner."

The man brightened and, as Ramirez left, he saw the heart patient reach for the buzzer that would summon his nurse. Nurses, Ramirez thought, had to be even more patient than cops.

Downstairs in the gleaming lobby with its shiny linoleum floor and its white walls, Ramirez found a pay phone, plugged in a quarter and dialed a number he had written earlier in his notebook. The phone buzzed three times and a woman answered.

"Yes?"

"Is this Southwest Creations Gallery?"

"Yes."

"Uh . . ."

"Nobody here. It's closed." The phone clicked dead. Ramirez dialed the number again.

"Yes?" the woman said again.

"This is the police," Ramirez said.

"Oh, Tony, I didn't recognize your voice."

"Connie?" he said. He heard her giggle, a high-pitched trill. "What are you doing?"

"Manning the phones. Fending off reporters."

"It didn't sound like you when you answered. Sounded like . . ."

"It's my Inn-yinn roots coming out." Connie giggled again.

"Look, when I was there earlier?" Ramirez said. "Some guy was at the door, guy in a cowboy hat, apparently was carrying on about pigeons."

"Yeah," Connie said enthusiastically. "Something to do with pigeon control. *Humane* pigeon control. He knocked on our door at home a day ago, or was it two? Time's all messed up. Kind of a creep."

"You got a name, an address?" Ramirez said.

"At home I do. Wait, here. He left the same card here. Ramón Tofoya. Want the phone number?" She read it off and Ramirez wrote it down in his notebook. "Why?" Connie said. "You got a pigeon problem?"

Ramirez thanked her and hung up.

The idea of Ramón Tofoya was like a chigger bite under Ramirez's belt. It was something oddly concrete in the midst of the opaque fluid events that had become Ramirez's business: three Anglo women killed and dumped in two weeks, one from nowhere, one from Olney, Illinois, and one from Southwest Creations. No connection except being Anglo. The gallery owned by

Elijah Potts, who had wowed the town—hell, the whole country, it seemed—with his announcement about those new O'Keeffe paintings. Worth a fortune if they were real, Ramirez thought, and now Potts would presumably get a hundred percent, not ninety, what with the Montague woman killed, which was what Ramirez should be looking into, of course, not this loose hair of a pigeon exterminator, but there he was, this Tofoya—around the neighborhood on the night a murder took place, at the gallery where the victim worked, even at the house of Mo and Connie, who were friends of some sort of Potts and the dead woman.

Guy didn't look Hispanic.

His phone number was nothing but an answering service: "This is Humane Pigeon Control. We're not here right now but if you'll leave your name and number, we'll get back to you as soon as possible. We're glad to be of help with our humane services to the community of Santa Fe." *Beeeep.*

Ramirez did not leave a message but soon enough reached the phone answering service. He found out from the manager of the service that no one had left any message for Humane Pigeon Control since the man Tofoya had hired them a week ago, that he had given as an address a number and street that, Ramirez knew, was a side street off Cerrillos Road, in a crummy neighborhood with a few old houses among the auto parts dealers and second-rate fast food franchises.

Ramirez now slowed down on Cerrillos Road. Up ahead, on the left, beyond the Squeaky Clean Car Wash and the Grease Monkey (LEGISLATORS WELCOME) was the New Mexico Humane Society, where they gassed dogs by the dozens every day and neutered anything with four legs. Hard to be humane in this world, Ramirez thought, and wondered if Ramón Tofoya, humane pigeon man, gassed his pigeons or what. Wondered also if it was an omen of some sort that he evidently lived within barking distance of the Humane Society.

For some unfathomable reason, traffic had come to a standstill on Cerrillos Road, and Ramirez tapped the steering wheel impatiently while he waited. In the lane next to him a woman with a mass of curly bronze hair was singing enthusiastically along with the radio, a Mexican song he recognized. In her passenger seat, Ramirez saw the top of a kid's head, and in the backseat the profile of a guy. The woman popped an unlit cigarette into her mouth and spotted Ramirez looking at her. In slow motion she grinned, removed the cigarette, and puckered up her lips in a silent kiss. Ramirez raised his fingers in salute, and she drove on, still smiling at him, the traffic jam having miraculously dissolved. Ramirez turned right at the Jiffy Lube, noted that no one needed a lube job right then—the place looked completely abandoned—turned right again and bumped along a dirt road for one block, pulling up at a low, run-down adobe building that looked like a bunch of brown shoe boxes tied randomly together.

Over a door that needed paint or stripping, one or the other, was the street address Ramón Tofoya had given the phone answering service as a place of business and residence, along with a sign that said THE KEYS TO THE KINGDOM COMMUNITY CENTER. In front of the Keys to the Kingdom was what he guessed was the biggest fleet of Harleys in New Mexico, presided over by three guys bedecked in every leather and metal cliché invented, thick sunburned arms protruding from black leather vests, shoulders and wrists darkened with nightmare tattoos. They were lounging around on a ramshackle porch, the three of them, indistinguishable, could be triplets, beards like birds' nests, shiny pates rimmed with hair down to their shoulders, like they washed their hair once every six months in axle grease.

Ramirez cut the engine and stepped out of the car. The three bikers looked over at him for the first time, moving only their eyes, not their heads. Their eyes followed him as he approached the porch. He wasn't going to get much help here, he figured. The grease triplets stared expressionlessly at him as he stopped some ten yards away.

"I'm Tony Ramirez," he said. "I'm—"

He startled inadvertently when all three of the bikers, in unison, said, *"Hi, Tony!"*

Oh, that Kingdom, Ramirez thought with relief.

"I'm here to—" he began.

"Everyone's welcome here, bro." It was the one on the left, speaking. "We're here for whatever bothers you. Got AA, rape, child abuse, drugs, even Alanon. You don't usually find Alanon and AA under the same roof. But here they meet in adjacent rooms. We're all grinding the same ax, brother, here in this life we got."

The biker paused, looked at Ramirez expectantly.

"Actually," Ramirez said, "I'm looking for a guy, gave this place as an address. Ramón Tofoya?"

"Oh, you're a cop."

"Sí. Santa Fe Police Department. Routine investigation."

"Yeah, spotted you as a cop, didn't we?" The other two nodded, smiled. "Some things you don't forget. Still can spot a cop in Times Square on New Year's Eve." The three men chuckled. "Even cops welcome here. We're all brothers and sisters. So. Ramón Tofoya, huh? Little guy with a mustache, like a little Kevin Costner got caught in the rain?"

Ramirez nodded.

"Came in for one meeting, what, about a week ago. Lives right over there." He gestured with his head. Ramirez turned and saw another old adobe building, smaller than the Keys to the Kingdom, more run-down, but of the same vintage—around World War Two. "We had a vacancy. Let guys stay there, three dollars a night, while they get themselves established. Not much, but it's better than sleepin' on a grate in God's outdoors, right, brothers?" The other two triplets nodded. "He ain't there, went off this morning, old Mustang loaded up with funny-lookin' traps. Saw something like 'em when I was in Maine. You know, them lobster pots. Quiet guy."

Ramirez hung around a few more minutes, finding that the big leather-and-chains triplets didn't know anything more about Ramón Tofoya but guaranteed they would see to it he got Ramirez's card, tell him to call.

"It's nothing serious," Ramirez said, and the three men nodded sagely. "Tell him the Steiners recommended him." Again the three men nodded. "Here, let me write that name down on my card. There. Okay? See you guys, and thanks."

"Sure enough. Come visit us sometime, Tony. Good fellowship here."

"Good idea," Ramirez said. He climbed into his car and headed for the station, feeling numb and tired.

It was bewildering. He could not make out any familiar patterns in the unaccustomed chaos overhead, the night gone mad, Coyote's work—yes, that old Indian story about the beginning of things. He lifted his feet, curling up in the suffusing heat, floating beyond gravity, and the world slipped away, breeze with a touch of ice inside his head. Suspended, looking up? Yes, up, watching silken tendrils of steam rise and vanish like prayers. Prayers to what? To the patterns of light in the mad sky, the immortals cast up—a wounded old centaur, a nymph too beautiful to bear—ha. Now there's a good one. The nymph Callisto. Too good to bear. Caught the lusty eye of Zeus, so his harridan wife turned her into a bear, and Zeus, in an act of pity, cast her up into heaven. So there she was, the Great Bear, Ursa Major, up among all those stars. So many stars here. All the usual constellations masked in the clear night's multitude, but up there nonetheless—thanks to Zeus, always getting rid of the evidence by hurling it into immortality up there.

Elijah Potts hung suspended in the water, 101 degrees Fahrenheit, and allowed his mind to roam the heavens while the frets of the day escaped through his pores and vanished into the night, will-o'-the-wisps, prayerful steam. No troubles here in this private spa under the stars. Is this what immortality is like—no body? Just floating in warm, silky formlessness?

It occurred to him to have another taste of the brandy he had smuggled into the premises in a silver flask in the large pocket of his Norfolk jacket. He doubted that the earnest, boneless young men who welcomed you to this place cared much if you broke that rule, and he wondered how they would remonstrate if they knew, so self-effacing were they, so polite, so discreet, up here in the trees, two thousand feet above the City of Holy Faith in the forest in the Japanese-style spa called Ten Thousand Waves. The brandy slipped down his throat and filled him with another kind of warmth, and he looked up again at the sky, so bedazzlingly filled with stars in the clear thin air. No moon. Its slivery silver crescent had slipped away. Just stars in the great black pelt of the sky, while he floated in the silence, attending the unspoken words that roamed his mind

the whispering together of girls

yes, waiting here afloat in the mist, a blur of sensation, brandy, the taste of the breeze, waiting

the smiles and deceptions

the delight, and the sweetness of love

yes, waiting here for Aphrodite to appear, his Aphrodite

and the flattery

He heard the gate latch lift, the gate open, saw the starlit white towel emerge, an hourglass in the dark.

"Elijah? Is that you?" Norah Vargas whispered.

"You've come," Elijah said. "The delight, and the sweetness of love."

"Who's *that* talking?" Norah said, and Potts could dimly make out the form of her body now, the towel now gone.

"Hesiod. The oldest of the poets."

"And who am I tonight?"

"Aphrodite, who else? She who inflames the souls of men. Slip in here, Aphrodite, I want to ravish you here in this warm eye of the universe, this amniotic sac. . . ." He strained his eyes and watched the black patch, shadow within a shadow, slip into the water, quicksilver stars dancing on the surface. . . . He reached out and pulled her through the water toward him and felt her legs around his waist.

"Amniotic sac? Isn't that an egg?" She laughed, a velvety sound that arose from her throat.

"The universe was born of an egg, a cosmic egg, fanned by the power of love. Everybody knows that. Want some brandy?"

"Are you a little smashed?" Norah asked, floating on his lap, her wrists draped over his shoulders.

"A little. Just floating here between the earth and the sky like a good boy. It's peaceful here, so peaceful, so quiet. One feels disembodied."

She laughed again, and swayed against him. "Funny, you don't feel disembodied at all. Maybe I will have some brandy."

He handed her the flask, watched her shadowy neck stretch upward. Touching the bottom with his toes, he spun her slowly around in the water, heard the water lap against them.

"So many stars," she said.

"So many you can't make out the ones you know."

"Like the sky has gone crazy."

"The world has gone crazy, I'm afraid," he said. "Anita."

"Yes. Christ . . ."

"But we don't have to talk about that, do we?" She raised her arms over her head, arched her back and fell luxuriously back into the water. Her teeth gleamed in the starlight. "Won't the world wait while we play here?" She pulled her knees up and sank below the surface, emerging a moment later with a splash. "Do you suppose dolphins have more fun?" she asked.

The water droplets on his face where Norah had splashed him were icy cold in the air. The nice equilibrium of heat, cold, and brandy was gone. He stood up in the water, shivered, and sank down again to his neck.

"The cops came by today. A Sergeant Ramirez, very polite."

Norah sighed. "I've met him," she said. "Nobody's fool. He was at the restaurant a few days ago, about Carolyn Marcy, the waitress. It was her they found. That's what I heard, in the recycling place. And now Anita. He's a busy man."

"He asked where I was last night," Potts said. "I suppose I'm a suspect." He snorted. "God, doesn't that sound like a soap opera?"

"That seems pretty farfetched, what with all these random killings of Anglo women. Or nonrandom. They're talking about the Santa Fe Trasher, a monster loose in the streets. And they're talking about how it could be some Hispanic group, making a statement, you know? That would seem more likely."

"Does that make you feel funny? You being . . . ?"

"My people think of themselves more as Spanish. We go straight back to the expedition of Juan de Oṇate, you know. Directly descended from Onate's trusted lieutenant, the poet Gaspar Perez de Villagra." The words rolled off her tongue like starlight on water.

"Aristocrats," Potts said.

"Sí." Norah laughed her velvety laugh.

"And all the others?"

"Mestizos," she said. "My grandfather was adamant about that." Her hands made submarine forays.

"It's almost impossible to concentrate when you do that," Potts said.

Norah sighed again. "So what did you tell the policeman?"

"I told him I was at Mediterranean Light, of course, until about nine-thirty, then went home."

"That's good," Norah said. "Are we finished concentrating now?"

"I've got a woman coming in tomorrow, a big shot from the O'Keeffe Foundation. Wants to see the paintings, of course. A real dragon lady."

"You met her already?"

"Not exactly."

"Should I be jealous?"

"Of what? Her hourglass figure? Her luscious, round melonlike breasts? Her welcoming dark caverns . . . ?"

"Hey, that's *me* you're describing."

"Sí." Potts looked up again at the stars and gave himself over to the watery heat that enveloped him.

"You know that boy Tofoya, livin' over there in the rooms? Droopy-assed boy with the mustache and all them lobster pots or whatever the hell he's got? Yeah, man, that's him, the little cocksucker the cop was askin' about this afternoon, left his card, Sergeant Anthony Ramirez, fucking homicide, man. Left his card for this here Tofoya, says he should call him. Well, Tofoya, he drags his butt in here about half an hour ago and I give him the card like the man said, and Tofoya? It's like someone run a thousand volts up his ass, he starts jiggin' and jumpin', turns white and then red like he's about to blow up, man. And he goes runnin' back to the rooms on them spindly legs like a roadrunner, you know, flat-assed out with his head down, and he stops, rips open his car door, thought he'd tear the door off that old Mustang. And he starts throwin' them lobster pots outta there all over the damn ground, don't know what the hell we're supposed to do with 'em, all layin' around out there, and he runs into his room, cussin' to beat hell, I never heard such cussin' since granddad got his dick slammed in the shower door, remember that? Oh, that was before you boys . . . ? Yeah, it was awful, man, awful, think of it. Haw, haw. Well, anyway, then this here Tofoya comes runnin' out with that duffel bag he came with, flings it in the Mustang, still cussin', and I swear to God if that little motherfucker didn't dig up half the damn yard, spinnin' outta here. You can see the ruts he made. *Vamos*, man. Hell no, man, I didn't call that cop about it. It's between them, man, none a my affair. Yeah, there they go, them Alanon people, that's the last of 'em. The rape people left a while back. It's near midnight. Guess we can close the place up now. Jason, you want to get the lights in there? Hey, good night, brothers, good night, sisters. God bless you all."

eight

On the western side of Mo Bowdre's enclosed yard, about thirty feet from the former mill house that served as his studio, a two-seater bench of concrete had been set in a semicircular garden of mixed perennials that were dormant at this time of year. This provided Connie Barnes with a peaceful outdoor nook where, most days, she sat waiting for the sun to make its presence felt in the eastern sky. For the Hopi, as for most Indian tribes, it is an important part of one's spiritual hygiene to greet the new sun each day, for it is a He, a supreme deity. The Hopi call Him *Dawa*, which means Father, and few things could be more important in this world, after all, than the daily arrival of the father of all things.

Connie sat in the predawn chill while the first tendrils of pink and peach light reached out overhead. She wore an ankle-length sheepskin coat Mo had brought her a year ago with all the pride of a cat bringing a wondrous mouse to its master, and a pair of sheepskin slippers. She felt no ritual need to wait for the Sun's forehead to actually appear over the mountains that lie behind Santa Fe. She had prayed and said welcome in the approved manner to Dawa's prelude in the sky, but she was content to sit on the bench a while longer.

Connie was, of course, well aware what astronomers said about the sun—the central feature of the local solar system around which the earth revolved, providing one with the illusion that the sun sets and rises over a stationary earth. She knew all that, but it did nothing to diminish her knowledge that the sun was also the living deity called Dawa. After all, even astronomers knew that without the sun there would be no life on earth. It *was* the father of all things, and if astronomers wanted to think of it only in terms of physics, that was fine with Connie. It simply seemed a bit narrow-minded.

The more time she spent in the white world, and the more inured she became to its strange and disconcerting lack of rhythm or poetry, the more intensely she felt the need to make these morning orisons. Like a compass or a gyroscope, or one of those other instruments whites use to keep track of where they are in the world.

This morning she was, as usual, happy to see the reassuring signs of Dawa's continuing paternity, but had wakened earlier with other matters on her mind, along with the always disturbing images from dreams still lingering but unreadable, like those patterns that haunt the periphery of one's vision, always floating so shyly away from direct observation. Suspended somewhere between sleep and wakefulness, her knees drawn up against the small of Mo Bowdre's back, she had watched what seemed to be a black marble rolling slowly along a silvery spiral path. As the marble approached the deep central part of the spiral—now black—it turned white and disappeared, but only momentarily because the spiral now opened up again. It seemed to her that she was floating along behind the white marble in an infinitely opening, expanding spiral, swooping along behind this ever brightening, round marble as it made its stately way into an increasingly black velvety place . . . always just ahead of her even as it became more and more urgent for her to catch up, to reach out and hold it. In the small white sphere, she sensed, were all the possibilities of the world.

And then it slipped away from her. Fully awake, she listened to the big man breathing beside her—inhalations and exhalations so long in duration that she could not match them. His lungs must be oversized, too, she thought. She put a hand over him and let it rest against his stomach, mildly surprised as usual that what looked for all the world like a typical paunch, a beer belly, was so firm. At her touch, he sighed once and went back to breathing in and out.

Five years, she thought. Five years we've been here. Yes, it's time. We'll have to talk about it. Don't want to scare him with the idea.

It was at that point that she had slipped out from under the down comforter, found her sheepskin coat in the closet, and gone outside to wait for the sun, thinking idly about how she would bring this matter up.

It was time they thought about having a baby. At least it was time *she* thought about it.

They had never talked much about marriage, just lived together. But for Hopi women, marriage was not a prerequisite for having a baby. Most Hopi women got married after that, in fact. But she knew that for Mo the idea of a baby would immediately bring up the idea of marriage, and she simply had no idea what he really thought about that. Probably, she imagined, he would writhe around like a trapped sheep. She smiled. There would be a monologue about antiquated social institutions, gender, liberty, the freedom of the imagination—it would be entertaining and also what he himself would call bullshit. The monologue would be in sections that would erupt over a period of, she guessed, three days, and at its end he would then actually confront the idea of paternity. What he would think, Connie had no idea. As well as she knew him, there were huge areas, great arenas, that eluded her.

Now she looked up again at the sky, filled with a pink glow, and was suddenly taken by another thought altogether. She was pretty sure—and she had no idea why—that the seven O'Keeffe paintings that Elijah Potts had found and shown the world were fakes. The word *fake* seemed to blink in her mind like an unfulfilled computer command.

She walked across the brown lawn as the sun peered over the mountains, and went inside, finding Mo in the kitchen, where he was hunched over a mug of coffee, wearing a plaid woolen bathrobe and a sleepy smile.

"Sun's up," he said.

"Yes."

"Coffee's good," he said.

"That's good."

He lifted the mug, a white one with fanciful lizards in black running around it in the style of a Mimbres pot.

"Now, tell me, what is it you got on your mind this morning?" he asked cheerfully, and took a sip. She watched him put the mug carefully down on the table and, with a forefinger, push his dark glasses back up the bridge of his nose. How did he know? she wondered.

"Those paintings," she said. "The O'Keeffes?"

"What about 'em?"

"They're fakes."

Mo's blond eyebrows danced above the rims of his glasses.

"What makes you think so?"

"I don't know," Connie said. "I don't even know why they came to mind. But I got this feeling or whatever while I was sitting outside."

Mo yawned, a long and luxurious process, and scratched his head. "Well, now, there's a can of worms for you."

"You think I'm right?"

"Hah—hah. Look here, you just got through telling me yesterday that this wasn't any of our business, so I put it out of my mind. *I* don't know if they're fakes. I can't see the damn things, not that that would do much good anyway. All I ever learned about painting wouldn't fill up the brain case of a deer mouse. But if you say they're fakes, then I'd have to guess they're fakes. Even though you don't know why you think that. And all of a sudden I got to think that all this *is* our business. Is that about right?"

"Well . . ."

"Good. I'm bored half to death. Let's us have some

breakfast. See how much we know about our friend Potts. Hah—hah."

There were times, Connie knew, when Mo Bowdre's staccato laugh wasn't a laugh at all. Sometimes it meant about the same thing as a male bison pawing the ground.

"On the road again," the voice sang adenoidally.

"*Shit!*" Ramón Tofoya said, snapping off the radio. "I got to sit here listening to that tax-evader? Hell no. Fucking criminal bastard, nobody's gonna throw *him* in the can, no, no, not him, a frigging celebrity. Guy owes millions—*millions*—and he's out loose on the road braying songs over the goddamn radio. If it was any normal person, they'd've trussed him up and thrown him into frigging solitary for two centuries. Willie Fucking Nelson. Big deal."

Ramón Tofoya realized he was talking out loud to himself and lapsed into silence as the flat colorless land flew past him at sixty-two miles an hour, the maximum at which he felt comfortable pushing his stolen Mustang, which sounded like it was going to throw a fucking rod and blow up in his face every time he got any closer to the goddamn speed limit of sixty-five, all these big arrogant semis steaming past him while the frigging Mustang shivered in the slipstreams, goddamn he hated this, eating other people's dust.

But what could he do? Slip one of these cocksuckers the bird as they hurtle by and they'll blow your damn head off with an Uzi, damn cokeheads, they should have rules or something.

Ramón Tofoya squinted behind his sunglasses as a

pain swelled behind his eyes. The sun glared directly through the windshield. Another two hours of this, he thought, until the goddamned sun gets above the windshield. What a godforsaken place. Nothing but this flat land going on forever, nothing, a big nothing. The pain behind his eyes grew and his eyes hurt, like they had sand in them, and he thought maybe he should pull over, get some z's, just for a while, but then there'd be this car—him—on the side of the highway and nothing else in the world but flat land, white sky, and this empty straight road, and some smart-ass cop, bored out of his mind, would stop and ask if everything was all right. . . .

It was another hour probably to Tucumcari, a bit more to the Texas border, maybe he could stop in Tucumcari, nothing but a strip of motels in the middle of nowhere. He was sick of this, this frigging big sky country.

New Orleans. That's where he'd go. Place with some class. Figure out a way to sell this shit and go to New Orleans, listen to the music, watch those Mardi Gras women wearing nothing but a string and a few beads, shaking their asses in public on those floats, black, white, brown women, all kinds, just wavin' it at you. He'd seen movies of it.

Ramón Tofoya had been driving for two hours now and he hadn't eaten since the night before. Besides his headache, it felt like his stomach was beginning to devour itself. It had taken him longer than he'd planned, getting out of Santa Fe. He hated changing plans like that, scam just getting going and all. Maybe it would work in New Orleans.

He had thrown the white business card with black

letters on the ground. The humongous biker sticking this card out at him in a big beefy fist, guy had fingers like pink sausages, and it said *Sergeant Anthony Ramirez.*

That was the *guy*, that was the same fucking cop as . . .

He didn't want to think about it.

On the run again. On the fucking run. Again. Ramón Tofoya wondered when the hell he was going to find someplace where he could stop, be at home, eat three squares a day, feel the sun on his face, maybe . . . maybe this time. Maybe in New Orleans or someplace like that. Something had to go his way. He was sick of running across the goddamn countryside in somebody else's piece-of-shit car. He wanted his own, something nice, a nice car, one hand on the wheel, the other hand tucked in there between the thighs of one of those Mardi Gras broads with their round silky asses, all warm—

He woke up as the Mustang's wheels lurched under him and he saw the desert coming obliquely at him, and a cattle fence. He yanked the wheel, slewed sideways in the dust. Ramón Tofoya said *shit* and heard a loud metallic sound as the car slammed sideways into the wire fence, then the motor raced like a banshee.

A quarter of a mile to the south in the brown scrubland, a cow jerked its head up at the sound, looked unseeingly in the direction of the highway, and put its nose down again into the dust.

The raven-haired woman seated at the other end of the table looked up from her plate—what was left of two fried eggs over medium, three thick slabs of bacon, two blueberry muffins, curlicued hash-brown potatoes—and smiled briefly in acknowledgment. Her hair, thick and shiny, obscured her face again as she looked down at the newspaper neatly folded beside her plate. She had a multicolored cardigan sweater—patches of oranges, yellows, reds, purples—over a white blouse. Black eyes, black eyebrows, a wide mouth behind that hair—a strikingly beautiful woman, short, voluptuous, about her own age. Samantha Burgess had seen her around town, but she could not place where or when. Maybe here at Pasqual's. Hair like that—so black and shiny—made Samantha jealous. Her own hair, she was all too aware, was thin and the color of a house mouse.

No one else besides the two women was at the community table in Pasqual's where Samantha occasionally came for breakfast to overhear what other locals were talking about, or even to chat with whatever acquaintances, or strangers, happened to sit down. Most of the locals had already eaten and left for wherever they worked. It was almost nine. Samantha took another bite of the thick blue-corn pancake on her plate and wished she could eat bacon like the black-haired woman. God, it looked good. But she knew what it did to her kidneys, so she put the temptation aside.

The woman was reading Samantha's backgrounder on Anita Montague in the *New Mexican*, mostly stuff pulled up electronically from the files, no time to do much else, and her partner Potts wasn't answering the phone. Just some dumb Indian woman at the gallery saying it was closed. No answer at his house. Stands to reason, Samantha supposed, but it was a pain in the butt. She swallowed the last of her heavy pancake, and helped it down with a final swig of orange juice.

The waitress approached the other end of the table. "Everything okay, Norah?"

The black-haired woman looked up, smiled warmly and nodded. "Perfect, Amy."

Amy looked over at Samantha. "Can I get you anything else?"

"Not a thing," Samantha said. She stood up and took her bill to the cash register, where two or three parties of tourists waited in line to pay.

"Out of curiosity," she asked when it was her turn, "do you know who that dark-haired woman is at the community table?"

"That's Norah Vargas. Works over at that new restaurant, Mediterranean Light. Hostess, I think. You been there yet? I hear it's kind of precious, you know? Like little portions for big bucks."

"Sign of the times," Samantha said.

Outside Pasqual's, Samantha turned right and walked along the narrow sidewalk toward San Francisco Street and the Plaza, where she turned left, feeling the temperature drop at least five degrees as she went out of the sun under the long portal that covered the sidewalk for the whole long block. She walked past the display windows, crowded with clothes, artifacts, expensive geegaws, real art, all clamoring for attention, and stopped in front of a bookstore window, now filled entirely with books about Georgia O'Keeffe. Big books, little books, art books, paperbacks. On the wall, an O'Keeffe poster for the

Santa Fe Opera, a huge red flower close-up, a cluster of waxy organs rising from its center.

The store was open and Samantha went in. The array of O'Keeffe books in the window was repeated on a table in the front. In the back, a clerk busied herself with one thing or another, and Samantha browsed among the O'Keeffe books, picking them up, laying them down.

In an oversized volume of O'Keeffe paintings, she found one from the pelvis series, *Pelvis with Pedernal.* It was dominated by the sharp hard lines of a section of a pelvis painted a pale ivory and shaded an indescribable lavender-brown, looking something like the innards of a gigantic ear, maybe a deformed conch shell. And beyond the pelvis, the hard-edged flat top of the mountain, a uniform blue against a lighter blue sky. Both pelvis and mountain simply floated there against the glowing blue sky, and the mountain bore a mysterious pink highlight on it—a modest Rorschach within a Rorschach within a Rorschach—all so brazen.

Even on the printed page the painting's mystery struck Samantha, made her uncomfortable. It seemed so impermanent, floating, ugly. She closed the book and continued browsing, choosing at length a paperback biography, *Portrait of an Artist*, from among several. It was by a woman, Laurie Lisle, and had a blurb on the front cover by Joyce Carol Oates. Probably more reliable, Samantha thought, than the one by Jeffrey Hogrefe, who seemed to be utterly and fashionably hung up on stories of Georgia's alleged abuse as a child.

She thumbed to the index, peered at the tiny print, and turned as directed to page 321. There at the bottom she began to read how in 1943 O'Keeffe found "a perfect pelvic bone in the mountains." On the next page, the biographer wrote:

> The bony frame often acted as a telescope—focusing the eye on the endlessly receding void of sky, or what the artist termed "the blue hole." In a burst of imagination and creative energy, she rapidly painted the hollow socket with familiar motifs—the Perdernal, flowers, the moon—trying the new shape with the old ones. And, as if unable . . .

Samantha looked up as the clerk approached. "I'll take this," she said. "I guess everyone has got Georgia on their mind these days."

"You bet," the clerk said. "It's like Christmas."

O'Keeffe, the quintessential loner, had nonetheless always had people around—even if just some local woman as a maid. So who, Samantha wanted to know, had been around in the 1940s? Maybe the biography would give her a clue. And maybe that person was somehow hooked to the guy Ricardo Gallegos, who had once owned Elijah Potts's little half-restored home away from home in Canones where the seven paintings had been found. And how many long shots was that?

Even if those seven paintings *had* been painted in the 1940s, the way all the scientific evidence pointed, Samantha Burgess, investigative reporter for the Santa Fe *New Mexican*, wasn't about to believe they were legit. The paintings, the paintings—they stuck in her craw. And the murder of Anita Montague . . . there's a Pulitzer in this, she thought, if I can just pull it all together, suddenly feeling in over her head.

On his way down Canyon Road at nine-thirty in the morning, Elijah Potts detected what he thought was a subtle change in the way the sun touched the nape of his neck, and a particular lilt in the air. The wintry mountain chill of early spring mornings, he predicted, was over . . . and with it, he prayed, the winds. He had enough wracking his nerves now without those wayward damned winds. With luck, the days now would be crystalline, calm, the sort of climate where the glass was half full, not half empty.

Once inside the gallery, Potts hung up his Norfolk jacket, thinking that he could put it away for the season now. He looked around his gallery as if for the first time. A slight film of dust lay on the antique table that served as a desk. He realized he didn't know the name of the woman who cleaned three times a week. It would be somewhere in Anita's desk—no, not her desk anymore. She'd been a bargain—a salary and ten percent of the gallery. A stickler for details, spit and polish, taking pleasure in the cascade of chores that came with running a place like this—chores Potts had no patience for whatsoever. Where would he find another . . . ?

It struck Potts that these were not the proper thoughts for a man grieving over the violent murder of a friend and junior partner. But here he was, without help, in this gallery that now felt like a prison. He was pinned down here. Everywhere he looked, he saw chores, chores he didn't understand, arrangements to be made that he had never had to arrange himself. He yearned to click his heels and take flight. He was Gulliver, lashed to the ground by too many tiny strings. Soon enough, he intoned to himself, soon enough I'll be free of all this.

First thing was to close the gallery indefinitely. After all, there'd been a tragedy. Well, no, he'd have to open it again for the O'Keeffe show. Then close it, sell the place to the highest bidder. Who needed this albatross? No, the first thing was to cancel that damned monthly series of talks—"Art from the Interior: the Work and the Soul." Potts snorted.

A lot of pap served up to the cow-eyed dilettantes, part of their pathetic pilgrimage along the comfortable path to Beauty, to Community, to some vague and narcissistic notion of personal self-fulfillment. What bullshit. And where were they now, this community of truth-seekers? Potts wondered. Now that he had suffered this unspeakable tragedy? A few embarrassed words of solace for the bereaved.

A murder? That was too bloody, too ugly, too real for his fair-weather community of well-financed pilgrims. Look the other way. Hold your nose. Keep it at arm's length. A dead woman, flesh and guts beginning to putrefy in some drainpipe. How artless. How inharmonious. What a rude interruption of perfect lives lived perfectly in this perfect city under a perfect sky.

Elijah Potts, standing immobile next to the slightly dusty antique desk with its antique telephone and its elegant tooled-leather album stamped with VISITORS in gold leaf, allowed himself a pleasurable wallow in cynicism.

In the last analysis, he had recognized years earlier, we

are all alone. He knew that life among humans was nothing but an array of practical arrangements, momentary deals, unspoken contracts of convenience that were entered into and broken as needed, and the craftiest negotiator won. To think anything else was to believe an illusion. There *were* no fairies out there in the garden, dancing in the morning dew.

For a time, now so long gone, when he had been a student of art history, he had lived in a state of perpetual elation as each day a new work of art had opened his senses even further to the limitless ways of beauty, each so pregnant with meanings that defied actual words—composition, texture, the sculpting of light, all embodying eternal stirrings. . . . And for a time he was able to pour into this sensual flagon the clear rich liquid of myth, history, civilization, seeing it all as whole, seeing himself as sharing in this shining potential of the human soul. It was like sharing in immortality. In those days, he could soar on a plane well above the run of common understanding, the sorry impurities of the mere world.

Well, yes, that had been a halcyon time, hadn't it?

But soon enough he had needed to mine this golden ore to make a living, and so it had become just that—a vein to be mined. And so he had become another salesman, another hustler with a product. And he was tired, now, of that, as bone-tired as anyone who had ever honestly confessed to himself the loss of innocence.

The paintings . . . the paintings. These were his gift from the all-giving, all-taking goddess known as Lady Luck. And if there was one thing a student of mythology knew, it was this: when she reaches out, plucks you for whatever reason and opens herself to you, you have no choice. You dance.

Very carefully, you dance in her embrace.

How careful, how measured, how precise he had been in the months and months involved in authenticating these seven paintings, this formal minuet where each step was a potential trap. And now, just one more step. This Mansfield woman, with her damned catalogue raisonné. Fredericka Ball Mansfield. Another crabby little expert to be assuaged, reassured, persuaded.

Well, the paintings spoke for themselves, didn't they? The real thing. All documented. Now, one more time, they would speak for themselves. This Mansfield woman, with her rude patrician phone manner, was due at the gallery at two this afternoon. The dessicated old maid, he assumed, married early to Art, like a nun. He took a deep breath, and sighed.

Fredericka Ball Mansfield would have her private viewing—he would make it seem the great honor it was. There, in the back corner of the gallery with the perfect lighting, he would hang the seven paintings, now upstairs in the vault. He would move the eight-paneled screen across . . . yes, to give them their private place, to reveal them to the woman as she came upon them all at once, in a burst of . . .

Words failed Elijah Potts, soaring momentarily again on a plane above the run of common understanding, above the sorry impurities of the world.

"See, three of us are arachnids," the woman said over the phone with what Sergeant Anthony Ramirez knew was a big grin. The woman was very pleased with herself.

"Arachnids? You mean spiders?" Ramirez shuddered.

"I mean weavers. Wool people. Like spinning, weaving. It's like a little club down here. Fiber arts, Anthony. Our logo is a spider, and we call ourselves arachnids."

The whole idea gave Ramirez the willies. Here was this pleasant woman, Gina Spicer, one of the state's medical investigators, spends her days poking around corpses, doing autopsies, and on her off-time being a self-styled arachnid. There were three of them. Spiders, centipedes, all those things gave Ramirez the willies.

"And if there's one thing we know," Gina Spicer said, "it's wool."

The call had come in a few minutes before ten, a preliminary report from the M.I.'s office on Anita Montague. Ramirez had just returned to his little cubicle of an office after listening to his boss, Lieutenant Ortiz, pass down the chain of command the hiding he had just received from the chief. And the chief had no doubt been hearing from the mayor, who wanted these damn murders of young women in Santa Fe stopped, solved, the perpetrator found, arrested, the whole damn thing behind them. The usual hysterics.

Ramirez knew the mayor was a fundamentally good person, as concerned as anyone with the actual tragedy of people dying, as aware, too, as anyone that crime, murder, whatever, was all part of the deal—what did the bumper sticker say? Shit happens. But this sort of thing was not good, either, for the image of the city held in the minds of countless art buyers, travel writers, and all those tourists sitting at home in Wabash, Illinois, or Berlin, Germany, or wherever, making their summer vacation plans, booking reservations in the posh Santa Fe hotels—all that. So the pressure was on.

When *wasn't* the pressure on?

So Gina Spicer calls at 9:48—Ramirez had looked at his watch—and launches into this amazing forensic tale, bubbling with an enthusiasm that normally does not accompany the clinical details of death. And Ramirez had to laugh to himself, in spite of his abiding distaste for creatures with more than four legs.

Among the fibers plucked from the body and clothing of Anita Montague were the expectable—threads from an Oriental-type rug, that sort of thing, the normal material that adheres to people in the course of their days. But there were some fibers, mostly from the upper part of the cycling outfit around the neck and shoulder area, that were clearly Harris tweed. More important, these same fibers were found under the fingernails of three fingers on her right hand.

Gina had explained to Ramirez that Harris tweed was a special tweed traditionally made on a few Scottish islands, very special stuff, in great demand. In fact, demand had far outstripped the old ways of making Harris tweed, so now it was made by machine on those same islands, a tragedy for the purist, but even old Scottish weavers had to make a living after all.

But *these* Harris tweed fibers—they were the real thing, Gina had known as soon as she saw them. Wool people know this stuff, she said. They were hand spun, hand-woven. She could tell by the irregularities in shape. Had to be hand spun. Olive, gray, and black in color, unlike any she had seen. So she had conferred with her two fellow arachnids in the M.I.'s office.

At this point in Gina's monologue, a picture came unbidden to Ramirez's mind of three women, sitting in a circle like the Fates, weaving the world into existence, cackling amongst themselves.

"And Janet remembered reading in one of the wool magazines, maybe it was *Spinoff*, that some posh American clothing outfit had specially commissioned some of the old guys to do up some Harris tweed the old, authentic way, for one of their products. It didn't take us long—it was this outfit in Kentucky, the J. Peterman Company, they sell only by catalogue, and they commissioned some Harris tweed, sort of peaty-colored, olive, gray, and black, for what they call a Norfolk jacket. It's got a lot of pockets and a tweed belt, very smart. It costs $275. Plus postage."

"Whew," Ramirez said.

"Hey, that's a bargain."

"So all I've got to do . . ." Ramirez said.

Gina giggled. "We already did it. Hope you don't mind us muscling in on your bailiwick, but we were really excited. We called up this Peterman outfit and they're FedEx-ing us some of the tweed, we'll have it tomorrow, but they're sure the only source of it is their Norfolk jacket. So I asked if they sold a lot of these things in New Mexico, and the woman said most of their customers were in New York and California, she could run a computer printout and give us the names of everyone in the state of New Mexico who had ordered a Norfolk jacket. It's a new product so there wouldn't be very many, she guessed." Gina paused for breath.

"And?" Ramirez said. He was feeling great, just great. These women . . . Jesus, were they great or what?

"And there are altogether eight people in the Land of Enchantment who have ordered a Peterman Norfolk jacket, what they call a Drummond Norfolk after some Brit who sent them one to copy. This is a very chichi outfit, Anthony. The woman was telling me about their Bumpy Sweaters, knit by hand in Montevideo from Uruguayan sheep. They got Italian moleskin shirts for men. Must be like a shirt made up of all these tiny moleskins. That kind of thing. Anyway, the good news: we got two people in Taos, three in Albuquerque, and three in Santa Fe. We have their names."

"And? The Santa Fe guys?"

"The bad news is that two of them are recently deceased—old guys in their seventies and eighties who died in the past month, and the third is a movie actor with a part-time residence outside of Tesuque. He's been in Europe for the last three months. Making some movie, I read."

Ramirez felt like a balloon that had just sprung a leak. "No one named Potts," he said.

"We thought that was the guy you'd be looking for, the Montague woman's partner."

"Damn."

"Cheer up, Anthony, honey," Gina said, the effervescence rising again in her voice. "We asked the Peterman people to run the whole list, everyone who'd ever ordered one of these things. Anywhere. And there's a woman who lives in Key West, Florida, ordered one last November as a Christmas gift. Her name is Claudia Potts."

Gina paused again.

"Claudia Potts is also known, on her American Express gold card, as Mrs. Elijah Potts. Do you love it, Anthony?"

"I do, I do. I am your faithful servant. Forever."

"We thought you'd like to get this right away. The paperwork'll be along soon. I mean, is this great?"

Ramirez assured the woman of his undying love and gratitude and hung up the phone, elated. Five minutes later he watched the lugubrious face and tired eyes of Lieutenant Ortiz break into a rare smile, a nearly unnoticeable turning up of the mouth, a crinkling around the eyes.

"I wonder how many places there are," Ortiz said, "where the M.I.'s are weavers. Maybe this *is* the Land of Enchantment. We just saved about two weeks." He shook his head. "But you said this guy Potts was somewhere else at the time of death."

"He said he was at that restaurant, Mediterranean Light, till about nine-thirty. The hostess there, woman named Vargas, said he was. I talked to her on the phone this morning. She said, yeah, he was there, left around nine, nine-thirty. I'll get her in for a statement."

"But he could've done it anyway, right? There was time?"

"Well, he could have, yeah. Barely. It's hairy."

Lieutenant Ortiz looked up at the ceiling.

"Yeah, it's hairy," he said. "Another problem. This guy Potts, they say he was banging the Montague woman. Why wouldn't he get this stuff on her, these fibers? Maybe they had a quickie before he left the gallery—a real quickie, him in his jacket."

"There are rumors about him bonking her, but he says no. And he's probably telling the truth."

"Why do you think so?"

"She was a lesbian."

"So get him," Ortiz said. "Bring him in for questioning. Suspicion. Find his jacket, this Drummond Norfolk jacket. Bring it all in. I'll tell the chief. He can tell the D.A. and the mayor."

"And the mayor can tell the governor," Ramirez said.

Again Lieutenant Ortiz looked at the ceiling, and Ramirez turned to go.

"Oh, yes. Another . . . a delicate matter, amigo," Ortiz said.

Ramirez paused at the door, and turned to face the Lieutenant. "The chief has raised this before."

Ramirez waited.

"And he mentioned it to me this morning."

Again Ramirez waited.

"He believes that the Santa Fe Police Department should be able to handle such matters on its own."

"Yes?" Ramirez said. "Why would anyone else be involved? This is our jusrisdiction. Who . . . ?"

Lieutenant Ortiz reached out and plucked a ballpoint pen from a coffee mug on his desk that held two others along with a nail file. He tapped the pen on the edge of the desk. "There are those paintings Potts found, the O'Keeffes."

"Oh. Yes," Ramirez said. "The paintings. My understanding is that they've been authenticated." He shrugged. "Who knows with that kind of thing? Why, our friends at the Attorney General's Office involved with that?"

Ortiz continued to tap his desk. "No. Anyway, there's no fraud until someone sells something, that's how that works. No, the chief was referring to your friend."

Ramirez again waited.

"The blind man, Bowdre. The artist. This is the sort of thing he . . . you know, art and all that. The chief made one of his cracks again this morning. About the homicide department needing help from amateurs."

Ramirez felt his neck redden. "On two occasions in all the—"

"The chief is very jealous of the department's reputation."

"You mean of *his* reputation," Ramirez said. "I suppose one of his golfing friends gave him the needle, huh?"

Ortiz shrugged. "Maybe something like that. Anyway, I know Bowdre has been helpful sometimes, but—"

"He hasn't got anything to do with this, Lieutenant. Does that make you happy?"

"Anthony . . ."

"So, if you'll excuse me, sir, I've got a collar to make. Right?" Ramirez saluted and left the lieutenant's office with part of his mind trying to calculate the current value of his pension plan.

nine

Sitting in an oversized chair cleverly constructed from some two dozen gnarled pieces of root and branch culled from the arroyos of northern New Mexico, Mo Bowdre listened to the clicking of plastic keys emanating from the room off the living room that served Connie Barnes as an office. His left hand idly stroked a smoothed piece of cedar root that formed part of the chair arm, a piece of cedar sculpted by accidental forces—the wind, the abrasion of sand. Then plucked out of the arroyo and tacked to these others to make this chair, and to be further smoothed by human use.

Mo Bowdre allowed his mind to dance like an electric current between two poles—here was an art form under his hand, a chair assembled from pieces of nature. In the other room, impelled into existence by the tapping of keys, was information arising from somewhere—cyberspace, another dimension in the world now. There was information, too, in the tangled roots of his chair—the history of its components, the urges of seedlings, all that.

Ridiculous. It was, Mo thought, a stupid way to think

of a chair, to think of it as a package of information. How pale. It was solid, real, comfortable, part of the earth. On the other hand, the new world was information, all out there like some odorless, colorless gas, floating around somewhere like electronic dandruff given off by any and all human activity. He hated the thought of all his own private dandruff floating around out there, waiting to be assembled by electronic wizardry into a personal, private story of his own life, there for anyone to ogle. Better to have secrets, hidden places, things about oneself that no one can ever know, the way the roots and branches of this chair did.

Surely they were going to find plenty of such secret places, such gaps, in the life story of Elijah Potts that Connie was in there assembling out of the Big Brotherly ether with her magic computer. And those would be the most interesting parts, Mo assured himself with the odd sympathy and respect a country boy out on a deer hunt has for his prey.

Mo stood up, stretched, and stepped across the room to the door of Connie's office. He waited until he heard a pause in the plastic clicking, and the curious sighing sound with which Connie's printer confronted any new task it was given.

"More tidbits?" Mo asked.

"College," Connie said.

"My God. How do you—"

"Some of it's in standard data banks, you know, like *Who's Who in the West.* Some of it comes from other sources . . . call it a network."

"I don't want to hear about it, do I?"

"Me neither," Connie said. "In fact, I don't really know how all this gets from there to here."

"Oh. We are covering our little electronic ass?"

Connie giggled. "I guess you could say that."

"Well, that's a relief. So what have we got on this boy now?"

"Sit down while I sort his stuff out of all this other stuff that came. Then I'll give you what we've got in order."

Elijah Potts was born in 1951, the second child and first son of William and Emma Potts, in Morehead City, North Carolina, a small town located leeward of some of the sandy barrier islands that protect the state's entire shoreline from most of the battering and scouring of the Atlantic Ocean. Even in those days—the Fifties—the population of Morehead City tripled every summer, bringing vacationers to the rows of clapboard houses that lined the beaches, and bringing in more than three-quarters of the city's annual revenues. William Potts had owned a furniture business in Morehead City that provided his family with a modest income. His daughter, Rachel, who was two years older than Elijah, attended high school, became a clerk in one of a dozen real estate firms that specialized in summer rentals, and was run over by a truck on her way to church in the same autumn that Elijah, age eighteen, left for Providence, Rhode Island, the first product of Morehead City ever to receive a full scholarship at Brown University.

"Now that's plain amazing," Mo commented. "Are you sure about this? I mean, you can always tell someone who grew up in North Carolina. Especially the eastern part. Those boys got an accent that sticks to 'em like the stigmata. Potts must've worked awful hard to get rid of that accent. Got a voice on him now like a radio announcer, you know, comes from nowhere."

Potts spent five years in all at Brown University, graduating cum laude in 1974 with a bachelor's degree in art history, having minored in European literature. The university and the local papers had no record of any involvement by Potts in the antiwar activities that occasionally disrupted the campus in those years. It appeared that he was kept busy by a rigorous extracurricular work schedule that was part of his scholarship, working afternoons as a clerk in the dean of student's office and, in his senior year, for the university's art museum as an aide to the conservator.

In his fifth year, when he was working toward a master's degree in art history on partial scholarship, he was arrested and held overnight in jail after an early morning raid on a club called Bimby's, where he was employed part-time as a male stripper. According to the Providence *Journal*'s brief story on this incident, it was ascertained that none of the male entertainers had exceeded the legal limits of undress and they were all released in the morning, along with the club's manager and owner, who accused the police of "blatant harassment" and let the matter drop. Soon afterward, Potts left his master's degree unfinished and lived for two years in Provincetown, Massachusetts, an art colony on the very tip of Cape Cod and also long a summer magnet for the Boston homosexual community. In 1975, Potts married

Claudia Ergstrom, a local painter originally from Greeley, a town on the plains of eastern Colorado, and a graduate of Smith College.

The wedding service was held on Provincetown's north beach, part of the Cape Cod National Seashore, within a hundred yards of the site where playwright Eugene O'Neill had had a shack many years earlier. According to the account in the local paper, the wedding was in the manner of a costume party, attended by about two hundred people, and lasted through one entire night and the following day, ending before sunset when National Park police arrived and sent the celebrators straggling home across the dunes.

"Hah—hah," Mo said, "costume party, my ass."

For the next decade, Claudia and Elijah Potts lived in Camden, Maine, southern France, and Carmel, California, earning a relatively comfortable existence from her painting and his occasional articles in mostly regional art magazines. In one of these, which caught the attention of the people at National Public Radio, he had dwelled on the spiritual connection between a northern California group of multimedia still-life innovators and the unknown shamans who had painted huge and mysterious animals in the Lascaux caves in the late European Paleolithic. Potts had suggested that the Lascaux artists were female. For two years he reported monthly on the West Coast art scene for NPR's *ArtChat*, and in 1981 published his first book, *Shaman Quest: Four Women in Art*, with a small San Francisco publisher.

"I remember that book, I think," Connie said, interrupting her monologue. "One of the four was a Kwakiutl woman. A sculptor. I didn't remember that Elijah wrote that book."

"How was it?"

Connie giggled. "I couldn't read it all the way through."

"Artspeak?" Mo asked. "Grand flights of sesquipedalia."

"Sesqui . . . what? It sounds almost like a Hopi word."

"It's a big word that means big words."

Connie giggled again. "Real big words. I wonder if that Kwakiutl woman understood all that stuff he was saying."

In 1982, Potts accompanied his wife to Greeley, Colorado, where they lived for six months, settling the estate of her father, who had died, a widower, at the age of seventy-two. The estate consisted entirely of a house, mortgage-free, and its furnishings, all of which Claudia sold for $122,000. In the following year the Pottses traveled to Europe, staying mostly in France and Greece, with extended side trips to Egypt and the Middle East, where they visited archaeological sites, particularly those in what is now Iraq along the Tigris and Euphrates rivers.

They returned to the United States in time for Potts to undertake a modest author tour for his second book, another semischolarly work, entitled *Astarte's Daughters: The Revolutionary Vision*, published by Praeger in New York City and Thames and Hudson in Great Britain. The book received a favorable, if brief, note in *The New York Review of Books*, and Potts and his wife moved to Key West that autumn, where she bought a small house, using what was left of her father's estate as a down payment. It was the first piece of real estate either had ever owned, and the couple went to elaborate legal lengths to assure that it belonged solely to Claudia Potts.

"Like some kind of postnuptial, prenuptial agreement, huh?" Mo said. "You'd have to guess old Potts wasn't too happy about that one."

Within a few months Claudia had arranged for her paintings to be carried exclusively by a Key West gallery called Gulf Works, and her still lifes of single fruits—pears, kiwis, small red bananas—were being locally praised for their technical proficiency and "an astonishing range of mood, a heightened intensity of objective being, and a mystical unity of time and timelessness reminiscent of the Dutch painters of the seventeenth century."

"Hah—hah," Mo said. "And what was Elijah doin' all this time?"

A year after the couple moved to Key West, Potts sued his publisher in a New York District Court, seeking the return of all rights to *Astarte's Daughters.* In his suit, according to *Publishers Weekly*, he asserted that the book had been "criminally underpromoted even in its obvious markets." The Florida chapter of a national literary group called PEN joined the suit as a friend of the plaintiff along with two West Coast women's associations, but Potts, predictably, lost the suit. In spite of having thereby gained the reputation in the publishing world of a troublemaker, Potts had become a minor lion with some fairly powerful connections in the world of quasi-academic arts and letters. His newly aquired literary agent in New York, a woman named Pressburger, managed to talk the art publisher Rizzoli into contracting with him for a major illustrated work on the Virgin Mary in twentieth-century art and psychoanalysis. Research for this volume took him far afield from Key West—chiefly to New York, Chicago, Santa Fe, and to San Miguel de Allende in Mexico, and within a year he had rented a small house off Canyon Road in Santa Fe, where he stayed first for months at a time, and soon for nine months out of the year, returning to Key West in the winter.

His book on the Virgin Mary was published in 1988, by which time he had bought a failing gallery on Canyon Road from a couple in their seventies, renamed it Southwest Creations, and begun selling the work of mostly local artists, though he represented two from Key West.

In 1990 he began his annual series of lectures at the gallery, usually one a month, including four guest lecturers, which had become a well-attended subscription program over the years, and from which Potts had produced two videotapes on art, myth, and healing, distributed by a Jungian think tank in San Francisco.

He refinanced the gallery twice in the intervening years with Sunwest Bank of New Mexico, the second refinancing being contingent on a more thoroughly worked-out business plan and the employment of a general manager, who, it came to pass, was Anita Montague. The gallery was appraised at the time as being worth upward of $400,000—based almost entirely on its real estate value—and had been showing modest profits since then. The mortgage—currently $279,000 at an interest rate of eight and a half percent—was now held by a mortgage company in Des Moines, Iowa, and included a standard commercial insurance policy of $287,000 against loss of or damage to any artwork on the premises. This policy had been raised six months earlier from $150,000.

"Around the time these O'Keeffe paintings showed up," Mo said. "Seems kind of low, doesn't it, if they're all they're cracked up to be. And if they aren't all they're cracked up to be, they aren't worth a bucket of white-wash. So what's this funny number—$137,000?"

"I'd guess it's what he could afford," Connie said. "It's just an increase in his general policy. It doesn't mention the O'Keeffes. They hadn't been authenticated by then, and there wouldn't have been any way to really value them."

"So you'd have to guess that Potts's gallery isn't what they call a big-time cash cow," Mo said.

"No, I guess not."

"And he'd bought that place out in Canones, too," Mo said.

"Last summer," Connie said. "From the bank. He put down ten thousand dollars, picked up the note. Little over three hundred a month. That's a pretty good deal."

"Okay," Mo said. "So here's a man from Rinky-dinkville, North Carolina, invents himself out of whole cloth, whips up some fancy tastes, a trendy rap, finds a little pond here where he can be a semi-big fish. But after twenty, twenty-five years he's still scramblin' his ass around making payments, right? On the gallery, on his rent, on this Canones place. Always hoping. Always smelling the pot of gold out there, it's just *got* to be out there. World holds out a lot of temptations to a man like that."

Mo sat erect in the chair next to Connie's desk, chewing at his mustache, thinking. "You remember that big fuss a while back about those fancy Eastern colleges making photographs of each of the incoming students standing naked? Some quack idea at the time about *posture* and science."

"Yes, I remember." Connie giggled. "Wasn't there something about maybe the President had been photographed like that when he was a student? When he was at Yale?"

"And his wife. Hey, I wonder if they did that stuff at Brown, too. Maybe they got old Elijah standing there straight out of Morehead City, wondering what he'd got hisself into? And a few years later he's prancing around at Bimby's Cultural Uplift Emporium tucking dollar bills in his G-string. Hah—hah. How you gonna keep 'em down on the farm?" Mo scratched his ear. "Well, what I was getting at is, I guess we're all like that now, like it or not, standing naked as a jaybird in cyberspace. Side view. Front view. Back view. I mean, some damn snoop could find out this kind of stuff about *me*, right?"

"Some of it, I guess," said Connie. "But there's a lot of your life where you didn't leave much of a trail."

Mo's eyebrows danced above his dark glasses, and he nibbled at his mustache. "Good," he said.

At eleven-fifteen Elijah Potts noticed himself in the mirror in the back room of Southwest Creations, and admired the way the white cotton shirt looked on his frame. Made in Ecuador. Collarless, pleats down the four-button placket, tiny wrinkles and creases—neither starched nor disheveled. It gave him a bit of the look of a pirate, he thought, swashbuckling. But dignified. He rolled the sleeves two folds up on his wrists and plucked a blue muslin smock from the clothes tree where he had hung his jacket earlier that morning. With the fresh white shirt protected, he turned and opened the door to the stairs that led to the second floor storage area, ducking his head as he went through the low doorway.

His feet clumped on the raw wooden stairs and he ducked his head again where the stairs turned back on themselves and led up another eight steps, opening out onto the second floor. The old couple who had owned the place before Potts told him they had intended to turn the long rectangular attic under the peaked roof into living quarters for themselves, but they had never gotten around to it. It had simply been finished off with wallboard, plastered and painted. Potts himself had built in the shelves and racks now filled with various prints and sculptures that were revolved in and out of the exhibit space downstairs, and he had also built the oaken closet that served now as a vault, hooked up with its own alarm system to an ever vigilant telephone in Minneapolis where, twenty-four hours a day every day of the year, someone waited, alert, to send the Santa Fe police scrambling into the gallery and up the stairs if the alarm went off. It seemed bizarre to Potts, this elaborate intracontinental system, but the people at American Security Systems had told him it was top of the line, and it certainly cost enough to be top of the line.

Potts crossed over to the oaken door and pressed the shiny chromium buttons. *Four. Three. Two. One.*

Then *Disarm.*

The door swung open on silent hinges, and Potts leaned in, and the world came to an end.

The vault was empty.

Empty.

He couldn't breathe. He sank on his knees, holding onto the door with one hand. He rocked backward off his knees, sat on the floor, his head between his legs, and opened his mouth and tried again to breathe.

So this is what it's like, dying.

Just one. Just one breath, he pleaded, and it burst violently into his lungs. Then another. And another. The paintings. The O'Keeffes.

Another breath.

They were gone.

Holding onto the open door, he pulled himself to his feet and looked in again. Nothing. He spun around, eyes sweeping wildly over the racks and shelves . . . maybe, maybe.

Maybe nothing. He slammed the door and crossed over to the stairs, clattering down, smacking his hand on the low ceiling where the stairs turned back on themselves, and burst out into the back room of his gallery.

He stopped, looking around the room, everything looking unfamiliar, and in the blur his eyes focused on the plastic phone receiver lying belly up on the desk. He grabbed it and punched out 911.

A long ring. And another. Five long rings. A voice, a woman's voice, and words tumbled out of him—Elijah

Potts, a robbery, Southwest Gallery, yes, on Canyon Road. No, it's not in progress, for Christ's sake, no, I've been robbed, invaluable . . . Yes, yes. Please. Please hurry.

At 11:38 Sergeant Anthony Ramirez arrived at the door of Southwest Creations with a uniformed officer, young Jameson with the freckled face, in tow. He glanced at the delta-shaped shaman that presided in the window. Its lugubrious visage reminded him of Lieutenant Ortiz.

Behind the glass of the gallery's door a sign said CLOSED, but through the reflections on the glass he could see someone pacing in the rear of the gallery, a man. Potts. Ramirez knocked on the glass three times. It had turned cloudy again, a cold breeze had stirred, and Ramirez shivered as Potts's head jerked up and he came toward the door in long, rapid strides.

Potts fumbled with the lock and swung the door open. His face was pale, and, to Ramirez, his eyes looked hollow. Like a man who had a concussion.

"Officer, yes, come in," Potts said. "What took you so long? I mean, thanks for coming. Here, please . . ."

Halfway through the door, Ramirez stopped, and the uniform behind him bumped into him. "You're glad to see us?" Ramirez said.

"Well, yes, there's been a robbery. I called 911." Potts stopped and pushed his hair away from his forehead. "But what are you . . . ? You're with . . ."

"Homicide," Ramirez said.

"I don't understand," Potts said, his eyes looking from Ramirez to the uniformed cop behind him. "The gallery has been robbed. The paintings, the O'Keeffes, they were in a vault upstairs. I went up just now, a few minutes ago, to bring them down. There's an important scholar coming to look at . . . oh, Christ." Potts looked at his watch. "I don't understand any of this. Sergeant Ramirez is it? Sergeant, what the hell is going on?"

"May we come in, Mr. Potts?"

"Yes, sure. Of course. Maybe you can . . ."

The two policemen walked into the gallery and the uniformed cop closed the door behind him.

"Mr. Potts, I am here about the death of Anita Montague."

Potts plucked at the buttons on his shirt front, a stylized white shirt with pleats. It looked foreign to Ramirez. South American.

"But I called 911 about a robbery! Don't you understand? The O'Keeffe paintings, seven of them. They've been stolen. This is a catastrophe, a nightmare! We need to do something right away, find . . . Sergeant, this is a terrible blow. And some other police are on their way. Can't we talk about Anita a little later? I'll be happy to answer any questions you have, but this robbery. I mean, we've got to . . ."

The man looked like he was about to burst into tears. Ramirez took him by the elbow and steered him toward the rear of the gallery where two armchairs flanked a delicate table.

"Mr. Potts. Why don't you sit down over there and we can try to straighten this all out." Potts slumped into one of the chairs, his head in one hand.

"This is crazy, man," Officer Jameson said.

"Very. When the others come, tell them to seal the place off." Ramirez turned to face Potts, then sat down in the chair next to him. "Mr. Potts, this is very regrettable. . . ."

"Regrettable? It's a nightmare. Those paintings—"

"No, no, it is worse, I'm afraid. You see, the medical investigator's office and the forensic people have found evidence linking you to the murder of Anita Montague, and so—"

Potts exploded out of the chair and stood before Ramirez. At the other end of the gallery, Officer Jameson spun around, and Ramirez gestured for him to stop with a wave of the hand.

"What?" Potts shouted. "Me? That's ridiculous!"

"This *is* all very strange," Ramirez said as he rose from his chair. "We got two matters here." He talked slowly, as one might to a child. "The first is this. I must tell you that we are going to take you to the police station for questioning about this murder. You are officially under arrest for suspicion of homicide."

"I've told you everything I know about that. Yesterday," Potts said.

"I think not."

"Jesus Christ, Sergeant, you can't . . . this can't be happening. Those paintings upstairs . . ." Jameson had approached Potts and took a set of handcuffs from his belt. "Handcuffs? *Hand*cuffs? Look . . ." As he pulled his hands behind his back, the officer recited the familiar statement of rights in a monotone, while Potts continued, ". . . can't we sit down and deal with this goddamned robbery first? I didn't have anything to do with this murder, for God's sake, you'll find that, but those paintings . . . why would I want to harm Anita?"

"To increase your ownership by ten percent."

"Ownership of what, for Christ's sake? This gallery? It's barely worth—"

"But the paintings," Ramirez said.

"That's the point, Sergeant, that's the whole point! The paintings are gone!" Potts writhed miserably in the cuffs. "Jesus!"

"But they weren't gone two days ago when Miz Montague was killed, correct? Now, be still. We'll go to the station and talk. Here, the other officers have come. The paintings, they were upstairs?"

"In a vault," Potts said and seemed to shrink.

"It was secured, locked, of course?"

"Yes. There's a code."

"And it is open now?"

"Yes. No. I slammed the door."

"The code?"

"Four, three, two, one, disarm. It's the same for the other system, the gallery. . . ."

Ramirez shook his head. Four, three, two, one was the default code on most security systems installed by the manufacturer. More than fifty percent of people didn't take the trouble to change the code to one of their own. That was common knowledge among law enforcement people and, Ramirez imagined, other concerned parties. And half the people who did change the code used the first four digits of their birthday, and felt safe. There were so many numbers for people to remember these days, Ramirez reflected. Social security, bank card code, zip code, area code, on and on it went . . . But still. He marveled at the perpetual stupidity of his fellow man.

Two uniformed policemen entered the gallery, and Ramirez spoke to them at length in a quiet voice. Turning to Potts, he said: "Now, you come along with us, Mr. Potts."

"But the paintings—"

"That will be dealt with."

"I get to call—"

"Of course. At the station. Come along now, Mr. Potts." He paused, his hand resting on Potts's arm. "Oh, yes, it's gotten cold again out there. It looks like it might snow again. Did you have a coat?"

"Yes. Back there. In the back room."

"Get it, Jameson."

The policeman disappeared into the back room, emerging a moment later with a peat-colored jacket of fine herringbone tweed. Ramirez took it from him and, allowing himself a narrow smile, draped it over the slumped shoulders of Elijah Potts and led him to the door. Outside, it had begun to rain lightly.

ten

By early afternoon the clouds that had been building up all morning over the Sangre de Cristo Mountains behind Santa Fe turned battleship-gray and began dropping snow silently into the parklands of spruce and ponderosa high up on the peaks. Before long, under cloud cover that had extended to the horizon, the lower piñon-juniper forest began to fill with a dusting of white, whipped and tossed by an increasing wind from the north. And soon, the rain in Santa Fe itself turned to thin snow as well, melting upon contact with the glistening streets. As the mercury dropped further, the soft curves of adobe walls and rooflines in Santa Fe were lined with white and the city took on something of the appearance of a photographic negative, an emulsion of gray, black, and white.

Residents knew that this snow, the last gasp of winter, or maybe not the last, would be gone by morning the next day when, the forecast said, temperatures would rise almost thirty degrees to the sixties and the sun would put color into the City Different once more. More winds were also in the forecast, but who could really tell about that? Early spring in Santa Fe is like a schoolchild with attention deficit disorder, good-natured enough at heart but not to be pinned down to someone else's curriculum.

Samantha Burgess of the *New Mexican* spent the afternoon sifting through the disorderly annals of Rio Arriba County, looking for further traces of Ricardo Gallegos, who had won a house in Canones in a poker game, lived there in the 1950s, and then disappeared. Or so it had been said. The woman in the old courthouse who silently presided over such records watched Samantha with undisguised suspicion, adding what Samantha decided to think of as zest to her quest.

Someone named Ricardo Gallegos had indeed owned the house during the period in question, but there was no record of who had owned it before, or when, in fact, it had been built. In the communitarian world of a northern New Mexico village, such things just happened in those days without particular reference to the interests of so distant and irrelevant an entity as a county government. There was no record, either, of this Ricardo Gallegos having been born, baptized, licensed to drive, married, divorced, employed, arrested, or elected to any county office, though Samantha knew he might have experienced many such rites without it having been recorded by the county. State records, she had already found, were equally innocent of the presence of this Ricardo Gallegos. No doubt he lived on, however wispily, in oral history, old stories, but she had already found that no one was likely to tell them to a young Anglo reporter from the newspaper in Santa Fe.

By the time she gave up on Ricardo Gallegos, her car was covered with two inches of wet snow over a thin film of ice, which her anemic windshield wipers were not equal to, forcing her to scrape it away with the edge of her Visa card, held in her bare hand.

It was just such days—gray and cold and frustrating—that Samantha had hoped to escape when she moved from Wisconsin to Santa Fe and took up the life of the freelancer, soon enough landing her job with the *New Mexican.* Bad weather and fruitless searches depressed her, and at such times she seriously thought about Prozac.

In the Santa Fe Police Department, Sergeant Anthony Ramirez completed the paperwork legitimizing his arrest of Elijah Potts. At one point a young woman cop named Maria dropped a thin sheaf of papers on his desk with a saucy smile, and Ramirez sifted through them, noting a copy of the phone records of Southwest Creations for the month before the murder—records he had routinely ordered up the morning after. No real need for them now, he thought, his eye idly skimming over them. But then he stopped, looked again, and called a familiar number at the phone company. A moment later he put the receiver down, leaned back and looked at the ceiling, thinking, maybe he'd go around to the cells and ask Elijah Potts a few questions.

But no. No point yet. Potts was in a windowless but clean holding cell, adamantly exercising his right to say nothing to anyone until his attorney made an appearance. His attorney, Philip Arguleta, a locally prominent graduate of the University of New Mexico law school, was in District Court for the day, waiting his chance to argue a motion for a court-ordered halt to construction of a ceramic tile manufacturing plant on the fringe of the old Hispanic neighborhood along Agua Fría. Tomorrow, Ramirez thought, was time enough to talk to Potts. He looked at his notebook, and picked up the phone again.

Upon finding Southwest Creations Gallery closed at the time of her appointment, Fredericka Ball Mansfield, art expert from New Orleans and composer of the now nearly complete catalogue raisonné of Georgia O'Keeffe's works, blew up. Back at La Fonda she called her office, explained to her secretary that so far as she was concerned Santa Fe and all its inhabitants were flakes, poseurs, frauds, or criminals. She went on to say that the newly discovered (but yet unseen by her) *alleged* O'Keeffe paintings were surely some sort of puerile and opportunistic scam that might excite the provincials but not her, and she was damned if she would legitimize them by even considering such an obvious sham for inclusion in the catalogue. She thereupon hired a car to take her the sixty miles to Albuquerque's airport and a plane back to New Orleans, where, among other things, it did not snow.

Some three hundred miles east of Santa Fe, in a Motel 6 located on the eastern outskirts of Amarillo, on an ever-widening and sunbaked plain, Ramón Tofoya woke up with a severe headache, bathed in sweat from his turbulent dreams of lying on a gurney while dark-skinned surgeons, speaking in rapid Spanish and visibly grinning behind their green masks, removed glistening pink things from a gaping and oddly painless incision in his stomach.

Only partly awake, and with the dull weight of daytime sleep in his skull, Tofoya stared at the cracked plaster ceiling and tried to imagine where he was. He put one hand on his stomach to reassure himself, stood up and went into the bathroom. Standing over the toilet, waiting for his bladder to obey, Tofoya began to piece together his last twelve hours or so, remembering that he had managed to bring into the motel room from the back of his now nearly terminal Mustang seven sixteen-by-twenty paintings of some fucking bones and blobs floating in a blue sky near some mountain, the blobs on some of the paintings looking like some kind of . . . what? Medical shit.

Finally relieved, he went purposefully back into the dim room where a plastic curtain was drawn against the torrid Texas sun. Outside, all around the motel, lay the same kind of flat, featureless, unrelentingly dull landscape that had so inspired a young artist almost a century earlier and had eventually led her, as if impelled by fate, to the open skies of New Mexico. But Ramón Tofoya knew none of this. Though a child of the plains some thirty years earlier, he preferred not to look at them. In his darkened motel room he turned on a light.

"I better have another look at those things," he said out loud, and winced at the subtle increase in pressure the act of speaking put on his aching temples. He loosened the string he had lashed around the seven canvases and peered at them. The stark lines were unappealing to him, the repetition of subject matter meaningless. He had seen stuff like this somewhere. The more he thought about it, he remembered seeing things like this in posters here and there around Santa Fe, in restaurant bathrooms, places like that. These ones all had this weird blob in the hole of the big white bone. More and more detailed, if that is what you called it. On one, the blob looked like . . . like what? Like some kind of pro-life propaganda. Tofoya looked away.

Gross, he thought. Maybe he had junk here. But then, they *had* been in that vault. People don't put junk in vaults.

Jesus, he thought to himself, none of these fuckers are signed. Junk.

He shoved the nearest painting, and, like dominoes, they all fell on the floor.

Fucking junk.

Then Ramón Tofoya noticed a mark like a brand had been painted on the back of one of the canvases. It was an *O* with a *K* inside. He turned the other six over and saw the same brand.

O-K. O-K. O-K.

It began to dawn on Ramón Tofoya just what he had in his crappy room in this crappy Motel 6 on this shit-eating flat plain in the panhandle of Texas. O-*Kay*. He had a fortune. A fucking fortune!

While the snow drifted down in Santa Fe early in the afternoon, Connie Barnes remained in her office in the adobe house on Canyon Road, trying to pluck additional tidbits about Elijah Potts out of the electronic ether. She was particularly interested in finding more out about Potts's years in Provincetown, right after his time at Brown University and up to his wedding on the beach.

She and Mo had eaten lunch earlier at the kitchen table, both silently pondering the emerging biography of Elijah Potts, and eventually Mo had said: "A nomad like that, he doesn't make many real friends in this world. He comes and goes among a lot of people. Charms 'em for a time, then goes off. May stay in touch, call 'em when some itchy need reminds him. But no real friends along the way. Does Potts have any real close friends here in Santa Fe that you're aware of?"

Connie had said no, none that she knew of.

"If a man like that has any real friends, he made 'em early. Maybe in college, but he sounds like he was kind of a loner there. Probably in the years right after that. I'd be willing to bet my dinner that those days in Provincetown were the happiest days in Elijah Potts's life. It's then you make your life friends, if you ever do. You know, the people you can always pick up with, depend on, even if you haven't seen 'em for years. It'd sure be nice to know who all those people were, dancing around bare-ass on the beach when Elijah got married."

"What makes you think they were all naked?" Connie had asked.

"Hah—hah. I don't know that for sure. But I reckon I would've been."

Connie clucked her tongue, grinned to herself, and went back to her computer.

By four o'clock the snow had stopped in the city, though it continued to fall in the higher elevations, and the word was out in Santa Fe that Elijah Potts had been taken in for questioning or maybe even arrested on suspicion of murder in the case of Anita Montague. This was soon followed by a murky rumor that the seven paintings Potts had found and had announced were by Georgia O'Keeffe had in some unspecified way been tampered with. The Santa Fe Police Department was yet to make any official announcement about any of this, which made each morsel of the news all the more delectable.

Sergeant Ramirez let the motor of his vehicle idle while he gazed at the one-story adobe house with its small metal windows, twin front doors, and two macadam paths leading up to them from the sidewalk. The right side of the house had been rented by the late Carolyn Marcy, waitress from Illinois, and now in the scraggly brown grass beside what had been her front door was a hand-lettered sign saying FOR RENT. Life goes on.

The left side of the house was rented by the outstandingly beautiful Norah Vargas, from one of the old families of the north, and currently hostess at Mediterranean Light, with whom Ramirez had spoken this morning. She confirmed by phone that Elijah Potts had been at the restaurant the night of the murder and had left at nine, nine-thirty, making it barely possible he had committed the murder.

Opportunity.

It called for confirmation, of course, and instead of asking the Vargas woman to come to the station as he had said he would, Ramirez decided to talk to her at her house. There is much to be learned by seeing somebody's house, especially when the visit is unannounced. It was not merely a commitment to routine thoroughness that had brought Ramirez here. Something else was bugging him—two something elses, in fact, and one of them was a legitimate police question to be cleared up.

He listened to his engine purr in neutral. It sounded smooth enough. He revved it lightly, and let it return to idle. Cylinders sounded fine to him. Manuel Trujillo, master mechanic and low-rider king, was probably full of shit. Ramirez smiled. Who isn't? He flicked off the ignition and walked up the macadam path.

Next to the door was a worn doorbell button, and Ramirez thumbed it two times, hearing it buzz inside. He waited awhile, then buzzed it again, supposing he should have called first. But he had wanted the element of surprise. It never hurts to put people a bit off balance. He buzzed again, and turned to face the street. Two kids went by on bicycles, maybe eight-year-olds, and an old woman with two brown grocery bags clutched in her arms shuffled down the other side of the street past houses that looked almost exactly like the one where Ramirez was waiting. One of the kids fell off his bike with a yelp, and the old woman watched attentively as he got up, looked around, and remounted. Only then did she continue on her way.

Ramirez was about to give up hope of putting anyone off balance, when he heard the lock click, and turned to see the door open an inch or two. A black eye looked out at him from under a few strands of very black, very wet hair.

"Miz Vargas?" he said. "Sergeant Ramirez. We talked earlier this morning."

"Oh yes," she said. "I was . . . well, come in." The door opened, and Ramirez swallowed rapidly twice.

Norah Vargas was smiling up at him, black soapy hair streaming down her cheeks and shoulders like rivulets, wearing only a white towel that was wrapped around her torso. Despite his training and his natural courtesy, his eyes quickly raked downward, sweeping past the top of her breasts, squeezed so pertly together by the towel and glistening with shampoo, and down to the coffee-ice-cream-colored hips and legs, dazzling with soap and droplets of water that emerged from below the towel. Her toenails were painted a deep crimson, and soapy water running off her ankles and her feet was making a small puddle on the carpet.

"Uh," Ramirez said, looking up past her head into the room.

"I was in the shower. It took me a while to get to the door." She smiled. A bit of mischief in the smile, Ramirez thought. A generous mouth and perfect white teeth. She looked just like some movie star, but who? "What can I do for you?"

"A few questions, Miz Vargas, if you don't mind."

"Oh, yes, come in," she said, stepping back to open the door farther. Ramirez stepped inside. "I won't be a minute," she said. Ramirez watched her retreat across the living room. Her long black hair hung down past glistening shoulder blades and about six inches past the upper edge of the towel, and her hips moved with a confident sway under the white terry cloth.

I sure got *her* off balance, Ramirez thought to himself as she disappeared into what he supposed was the bedroom, leaving the door open. Who *was* that movie star? She's a dead ringer. He looked at the wet footprints on the carpet leading from and back into the bedroom, and sighed.

"Make yourself at home, Sergeant," she called from the bedroom. "There's some coffee on the stove." He heard the shower come on and a shower door clank into place.

He was standing in the middle of a tan-carpeted living room some fifteen feet square, furnished with two comfortable-looking easy chairs covered in a mostly barn-red print, facing a small sofa upholstered with some kind of nubby orange and yellow material. They looked new, at least the upholstery did. To their left was a fireplace with a wooden mantelpiece, over which hung a large painting of a kachina rising above an old pueblo village in a pink sky that glowed as if it were truly dawn. A tidy fire of cedar logs sizzled in the fireplace.

A hardcover book was open on the seat of the easy chair nearest the fire. He stepped over to the chair and picked it up. A romance novel, as proclaimed by a bare-chested, black-haired Adonis holding a cutlass in one hand while, with his other arm, he clasped the waist of a gorgeous young redhead. She wore a ruffly purple dress that barely covered her bosom, now swollen with passion for Adonis, while some kind of battle evidently raged around them in the light of a dying sun.

Ramirez put the book down and stepped over to the fireplace, confirming that the kachina painting was by Dan Namingha, the local Hopi artist, a big shot, worth a lot of money, though how much Ramirez couldn't say. On the other side of the room, the near doorway led into a small, tidy kitchen and the far one into the bedroom.

The layout was a reverse copy of the one next door where Carolyn Marcy had lived, but her place had been furnished sparsely with the kind of secondhand stuff and wall posters of a college kid.

Ramirez glanced a bit furtively into the bedroom, which seemed to be taken up mostly by a bed with a yellow dust ruffle, a yellow comforter, and a lot of colorful pillows. He looked away, letting his eyes wander around the living room, noting a recessed bookshelf above the sofa, which housed two wooden santos, a small array of paperback books—all of them read, judging from the creases in their spines—and a few large-format hardcover books, art books of some sort, their jackets a bit ragged. Relics of college, maybe.

He looked back at the santos. One, dark-featured, standing within a delicately carved full-body halo and on an upturned crescent, Ramirez recognized as Nuestra Señora de Guadalupe, the popular patroness of all the Mexican and Indian peoples. The other, more crudely carved, and adorned in a faded red robe with a crucifix in one hand and a lamb in the other, seemed older. He had no idea who it was. His mother had some twenty santos in her house, every niche and cranny, but he had never seen this one.

Turning away from the two icons, he looked back at the front door. Beside it was an old-fashioned coatrack of curved, dark wood on which a puffy light blue parka hung, probably filled with down, along with a longer woolen jacket of dark purple material with a thick knap—probably wool. They both looked expensive. He stepped over to the coatrack and idly scratched the collar of the purple jacket with his forefinger. It smelled strongly of perfume. On the wall behind the coatrack was a black-and-white photograph of an old masonry building like those one sees in any number of old northern New Mexico towns. It had a shallow peaked roof of tin, and a narrow portal across the front, also of tin and supported by two whitewashed round poles. Above the tin portal it said VIGIL'S STORE, and under the portal, painted on the wall to the right of the front door, was an almost exact duplicate of the santo across the room, the one with the crucifix and lamb. On the other side of the front door it said:

SANTOS
WOODCARVING
POPSICLES

Ramirez turned when he heard Norah Vargas enter the living room. She was dressed totally in white—loose white slacks, a loose white shirt with a revealing scoop neck, and white sandals—except for a brightly colored cloth belt tied around her waist, its ends dangling at her hip. Her long wet black hair clung closely to the side of her head before plunging straight down the back. She smelled fresh and good.

"This is a very nice place you have here, Miz Vargas."

"It's cozy," she said, smiling again. "Would you like to sit down, Sergeant?" She gestured to one of the easy chairs, and as he sat down, she took a seat in the middle of the sofa, crossing her legs.

"The santo there, with the lamb," Ramirez said. "Who is it?"

She laughed. "Nuestra Señora de los Angeles," she said. "One of my uncles carved it for me when I was little. I used to be scared of the dark, and he made it for me to keep me safe. She is in charge of all the angels and is very effective at monster control. Were you scared of monsters when you were little, Sergeant?"

"Only the ones under the bed." He glanced at the narrow foot with red toenails bobbing in his direction, wishing he wasn't a cop with duties and rules of professional behavior that prevented him from reaching out for that foot. He cleared his throat.

"Well, this morning on the telephone you told me that Elijah Potts had dinner at Mediterranean Light on Sunday night."

"Yes, I showed him to his table, and afterward he paid me at the cash register."

Ramirez's eyebrows lifted. "He didn't pay at the table?"

"No. We were shorthanded that night and service at the tables was a bit slow."

"Ah. And did he seem in a hurry?"

"No. Not at all. We talked at the cash register, chatted."

"He paid with a credit card?"

"Yes, I forget which. We take them all. Oh, yes, there's a record of it, of course."

"He ate alone?"

"Yes, he was reading a book."

"You know him well?"

"To talk to. He's very charming. Very witty. I've been to his gallery a few times, and he comes to the restaurant quite often, maybe twice a month."

"Ah. But he's not . . ."

She grinned, a lovely sight. "He's not my type, Sergeant. Wouldn't you say he's in his mid-forties? Quite good-looking, but . . ." She shrugged, still grinning.

"This afternoon," Ramirez said, looking directly into her eyes, "we took him into custody. Suspicion in the murder of his partner Anita Montague." He watched the grin fade from her face, frown lines crease her forehead.

"My God." She looked around the room, uncrossed her legs, recrossed them. "But he was at the restaurant. . . ."

"Until nine or nine-thirty, you said. Which was it?"

Her eyes widened, black pupils rimmed entirely by the whites. She was all black and white, Ramirez noticed, black features and white clothes, against the orange and yellow sofa, immobile, like a picture from one of those snappy shelter magazines.

"It was very busy," she began. "Very busy, but I think . . . let me see. I know it was after nine, yes, someone called a little after nine to see if we were serving dinner still, and it was after that. . . . It must have been later, about twenty past?"

"And you chatted for a moment when he paid his bill."

"Yes, we talked about those O'Keeffe paintings, the new ones. Everyone has been talking about them. And after that, he *killed* . . . ?"

"Yes, that seems to be the case. And you see, Miz Vargas, I am just trying to get all the details, all the timing of things that night down clearly in my head. Can you tell me what time you arrived at the restaurant that night?"

"Of course. It wasn't that night. It was at eleven-thirty that morning. I work both lunch and dinner there."

Ramirez nodded. "Oh. Yes. Do you get a break in the afternoon?"

"An hour or two. Not really enough to do much of anything," she said with a mild pout. "I have to be back there by five, and sometimes the last lunch crowd hangs around until three, three-thirty, even four. It's really not a very good job. Kind of boring."

"But it pays well enough?" Ramirez said.

She shrugged. "You want to know what I earn?"

"No, no. That's okay." Ramirez nodded, as if to himself. "So, of course," he said, glancing briefly over at the Namingha painting, "you weren't at home that evening—say, about seven-thirty or eight. You were at the restaurant."

"Yes," she said, a look of surprise on her face. "Why?"

"You have an answering machine?"

"Yes, it's in the kitchen." She recrossed her legs again.

"Did you find any messages on it that evening? When you came home after work?"

Norah Vargas blinked, pulled her knee up toward her. "Let me think. That night, I came in late and went to bed right away. I didn't check the messages. But, let's see. Yes, in the morning I listened to the tape. There were two messages. One was from an old friend of mine, he's in Colorado now."

"And the other one, the one from Southwest Creations? Who was that calling you?"

Norah's eyes looked steadily into his, no flinch, no sign of anything. "It was Anita Montague," she said. "She wanted to get together."

"About what?"

"She didn't say. Just said she wanted to get together, maybe we could have breakfast one of these days, you know? She knew about my schedule at the restaurant." She paused, plucked at her sleeve. "I hadn't thought of that, put the two things together. She called me the night she got killed. That's real spooky. Awful."

"In fact," Ramirez said, "the phone company's records show that you got a lot of calls from the gallery over the last month or so."

"Well, sure. We're—We were friends. See each other now and then."

"But not—"

A short laugh burst from Norah Vargas's pretty mouth, and she leaned forward, quite obviously inviting Ramirez to enjoy a glimpse of her excellent breasts. "Oh, Sergeant. For heaven's sake! I am definitely not one of *them.* I think that's fine if that's what you like but, believe me, I'm one of your traditional, hot-blooded passionate Spaniard ladies. Hetero as they come." She leaned back on the sofa. "Very romantic. Like the woman on the jacket of the book you looked at."

Ramirez nodded. "I didn't mean to—"

"Sergeant, you're kind of cute when you're embarrassed. Are we, um, done with the questions now?"

"One other, actually," he said. "This is your day off." He paused, and Norah Vargas sat back and crossed her arms around her. "I'm curious why you were at the restaurant this morning, this being your day off, when I called this morning to talk to the manager or whoever about when and if Elijah Potts had been there that night."

Her eyes bored into him. Expressionless. She tightened her arms under her breasts. "I went back to the restaurant to get my clothes. I changed at the restaurant last night. I had a date after work. In fact, I was gone all night. So I went back this morning on my way home and got them. When you called there, I was on my way out. There wasn't anyone else there but the cooks. Luis—he's the manager—he doesn't usually get there before ten-thirty. Anything else?"

"I'm sorry to intrude in private things, Miz Vargas. Into your lifestyle." He shrugged. "Murder investigations have their own necessary dialectic."

"I understand."

Ramirez stood up. "I'm glad you were truthful with me."

She remained seated.

"It's the one who fell off the boat," Ramirez said suddenly.

"What?"

"The actress, the one who died when she fell off a motorboat."

"What are you—"

"That's who you reminded me of today. I can't think of her name, for the life of me."

"You mean Natalie Wood?"

"Sí. That's the one."

Norah Vargas stood up, tugged her white shirt down under the belt. "Sergeant, can I tell you something?"

Ramirez nodded. "Sí. By all means."

"Women don't like to be told they look like someone else. Even someone beautiful like Natalie Wood. We like to think we're each uniquely breathtaking. Sí, Sergeant?" She flashed him a big smile with perfect white teeth. "Here, I'll see you out."

Ramirez raised both his hands. "Please," he mumbled. "It's not necessary."

As he closed the front door, he looked back into the room. Norah Vargas wasn't there. Gone into one of the other rooms. A formidable young woman, Ramirez thought. Very classy.

But not up on her santos. Our Lady of the Angels had a blue robe, not a red one, and carried a sword and a dove, not a crucifix and a lamb. She presided over a room in his mother's house, keeping the monsters at bay, and Ramirez knew her well.

A beautiful woman, Ramirez thought as he stepped into his vehicle and fastened his seat belt. Like Natalie Wood, but more . . . what? Ample.

And a very accomplished liar. Aristocratic, yes, but surely not descended from the conquistadors as she would have us think.

It took Ramirez fifteen minutes to get back to the station. Cerrillos Road was experiencing one of its ever more frequent tie-ups. The city was growing. No, the city wasn't growing. That was the problem. It was staying the same size and too many people were filling it up. As he approached the door to his little cubicle, the diminutive cop, Maria, looked up from her desk and flagged him down.

"Your friend called. The sculptor? He tole me to tell

you he wants to celebrate"—she looked down at a pink piece of paper—" 'your great criminological triumph.' He said to meet him at Maria's at six-thirty if you wanted. He's cute, that guy," Maria said.

Ramirez looked at her, puzzled. She stood five-one if that.

Cute? Bowdre cute? Cute like an ox.

"You really think he's *cute*?"

"Damn right. You don' want to go, I'll take your place."

"He's taken, Maria."

"Yeah, I know," she said. "Damn shame. Let me know if that big Hopi woman blows it, okay?"

Ramirez went into his office shaking his head.

eleven

“We got to stop meeting like this.”

“Hey, Tony. Sit down.”

“Hi, Tony.”

“Hi, Connie.”

“What do you mean, we gotta stop meeting like this?”

“Chief says so.”

“How come?”

“He says it looks bad for the department we get help from amateurs.”

“Help on what?”

“Like homicides. He says we should be able to do this stuff without getting help from private citizens.”

“Uh-huh. You know there’s a fable of some sort about a bird that was doomed to fly in ever-diminishing circles until it flew right up . . . well, beg your pardon, Connie.”

“My sentiments exactly,” Tony Ramirez said.

“Anyway, who says we’re even interested that you people arrested Elijah Potts for suspicion in the murder of Anita Montague? Just another fellow human being.

No damn concern of ours. You want one of these here margaritas?"

"Sí. Why don't you choose one for me, since you're paying?"

"Miss? We'll have one number thirty-six margarita for Sherlock Holmes here. Tony, you know what a margarita is?"

"Of course. Tequila, triple sec, and lemon or lime juice. Ice. You got to use real tequila, made from the heart of the blue agave plant. A lot of your cheap American tequila doesn't have enough of the agave stuff in it. It's an old Mexican drink."

"Hah—hah. Maybe not."

"What do you mean?"

"See, I was askin' them here about that before you came. It seems that some boys visiting Palm Springs after the war—that's World War Two—took to snorting a shot of tequila with some lime and a lick of salt like the Mexicans do. Then the wives showed up and didn't like that so much, seemed a bit inelegant or whatever. So this bartender got an idea, poured the tequila on ice, threw a little triple sec in there, some lime juice, put some salt on the rim of the glass all pretty, and the wimenfolk thought that was just beautiful."

"So you're saying that this Mexican contribution to civilization is really another gringo invention, huh? And tamales? I guess they really came from Boston along with the refried baked beans."

"Well, the bartender was probably from Mexico, wouldn't you bet? Man's name is lost to history. And isn't that just typical? We know all about Thomas Edison and all those guys, but people who invent the really important things . . . So tell me, what makes you think Potts killed that woman? That boy is about as likely a murderer as Wee Willie Winkie. Couldn't it be a random piece of violence like we're all getting accustomed to here in the Land of Enchantment?"

"I was wondering when you were going to ask. In the first place, my sources say there were some roaming scumbags, come in from Texas, that might have done the Marcy woman, maybe the other one. But not Montague. I'm inclined to trust this particular grapevine."

"Oh. Can I inquire as to who . . . I mean just as a matter of curiosity?"

"It's Manuel Trujillo. You know, the guy who makes hydraulic systems for the low riders. He keeps his ear to the ground."

"I know him," Mo said. "Old Manuel. There's a boy with real cojones."

"And as for Potts," Ramirez went on, "for starters we got motive, opportunity, and forensic evidence tying him to the dead woman."

"Oh."

Mo Bowdre's dark glasses stared at Ramirez across the wooden table in Maria's bar. In the absence of conversation at the table, they all listened to the strains of Leonard Bernstein's music for *West Side Story*, which was playing quietly over the loudspeakers. Someone was singing Maria, Maria, Ma-reeee-ya.

"Anything else you want to know?" Ramirez asked.

"Nah."

"Good. You know the chief and how he—"

"Right. The chief. But, say, I thought Potts said he had an alibi," Mo said. "Wasn't he at that Mediterranean Light place that night?"

"Yeah, but it seems like he left around nine-twenty, which gives him time to get over there."

"I see. He takes his bicycle chain to Mediterranean Light, keeps it all coiled up on his lap, maybe wrapped up in a little shopping bag to keep the grease off his new cavalry twill trousers from the Peterman catalogue while he eats his tabouli, and then he nips over to wherever Anita might be that night, out riding on her bicycle somewhere in the middle of Santa Fe."

"All I'm saying is this woman at Mediterranean Light, Norah Vargas, a hostess, she says he left at nine-twenty, around then. And that gives him time. That Vargas woman is something, by the way. Looks like Natalie Wood, but plumper."

Connie sniffed. "I'm glad to hear the Santa Fe P.D. pays attention to that kind of thing."

"Well . . ."

"I was just thinking, Tony," Connie said, grinning wolfishly, "you sort of remind me of that Puerto Rican guy, the actor, played in *La Bamba*. Then they put him in that movie, *The Dark Wind*. Played an Indian. You're as cute as him but you're, you know, bigger in the chest? Real nice pecs."

"Okay, okay. Sorry. Anyway, this Vargas woman, she claims she's some kind of descendant of the first Spanish guys in New Mexico. But she isn't."

"Really," Mo said.

"Yeah. You get to recognize these things."

"Hey, an ethnic secret. Cool."

"No big deal, Mo."

"Elementary?"

"If you make a lot of noise about being part of those old conquistador families, you probably wouldn't have Our Lady of Guadalupe taking care of things in your house. A santo."

"You wouldn't? Why not?"

"She's more a patron for the mestizos—Mexicans, Indians. Common people. Riffraff. You know, like me."

"I see. Flotsam and jetsam. So this woman Vargas who lies about her ancestry tells you when Potts left the restaurant, establishing beyond the shadow of a reasonable doubt his guilt in a matter of life and death. This is terrific. You talk to the D.A. about this? Is she pleased?"

Ramirez ignored him. "So the Montague woman was out on her bicycle, and we had already figured it had to be someone she knew on the sidewalk waiting with this bicycle chain hidden."

"Good," Mo said. "In his shopping bag."

"Because she didn't go off the sidewalk onto the street. Like any woman would if she saw some stranger standing there in the dark. You know, with all the talk of these killings—the Trasher, all that. So she slows up, says hi or whatever, and the guy, this aquaintance at *least*, swings the chain, *whap*! and knocks her off the bike right there on the sidewalk. The scrape marks on the sidewalk are unmistakable. Then he snapped her neck while she was grabbing at his arm around her throat."

Mo held his glass up. "Congratulations. With stage

directions like this, they could make a TV movie out of it."

"See, she had fibers under her fingernails." Ramirez told about the fibers from the Norfolk jacket, about the alert work of the M.I.'s tracking the Peterman catalogue customer list. "So Elijah Potts is the only guy still alive in Santa Fe who owns one of these Norfolk jackets from the Peterman people. Q.D."

"There's a *E* in there."

"What?"

"It's Q.*E*.D. *Quod erat demonstrandum.* That's Latin for—"

"Right."

"Open and shut," Mo said. "Case closed." He held his glass up again in congratulations. "What about the paintings? They say they were stolen."

"Amazing. Same time we go to arrest Potts, he's called 911 about the robbery. So he's happy to see us, if you can imagine that. Until we tell him why we're there, of course."

"What about the robbery?"

"I don't know. Not my department. Someone went in and stole 'em." He explained about the failure to change the default code on the security system. "So anyway, they're stolen."

"You believe that?" Mo said.

"Yeah, why not?"

"So Elijah, good old smooth-talking Elijah, took you in."

"Took *me* in? I took *him* in. What're you talking

about? He was really upset about those paintings. Looked like he'd been hit with a hammer."

"Maybe he stole the paintings."

"From himself?" Ramirez snorted. "Why would anybody do that?"

"Beats me, Tony. And anyway, that's none of *our* business either, right, Connie? The chief said so. So what would you like to eat here? I recommend the posole, Connie. Got *cuerenos* in it."

"Cueritos," Ramirez said.

"Yeah, like I said, little bits of bacon. Tell us more about Norah Vargas, Tony. You get a funny timbre in your voice when you're talking about her."

"Interesting. That Montague woman at the gallery? She called Vargas at home the night she was killed. Around seven-thirty. Left a message on the answering machine that she wanted to get together with her sometime. They were friends."

"But not . . . ?"

"No way, man. Not her. I figure she's got a sugar daddy or whatever. Really nice little place she's got, a big Namingha painting over the fireplace. You don't buy one of those with a hostess's salary."

"You've been busy. Got your collar."

"Doin' the people's work," Ramirez said. "Here she comes with my margarita. Man, they're busy here tonight."

The phone was ringing when Claudia Potts let herself through the slatted gate from Petronia Street onto the narrow slate patio, and it continued ringing as she unlocked the door to her bedroom off the patio. As the fourth ring ended, she picked it up, expecting that the answering service would already have intervened, but said "Hello" anyway.

"Mrs. Potts?" An unfamiliar male voice.

"Yes." She looked back toward the door at Jimmy, who was closing it behind him. She shrugged as he looked questioningly at her.

"This is Philip Arguleta. I am calling from Santa Fe."

Alarms went off, clanging in Claudia Potts's brain.

"Yes?" she said. Jimmy sat down on the king-sized bed with its cheerful floral cover and began unlacing the front of his pale yellow shirt. Claudia had bought it for him the other day, a modified polo shirt that laced up from below the ribs to the throat. Very sexy.

"I am an attorney and I am representing your husband, Mrs. Potts. I have to report to you that he has been placed under arrest."

"What?" It was almost a shout, and Jimmy looked up at her. "What do you mean?" she asked, recovering her normal voice.

"Well, you see, Mrs. Potts, he's been arrested by the Santa Fe police and is in jail under suspicion in the murder of Anita Montague. You heard about—"

"Yes, yes, that she was killed. But Elijah?"

"I'm sorry I have to bring you this news, Mrs. Potts, but the police have amassed a certain amount of evidence that points to your husband's involvement in this crime."

"Involvement?"

"As the perpetrator."

Claudia was silent. Jimmy pulled the yellow shirt up

over his head and let it fall to the floor with a perhaps unconscious flexing of his chest and arm muscles. A rooster, Claudia thought with part of her mind as, with the rest of it, she tried to surround the new information coming at her over the phone.

"Excuse me, I didn't quite get your name, Mister . . ." she said.

"Arguleta, ma'am. Philip Arguleta."

"Thank you, Mr. Arguleta. Uh, I don't quite know what to say. How serious is this?"

"Homicide is a very serious business, and the police do have some evidence that definitely points toward your husband. It is circumstantial, of course, but damaging. Presumably, they'll be collecting as much more as they can to strengthen their case. They may feel they have enough now for an arraignment. If not, they will probably let him go on his own recognizance, but I seriously doubt that will be the case."

"Jesus," Claudia hissed.

"I have tried to, ah, force the issue by demanding a speedy arraignment, which is of course his right, so I should have more to tell you by tomorrow morning. But Elijah wanted me to let you know what the situation is as of now."

"What does he want me to do?"

"That, he didn't say, Mrs. Potts. But he also asked me to inform you that the paintings are missing. Evidently stolen."

"What?"

"Yes, a burglary of some sort, discovered earlier

today. Another department of the police is working on that. It's all a bit confusing."

Claudia Potts barely listened as the lawyer went on in a lawyer's monotone about the complexities of jurisdictions and God knew what else. She stared unseeing as a bare-chested Jimmy lay back on the bed, his feet up, and began to push his white cotton jeans down around his hips.

"Jesus," she said to herself, and then *"Stop that!"* as she reached out and smacked Jimmy's abdomen with the flat of her hand.

"Hey!"

"What? I beg you pardon?" Arguleta said on the phone.

"Nothing. Nothing. Hold on, please." She smacked Jimmy again, her other hand covering the receiver. "Goddamn it, Jimmy."

"What the hell did I do?"

"Put your goddamned clothes on!"

"What the fuck is going on here? Who is that?" He sat up with a pout.

Claudia spoke into the phone. "Excuse me, just one moment." Then to Jimmy: "The party's over. It's not your fault. I'm sorry. Sorry I smacked you. You've got to go now. *I've* got to go now. Get the hell out of here."

"Well, shit," Jimmy said. "This is really something." He stood up and zipped his fly. "This is really something, Claudia."

Claudia heard him still complaining as he slammed the bedroom door and then the gate.

"Mr. Arguleta, please excuse me. You say that the

paintings have been stolen and that my husband is in jail on suspicion of murdering Anita Montague. Is that right?"

"Sí. Yes."

"And this all happened on the same day? Today?"

"Mr. Potts was arrested today, yes, this afternoon. I would have called you earlier but I was before a federal judge until late this afternoon and only got to see your husband this evening. And I'm sorry to interrupt you so late in the evening—it's what? Ten-thirty in Florida now? As for the burglary, it was discovered today, yes, but it could have happened . . . well, who knows at this point?"

"How much of this is public knowledge?" Claudia asked.

"The arrest is public. The theft of the paintings is still under investigation, so I don't think it has been announced."

"Oh, God. Well, Mr. Arguleta, I'll see about a plane."

"Yes. If there is anything I can do . . . Have you met at the airport . . ."

"No, no. I'll take care of all that. I should be there tomorrow evening."

The lawyer left his telephone number and his address on Guadalupe Street, and apologized for being the messenger of so much bad news. After he hung up, Claudia Potts stared into the phone receiver for a moment until it began to squeal at her. She slammed it down, sat down on the bed with her fists clenched between her thighs and said, "Damn. Damn. *Damn!*" She looked around her nest.

Jimmy's new yellow shirt with the laces was in a heap on the floor.

"Damn," she said again, and picked up the phone.

In the thin light from the stars, Connie Barnes watched the big man open the gate into their enclosed backyard off Canyon Road and walk in measured steps toward the covered patio. Familiar ground. There were so many places for which Mo Bowdre had developed some unfathomable kind of internal map, where he could walk unhesitatingly and surely in the perpetual dark. Here in his own backyard it would be impossible for a stranger to tell that he was blind. And on less familiar ground, he could walk a half step behind a seeing companion and hardly ever miss a beat. In the first days, months, she had known him, Connie had wondered why Mo refused to use the blind man's stick, refused to own a dog. It was, it had seemed to her at first, what the psychologists called denial. But he rarely made any bones about his blindness. He wasn't interested in hiding it. Maybe it was a kind of arrogance. That was it, partly, she had concluded. That, and the challenge.

Once, as a young girl in her village on the Hopi mesas, she had climbed onto the roof of her uncle's house, where he had tethered a young eagle. The bird had looked alertly at her from one eye, its head cocked, as she approached a few short paces at a time. The closer she got, the larger the fierce eye loomed in her mind—golden orange and black, deep, glimmering, without expression, surrounded by tiny feathers that rose and fell in the breeze—an enormous eye, staring at her, and she had wondered: Just what does that eye see? She knew she would never know, never understand the challenges it faced in whatever world it could see, never know how that eye resolved such things into some useful form of reality. She couldn't remember at the time how long she had stood staring into the eye of her uncle's eagle—it could have been a minute, maybe much more—but finally it had turned its head, and she had woken as if from a dream. How could you know an eagle's world? You couldn't.

As hard as she tried, she couldn't know Mo's world, either.

She watched him pause, sniff the air in the weak light of the stars, and turn.

"I do believe we've seen the last of those damned winds," he said. "You want to sit out here for a while?" She followed him over to the concrete bench surrounded with perennials, where she waited most mornings for the sun. "These penstemons showing any signs of life?" he asked.

Connie sat on the bench beside him. "It's a little early," she said.

"I remember those red ones you get up in the mountains. You'd be walking along in the trees and there one would be, reddest damn thing in the world, a couple of stems blowing in the wind, those little red flowers like tubes up and down the stems holding on for dear life. Like pennants on a boat, you know, those flags they use, alpha, beta, Charlie, whatever. Cocktail time, all kinds of messages you can send with those little flags. Now, there's another language for you. Boat language."

Connie was accustomed to people talking about something else besides what they really were concerned about. The old men at Hopi would do that, circling in on something while they looked the other way. Mo sniffed again.

"What is he, about six foot? Six-one?"

"Who?" Connie asked.

"Potts."

"I guess. About that."

"Thought so." Mo crossed his arms on his chest and nibbled at his mustache. "That's what I thought," he said, and lapsed into a long silence, which he finally broke: "Sure would be good if there was some photographs of that wedding we could get a look at."

"We?"

"Hah—hah. What d'you mean *we*, white man? Is that it?"

"You mean Elijah's wedding?" Connie asked. "On the beach? With all those naked people running around. Why would *we* want to look at that?"

"Anatomy," Mo said. "I had a professor in college, he said you can look at some old bone, like a leg bone or an ear bone, and figure out pretty much the whole damn animal."

"I don't know what you're talking about, Mo."

He put a big arm around her shoulder. "Welcome to the club, darlin'. Let's go inside, is that okay?"

When she opened the door into the living room, Connie saw the red light on the answering machine blinking in the dark.

"Message," she said, and flicked on the lights.

Mo crossed the room and poked at the machine. The

tape whirred, clicked obediently, and a man's voice said: "Mr. Bowdre? This is Philip Arguleta. I'm an attorney and I've been retained by Elijah Potts. He's in the Santa Fe jail, as I'm sure you know, charged with suspicion of homicide. He asked me to tell you that he wants to see you. Not about the homicide charges, of course. About the Georgia O'Keeffe paintings. A separate matter. Please call me in the morning and I'll arrange a visit." He left his phone number, saying it slowly twice.

"Hah—hah—hah," Mo said. He rubbed his big hands together like a hungry man at a barbecue.

twelve

"Ah, Maria, it's you," Mo Bowdre said, feeling a light touch on his left elbow. The front hall of the Santa Fe police station was filled with comings and goings, the closings of doors. He leaned his head down toward the diminutive policewoman. "You smell as fresh as a spring lilac today."

"Mr. Bowdre, what have I told you about sexual harassment? Sergeant Ramirez told me to whisk you in, so come with me."

"Oh, the chief."

"Something about the chief. I didn't unnerstand it. The chief mad at you?" she asked as they went through a door.

"I never met the man."

"Left here. Say, can I ask you a personal question?"

"Sure."

"How come you don't have a dog?"

"Well, Maria, it's like this. I'm allergic to dogs. Used to have one when I was a kid, name was Hunter, big red hound without any sense whatsoever, and I spent my entire formative years clogged up and sneezing. Don't know which of us was the bigger slob. So when I got blind I decided a sense of smell would be worth more to me than a dog's idea about things. I been thinking maybe I'll get me a seeing-eye parrot. You know, teach him to say left, right, look out for that semi, that sort of thing."

"Like one of those old-time pirates, huh? Here we go, Mr. Bowdre. The prisoner is right in here. Other side of the table in the middle of the room. When you're finished, just come out here in the hall, someone'll get me."

"I'll just follow the scent of spring lilacs to wherever you are, Maria."

In the room was the metallic smell of old sweat and despair. Some things you just can't clean up from a place, Mo thought.

"Elijah, that you?"

"Yes. Thanks for coming. God, what a nightmare this is. I need to talk to someone who . . . This is all very awkward."

"Awkward. Well, I guess it is. They put you in them prison pajamas? One size fits all? That's hard on a man's ego." With his hand, Mo found the back of a small metal folding chair, swung it out from the table and sat down.

"No, no. It's not that," Potts said. "It's not even this damn murder thing. That's a nightmare, but I didn't *do* it, for God's sake, and I'm sure it will all be cleared up before long. Somehow. It's just that, well, I don't really know you very well but I couldn't think of anyone else. . . . I need help and it's something I don't want to get my lawyer involved with right now."

"Why not?"

"It's a separate issue."

"The paintings. Those O'Keeffes, right?"

"Yes." Potts's voice was subdued, arising from some deep-seated exhaustion. "With all this happening, you and Connie have been the only . . . well. It's complicated. And I need an ally."

Mo nodded, rocking back and forth on the little metal chair.

"And," Potts went on, "you've got this reputation for, uh, figuring things out, so I thought . . ."

Mo nodded again.

"I'm really pretty desperate here," Potts said.

"Hah—hah."

"I mean—"

"So you are proposing here a little temporary alliance to rescue your investment?"

"Yes."

"What's in it for me, if you don't mind my askin'?"

"Forty percent."

"Make it sixty."

"That's a lot of money," Potts said.

"It could be a lot of money. That's what I was thinking. But it's a lot of nothing until those paintings turn up again. And I got me a little whiff here"—Mo's voice fell into a nearly inaudible whisper—"that what we are talking about is not the kind of totally aboveboard piece of work that would make an officer of the court, like that Arguleta boy, feel all righteous. Is that about right? And my guess is that you don't feel too beholden to anybody else these days, like whoever else was in on this thing. Am I right about that?"

"Okay, fifty," Potts said.

"Good. Now I don't know how long they'll let me sit here shooting the breeze with a murder suspect, so why don't you just fill me in. You know, the truth? I mean about the paintings. I'd bet the ranch you didn't kill Anita Montague."

"Really?"

"Yeah. You're not built for it. So tell me a story, Elijah. The Story of Elijah and the Golden Eggs that Got Mislaid. Or is it Elijah and the Golden Fleece? Hah—hah."

Later that morning, Mo Bowdre asked Connie Barnes if she would drive him to someplace away from their fellow man, a place where they could talk without fear of any interruption of any sort. "Some sort of clearing," Mo had said.

An hour later the two of them were seated on an outcrop of rock on the edge of the ponderosa pine forest nine thousand feet up in the Sangre de Cristo Mountains. From the ledge, Connie explained, there was nothing to see—no sign of human life, no dwelling, only the green mountains stretching away from them eastward into the Pecos wilderness. During the ride from Canyon Road to this eyrie in Mo's old pickup truck, he had remained silent, as if lost in a dream.

"Well," Mo said, stretching his legs out on the rocky promontory. He pulled his black cowboy hat down over his dark glasses. "I am now part of a criminal conspiracy. It's amazing what it does for a man's adrenaline." He leaned back on his elbows. "See, Elijah wants a new partner. He's been betrayed."

"Why you?"

"He says I got a reputation for figuring things out."

"But still . . ."

"You know how some people think the good shaman can also be a bad witch—maybe if they're dealing with all this stuff, they go both ways. Hah . . . hah. I'm telling *you* about this, an Indian? Anyway, let's just say that a larcenous man is likely to sniff the same urge in other people. So I am now a bona fidey, certified member of the Elijah Potts Pot of Gold at the End of the Rainbow Society. We're gonna be rich beyond our wildest dreams, Connie. Dripping in money. Awash in money. Floating on a sea of money. Waves of money breaking over us like the surf. We might even want to trade in that old pickup. Get us a Range Rover like the Hollywood people. Go buy us a damn beach. Or a whole island. Lie in the sun and listen to the sound of the surf and the ocean breeze riffling through our piles of cash. Stick with me, kid. Whooo-ee."

"Mo?"

"Isn't that every man's dream?"

"Mo?"

"Okay, okay. I'll tell you the story. But first, would you tell me why you think those paintings are fakes? You had that *feeling* the other day, remember?"

Connie turned, lay down on her back with her head on Mo's thigh. "Women see things differently," she said, wiggling a bit to get comfortable on the rocky ledge.

"I'll say."

"I was half awake that morning," Connie went on,

"and kind of dreaming, thinking about babies." Connie paused.

"Babies."

"Well, those paintings are about babies."

"And?"

"I was following this little white thing, like a white ball, down into a real dark place. A spiral."

"This was in your dream?"

"Yes. I was floating along after the ball, down and down, and the black place was like velvet. It kept opening out."

Mo leaned back on his arms. "And that's why these paintings are fakes. Sure, I can understand that."

"When a woman thinks about that sort of thing down deep, she won't see it the way a man does, like something out of a book, you know, literal. Anyway, I suddenly got the feeling that the paintings were done by a man."

"I'll be damned."

"Later I was looking through a book of Georgia O'Keeffe paintings and I found one that was something like my dream. It had this little white ball or spot, tiny, in the middle of this curvy black place. She called it *Black Abstraction*. She was forty when she painted it, and that's about the limit for, you know . . ."

"Babies," Mo said. "And when you were lying there half awake you were visualizing in your head how someone like Georgia O'Keeffe might have felt deep down about babies."

Connie giggled, a high ripple.

"That's real interesting," Mo said. "I got to hand it to you."

They sat silently for a moment, listening to the low, irregular hiss of the breeze in the ponderosas behind them. Mo took off his hat to let the sun, now nearly overhead, shine down on his face. "You'll like this," he said.

It had been a busy year for Elijah Potts, commencing only a few days after his return from Key West following his annual period of direct, hands-on stewardship of his long and peculiar marriage to Claudia Potts. It was a delicate thing, this marriage, rather like a fine piece of Queen Anne furniture. It took careful polishing and it was best not put to heavy use. Nothing too weighty could be put in its finely curved drawers lest its thin and tapered legs snap off and the entire piece come crashing down.

Both partners knew all this perfectly well and approached the marriage with the hands of a curator, sensing almost simultaneously when its fine finish was at risk of abrasion. And at this point—approximately mid-April of each year—Elijah Potts bid his farewell to Key West and to Claudia Potts and left for Santa Fe, eager for the robust life of the West, well-rested, tanned, and randy as a goat.

It was only a few days after his arrival in April a year ago, while attending a reception at St. John's College for the retirement of its revered president, that Potts's eye had been struck by a raven-haired beauty across the room. In no time he had managed to be introduced to her and spend a happy few minutes exchanging memories of Madrid, from which she had recently returned and where

Potts had never been. Nevertheless he had spoken winningly of the few landmarks he had read about along with the paintings he knew to be in the city's illustrious museum, the Prado. He found her researches into her conquistadorean ancestors fascinating, and they had agreed to meet again. She was short—perhaps five-three—both trim and voluptuous, with the smile of a mischievous angel, and Potts was quite captivated. This was Norah Vargas.

They had met again, accidentally, a day later in the coffee shop near the plaza where Potts went each morning for café latte, a fresh-baked roll, and the *New York Times*. She had smiled winningly and with that hint of mischief from across the small room, and he had joined her at her table, admiring the fineness of her teeth, the pretty slope of her neck (she had her hair swept up on her head like a Gibson Girl that morning), and the elegant way her roomy, expensive silken blouse hung so beckoningly from her shoulders. They talked again of genealogy, old families, and old family traditions, particularly hers, and again of the classic art of Spain. Velasquez. El Greco. Goya.

They talked also that morning with the budding ebullience of mutual understanding, of imminent conquest, and it had been no more than three days after this second chance meeting that Elijah Potts found himself lying comfortable and momentarily spent between her aristocratic thighs on the queen-sized bed in her cozy little nest on Lovatos Street.

With playful sophistication they had agreed to see how long they could keep the flowering affair a secret from the good-natured prying of Santa Fe society, since secrecy always added a special zest to such things. And so, Potts's days that spring and summer were filled with a near-ecstasy of schemes and trysts, of absences and passionate comings-together in imaginative settings, of lovely tales dreamily recounted—tales of former travels, of adventures, of unusual people, of an old grandmother passing along the manners and secrets of an aristocratic past. These were days of golden light, velvet nights, halcyon excursions into magical places.

Looking back on it today, of course, from the vantage point of the Santa Fe Police Department's cinder block and steel cell block, Elijah Potts realized that he had been had, completely taken, that from the first the entire liaison—with its early accidental meetings, with the dancing dark eyes and mischievous lips, the delicious secrecy, the laughter and the soaring passion—had all been a thoroughly calculated plot devised by an icy siren of unspeakable malevolence.

In other words, Elijah Potts had fallen for the oldest con in the world. For all his sophisticated researches into the feminine divine, this dark-haired popsicle in her luscious late twenties had taken advantage of a man approaching mid-life, with its attendant hints of mortality, and, by holding out to him the sensuous fountain of youth, had grabbed him by the nuts and led him around like an obedient dog.

Early that summer, Norah began to entice Potts with hints of another secret they could share. Something her old grandmother was talking about a bit elliptically, the way old people talk sometimes. At the same time—this being about June of that year—they had begun to talk of Potts finding a quiet place, a second house, where they could spend weekends together far from the prying noses of the City Different, a place for nonstop revels in each other's arms. So Potts, with Norah's help, located the old house in Canones and began the languorous process of getting local help to fix it up.

Even in its raw and unfinished state, and with little more than a futon on the bare floors, it provided numerous marathon days and nights of flagrant delight that reminded Potts in some ways of the happier moments in Brando's underrated classic, *Last Tango in Paris*. Meanwhile, Potts had lent Norah various works with which to brighten the nooks and walls of her own little nest on Lovatos Street—an early Namingha painting and a few other valuable things from the collection of Southwest Creations Gallery. Through the summer and into the autumn they enjoyed bowers abounding.

One day while they lay cool and naked on the futon in Canones with a summer breeze flowing over them through the open windows, bearing the scent of evergreen trees from the mountains beyond, Norah explained that her grandmother had given her some paintings that had come into the family and that she wanted Potts to see them. The gift had been solemnly given just last week, a few days before the old woman had finally passed away, lying in bed in peace and piety, her silver cross clutched in her hand. The traditional funeral had been so beautiful.

Later that night, in the house on Lovatos Street, Norah cut the twine and pulled away the brown wrapping paper from seven sixteen-by-twenty oil paintings, studies of a white pelvis, the blue mountain called Pedernal, and the odd presence of what seemed to be a developing human child floating in space. Norah placed the paintings in a semicircle around the walls of her snug living room and the two looked on them in silence for a long time.

That they were O'Keeffean couldn't be more obvious. That they were actual O'Keeffes seemed possible. That they weren't very good O'Keeffes was also obvious to Potts's practiced eye. That they might be paintings she had tossed away, as was her wont, was a distinct possibility. And of course that they were fakes also crossed Potts's mind during those first few moments that he looked at them in Norah Vargas's living room.

Potts, it should be pointed out, didn't believe for a minute that Norah carried in her veins the blood of conquistadors. He was happily certain all that pose was entertaining nonsense, part of a delightful, perhaps childish game that Norah delighted in—like the secrecy of their affair and a number of girlish pranks she liked to play on him.

But the seven canvases were palpable, real. Potts was certain Norah's family had not bought them with whatever remained of an old aristocratic family's riches, as Norah would have it. Instead, surely, they had been picked up from some trash heap, just as in the well-known story of the fellow in Abiquiu who had taken one reject to the bank and secured himself a twelve-thousand-dollar down payment on a house. Potts could well imagine the inhabitants of Abiquiu watching O'Keeffe's every move with keen peasant eyes whenever the old woman ventured out from within her ascetic walls, hoping against hope that she would be dumping yet another failed painting or two and making their lives richer and more complete.

Or, again, they were out-and-out fakes. Good ones, to Potts's eye. It made little difference. The possibilities were nearly endless, and Norah had said—disingenuously—that she had no idea what one did with them. She needed the help of someone who knew about such things. How lucky she was for yet another reason that Potts had entered her life when he did.

Potts and Norah knelt on the floor that night, arms around each other in the semicircle of canvases, and the planning began, the fifty-fifty nature of the deal unspoken but patently clear in both their minds.

It would be best, they agreed, that the paintings be handled through the legitimizing vehicle of Potts's gallery, Southwest Creations. To be sure, Anita Montague owned a piece of the gallery, but Potts said he would take care of all that. This could be a special and separate matter. One thing that needed planning, then, was how they would come into Potts's possession, some accident. The Canones house, with its old outbuilding layered in cobwebs and spiderwebs, presented itself to them as a possibility. The paintings could simply turn up there. Wasn't there some rather mysterious person, Gallegos or whoever, who had owned the place for a while and disappeared?

But what if they really were fake? Then what? This could be ascertained. There were all kinds of technical means, tests performed in any one of dozens of laboratories. Perhaps they had better test them right away. It could all be done quietly. If they were fakes, well, there might still be possibilities. If they weren't, if the lab tests were positive, then experts would have to be brought in, experts from the world of fine art. Maybe one expert would do, so long as he—or she—had an impeccable reputation. And then . . . well, they could be worth a million. Even millions. Plural.

So Potts had located a laboratory in New Jersey capable of making the needed tests—infrared, X-ray, all the rest—and capable then of destroying its results. He had personally taken the paintings to the lab, then waited around impatiently for three days in a motel outside Newark while the tests were performed. It was clear, the results showed, that they had been painted over an O'Keeffean underpainting and not subsequently tampered with. For example, they were not paintings of the pelvis and the mountain to which some faker had added the mysterious swirl that resolved itself as the series went on into a fetus. They had each been painted of a piece, and with the materials that O'Keeffe had used in those days and, as best science could tell, in the period—the Forties—when O'Keeffe had been doing pelvises. The paintings then quite possibly—even probably—were discarded O'Keeffes. Discarded, but real.

Potts continued to probe gently about where the paintings had really come from, but he did this with the utmost tact lest he show any doubts about Norah's conquistadorean roots. But no, Norah had no idea how her grandmother came to have the paintings. The old woman had simply said they were part of Norah's legacy and had given them to her before she died. Potts was not about to let the matter go at that, and privately, without Norah's knowledge, researched the poor and skimpy records, poring through old county documents, leafing among dusty, incomplete genealogies in the state university's archives of local Hispanic history, making a trip to Yale, where many of O'Keeffe's letters and other documents had been housed after her death. He kept away from the O'Keeffe Foundation, of course, as a lamb would avoid a lion, and any other agency or people that could later trace him to these inquiries. At Yale he presented himself under another name, with credentials as a Peruvian scholar of twentieth-century women's art in the Americas.

In due course he had found that among the many housemaids O'Keeffe would employ and then peremptorily dismiss over some misunderstanding or other, one had been named Vargas before marrying a man named Vigil. She had worked in the artist's Abiquiu house for a period of some six months. And, once back in New Mexico, Potts had managed to locate a partial but telling genealogy of a Vigil family going back to the eighteenth century and forward through time to the 1930s. At that time an Antonio Vigil had married a woman named Inez Vargas, and they had lived in the 1940s in Abiquiu. After that, Antonio and Inez had moved back to his family's town of Ensenada.

Making a quiet visit to Ensenada, Potts asked at the quaint old Vigil's Store about paintings anyone in the village might have made in the old days of the revered saints—not carved or painted santos, you understand, but paintings. On canvas. He was a curator from a great museum in San Antonio, hoping to bring to light yet further examples of the richness and reflowering of the great artistic spirit of La Raza. At Vigil's Store they knew nothing of such paintings of saints, but did show Potts a few that one of their old uncles, Antonio, had made, some landscapes clumsy in line and form but painted with brush strokes so fine as to seem like a photograph. Potts expressed great pleasure in seeing such excellent works but apologized to the old man at the counter that they were not, of course, what he was seeking.

He left Vigil's Store quite certain about the seven sixteen-by-twenty so-called O'Keeffes Norah's grandmother had left her. It was, he imagined, like this:

While Inez Vargas Vigil labored in Georgia O'Keeffe's house, Antonio—probably a man of great peasant charm—had talked the old artist into giving him a few painting lessons. She was known to have such flashes of generosity. And so Antonio, by way of practicing, had whipped up a few quite good pelvis paintings on his own in the O'Keeffe manner and, with the Hispanic's sadness for a woman without issue, had generously provided the paintings with the glory and mystery of life, a Niño Becoming.

And, Potts reasoned, the clever copyist had imagined himself palming them off as the real thing and taking his fortune and maybe even his wife, the long-suffering Inez, off to some snazzy place. But, for whatever reason, Antonio Vigil's paintings had languished somewhere until Norah's grandmother came across them and passed them on to her in a blurry recollection of a far grander if imaginary past.

Whatever.

In any event, they were good enough to pass the test of science. It was time for the next steps of the plan.

The first was something of a flourish, conceived out of a kind of cocksure arrogance that had taken hold. One weekend in the Canones house, Potts sat down at his laptop computer and began making notes toward a lecture he would give next year as part of Southwest Creations Gallery's annual series—Georgia O'Keeffe and what she did not choose, from the purgatorial realms of her soul, to put on canvas.

Second, the two conspirators secreted the canvases in the broken-down outbuilding at Potts's Canones house, carefully inserting the metal box holding them between an outer wall and some spiderwebs—a delicate task. And then, on a fine weekend in early September, he suggested to his partner Anita Montague that perhaps she might want to bring her mountain bike out to Canones so that he could show her his new digs, she could have a picnic lunch with him and then do some cycling in the surrounding mountains. It was an accident, and a happy one to be sure, that Anita talked Connie Barnes into joining her that Saturday. Connie's implacable probity as a certified public accountant only could add an aura of authenticity to the accidental find.

"Hey," Connie interrupted.

"You were taken, my dear. Taken in."

"That's real lousy," she said.

Once the paintings were found—with the attendant excitement and, on Potts's part, well-rehearsed astonishment—and the finders sworn to secrecy, it was time to take yet another crucial step.

Potts arranged to take the paintings to Microbeam in Chicago, an analytical lab with a respected reputation in the art world, having helped expose numerous fakes in the past decade, and having authenticated numerous newly discovered works, including, most notably, a previously unknown landscape by Gauguin painted shortly before he went to Tahiti, a painting that sold for a record (at the time) nine million dollars. In due course, this second and official set of lab results came back as hoped.

Now it was time to see if they could pass the test of the practiced, scholarly eye. And Potts knew of such an expert. An old friend he hadn't seen for years. A man with an impeccable reputation in the world of twentieth-century American art. Nelson Adams Lockman. Norah was delighted that Potts knew such a man. This all looked like it would be so—well—easy, didn't it?

As each such step in the plan was completed—with each check mark on the list—a celebration was called for, celebrations of an ever more imaginative nature. Potts was, in short, utterly lost in the succulence of greed and passion, his days and nights filled with swelling promise and heightened rewards. He was, in that respect, blinded and deafened, inattentive to signals he might otherwise have taken note of. No muted tinkle of an alarm bell could be heard through the growing sense that he was in control of this golden game.

In Chicago, Nelson Adams Lockman was happy to hear from his old friend from their days in Provincetown, cackled on the phone about Claudia and Elijah's memorable union on the beach, but then turned stuffy and professional when he learned what Potts was calling about.

Before agreeing to look at the canvases, he wanted to see the lab results. After reviewing these, which took a couple of weeks, he called for the canvases and insisted that they be sent, rather than brought to him by Potts. A matter of professional probity, he said. So Potts nervously consigned them to the care of Wells Fargo and even more nervously awaited Lockman's response. By the time ten days had passed without a word from Chicago, Potts was in a near frenzy of anticipation. What with the added strain to his budget of the Canones house, his finances at this time were in a parlous state, and he had placed what might easily be his final bet on the paintings.

When Lockman issued a terse preliminary report, promising a more detailed account, that the canvases were almost certainly authentic, the work of the artist but quite likely castoffs, elation burst in Potts's soul with the brilliance of Chinese fireworks. He swept Norah off for a three-day revel at a small but elegant hotel with a little-trammeled beach on the ocean side of Baja California some fifty miles north of La Paz, which, of course, means *peace*.

Timing was of crucial importance in the overall scheme, and in this instance the glorious day that the canvases' existence should be announced to the world needed to coincide with the schedule of *Ars Longa*, the art institute's scholarly journal in which Lockman would publish a special "letter" about the canvases and their provenance. Given the usual languor with which scholarly publication takes place, it was all the more elating that the journal's editor guaranteed that Lockman's paper would appear in the May issue the following year. Thus an announcement in April, shortly after Potts's return from Key West, was scheduled.

Potts went through the normal routine of daily events in the ensuing period with what seemed to him a superhuman patience. But patience was possible because he had no doubt whatsoever that, once the O'Keeffes had been announced, their authenticity testified to by both laboratory and leading art experts, they would sell like the proverbial hotcakes. At least three, and possibly four, of the pilgrims in his lecture series on art, myth, and soul—yuppian women in possession of a virtually cornucopian supply of "new" money—would be buyers, he was sure of that.

That Norah never seemed the slightest bit put off by the fact that Elijah would soon spend three months, as usual, with his wife in Key West was one of the alarm bells that Elijah did not heed. The world was totally, perfectly, gloriously, and incontrovertibly his oyster.

In Key West, while he finished up his treatise on the Black Madonna, he spoke elliptically to his wife Claudia about a wonderful opportunity that had come his way, something that he would be sure of upon his return to Santa Fe. He let on that it had something to do with some newfound paintings from a dead artist, and let it ride at that. Claudia, with her usual sangfroid, had been happy for Elijah but uncurious. It was not the first time that Elijah had harbored a new fantasy of quick financial reward. That they never quite came to fruition was what lay behind her sole ownership of the Key West house.

She had long been determined that her future would not go up in the smoke of one of Elijah's enthusiasms.

Upon Potts's return to Santa Fe, everything had gone like a well-rehearsed theatrical production: the announcement to Potts's circle, and the announcement to the press the following day, with Lockman having flown in to make a dramatic and reassuring appearance. Potts had, in fact, been surprised (and of course delighted) when Lockman made tantalizing noises suggesting that the institute itself might be interested in purchasing one of the paintings. The next day, while the two men visited at Potts's Canones house, Lockman neither confirmed nor denied such an interest, but smiled happily and—Potts thought—conspiratorially when he brought the matter up.

That afternoon the two men had laughed when Lockman told Potts (who'd earlier gone inside to take a nap) that he had chased someone off the premises, a mousy-looking woman, presumably a reporter. Potts would have to get used to being importuned by the press now that he was a celebrity. Paparazzi. News hawks from *People* and so forth. Lockman nodded enthusiastically about the plan to put the seven canvases on exhibition in Southwest Creations in a few weeks before they went on sale. He said he would be most interested in attending. The two men left Canones later that afternoon, and Potts treated his old friend to an early dinner at a quiet restaurant in Espanola where Potts was not known. It would not do, Potts thought, for people to guess that he and Lockman were old, old friends. The professional nature of Lockman's expert opinion needed to be without question. Afterward, Lockman had left for the airport in

Albuquerque and Potts had gone home, arriving there at about eight-thirty. He turned on some music and reveled in his excellent planning and his good fortune, his brilliant minuet with gracious and alluring Lady Luck.

Of course, as he reveled, Anita Montague was being murdered—a terrible shock, a tragedy. Potts was genuinely devastated by the news the next morning but, he had to confess, even this did not diminish his certainty that he had won the game. Of course, still feeling that the world should not know too much about his and Lockman's old friendship, lest it somehow besmirch the authenticity of his report on the O'Keeffes, he made up a phony alibi on the spot—dinner at Mediterranean Light alone—when the police asked him about his whereabouts. Later that night, when Norah appeared in the gloom, the naked Aphrodite of the Hot Tub at Ten Thousand Waves, she had unquestioningly agreed to confirm the alibi.

And only now, reviewing all these events in the solitude of his cell, had Potts recalled the old poetry that filled his mind that night, Hesiod's song of Aphrodite:

the whispering together of girls,
the smiles and deceptions
the delight, and the sweetness of love
and the flattery

Yes, the smiles and the *deceptions*. The deceptions.

For it was now clear to Potts that he had been totally, viciously betrayed.

The bitch-goddess Norah had set him up for this from the very start. She had played innocent, knowing that he would take the bait and run with it, using all the expertise in his possession to set up the series of steps that would prove the canvases to be authentic O'Keeffes and let the world know of their existence in a way best calculated to take advantage of them. He would *create* their value.

He had done just that. Only to be betrayed. What was now obvious was that Norah, the evil sorceress, had shaved a few minutes off his alibi, just enough to make it possible in the police mind that he had had the opportunity to kill Anita. And since he was the only suspect, the police had arrested him to languish in this obscene jail cell while she took the paintings, burglarized the gallery! and took the damn paintings. Of course, she had arranged for Anita to be murdered while she herself was happily seating people at their tables in Mediterranean Light. It was no great thing to arrange a hit; surely she had ways of putting some hoodlum or another from the Hispanic community to work in return for a favor of some sort. Ha. A favor of some sort. The insatiable bitch almost surely had some stud panting at her feet, crawling on his knees, willing to do anything in the world for a taste of her perfidious . . .

So with Potts conveniently framed for murder and in jail, Norah had run off with the paintings. They would go on the black market soon enough, never to be seen again, while Norah rolled in money enough to buy whatever she had ever dreamed of owning. A Spanish castle, perhaps, even a title in keeping with her fantasies. It was disgusting.

And Potts, now desperate as well as utterly humiliated,

was asking Mo Bowdre to take matters in hand. Somehow. To recover the paintings. For fifty percent.

"Elijah told you all that? In just the few minutes they give you?"

"He gave me all the important bones," Mo said. "I fleshed them out with plausible detail. You know, the way us artists do."

"Do you think he told you the truth?"

"And nothing but? Well, who's to say?"

Connie fidgeted on the rock ledge. "Why do you think he didn't kill Anita? Tony said he's got all that evidence."

Mo leaned back on the rocky ledge again. A shadow flitted over his face.

"What was that?"

"A hawk," Connie said, watching it float down the side of the mountain. "A big one."

"That a good omen?" Mo asked.

"For who?"

"My theory, maybe. See, I've been thinking about how I'd knock someone off a bike with a chain like that. Someone like Anita Montague who was what, about five-six?"

"About that. Shorter than me, a little," Connie said.

"Right. So Anita spots someone up ahead of her on the sidewalk, and slows down, and then—like Ramirez says—recognizes him. Or her, of course. So what does Anita do? She stops, and puts one foot down on the sidewalk, so she's partly standing there on the ball of one foot, and also sitting on the bicycle seat. So let's say it's

Potts there with the chain in his right hand—he *is* right-handed—and he swings around at her like he's swinging a bullwhip or maybe even two hands like a baseball bat, aiming for her neck. *Whap!* Catches her right on the throat with a terrible force and the chain wraps around her neck and he yanks her off the bike. You visualize that?"

"Yes."

"She's standing there on the ball of one foot, resting her haunch on the seat, and this chain comes out of nowhere, hits her right in the throat. Or more likely on the side of her neck since she'd probably be turned a little bit toward him. Anyway, it slams her neck and the end slaps her again after it wraps around, and then next thing she knows, she's on the ground. Right?"

"Right."

"But it wouldn't be like that if it was Potts." Mo paused, sniffed, and made a small O with his lips. "Not with his height. He's about six-foot, and he'd be swinging the chain horizontally or maybe down a little. Like a sidearm pitch. Get some real force behind it. But they said the chain left marks on her neck and the end of it tore off part of her lip. The chain was wrapping itself around her from a low point, her neck, to a higher point. The lip. So it had to be someone her height or a little shorter, but not anyone who was taller."

Mo grinned, extremely pleased with himself.

"See it?" he said.

"I can see that, but . . ."

"But what?"

"What about those fibers that came from Elijah's jacket, the one's under her fingernails?"

Mo sniffed and waved a big hand, as if brushing a fly away from his face. "That's just a damn detail. Bound to be some explanation for it. Now we better get going. We got a whole lot of work to do. And some things I reckon we better get to real quick."

thirteen

Ramón Tofoya's stolen Mustang began emitting unmistakable sounds of mortality as he crossed the Oklahoma border into Fort Smith, Arkansas, an unpromising town, Ramón reckoned, probably full of upstanding Baptists who locked everything up, put chastity belts on their knock-kneed daughters and those goddamn alarms in their Buicks. So he limped on another 160 miles to the more urbanized, freer and easier city of Little Rock, where he abandoned the car in an empty lot near the Greyhound Bus station, expecting to make a handy switch. But nothing in the lot looked quite right, and Ramón was a man who knew full well it was wise to trust his gut instincts. With the seven paintings bundled under his arm, he decided to let Greyhound do the driving.

He waited calmly in the station for the next bus to Memphis, where he now planned to stop off and see the Elvis Presley shrine at Graceland and bow to the King before taking yet another bus due south to the Big Easy. He ate a cardboard chicken sandwich from a coin machine, and drank down a Diet Pepsi, and even that awful crap tasted good to Ramón Tofoya. When he got to

New Orleans, he'd get himself another name. Something classy.

Cool. Everything was cool.

Tofoya watched a man sitting at the other end of the worn wooden bench in the cruddy bus terminal nervously folding and unfolding a newspaper as if he were looking for something, some treasure, secreted between its pages. Eventually the man, a seedy little rube with nicotine-stained fingers, threw the paper down and impatiently stalked off toward the men's room. When the rube was out of sight, Tofoya casually picked the paper up off the bench and began to look through it even though it was a day old. On an inside page in a section devoted mostly to daily living in Little Rock, a lot of crap about lawn care and some goody-goody high school cheerleaders volunteering their time to read stories to some pathetic old bags in a nursing home, he came across a headline with the name O'Keeffe and a picture of the gaunt old dame. She looked like some wizened unisex Indian.

He read the article eagerly, discovering with growing, heart-pounding elation precisely the dimensions of the treasure that he carried with him, the cumbersome bundle of seven sixteen-by-twenty canvases that had been brought to light by this guy Elijah Potts in the gallery called Southwest Creations in Santa Fe. *Yes!* It was an AP story that quoted a lot of guys from the art world, guys with three names, and their speculations on the paintings' value. Seven figures per, one said. Seven fucking figures.

His, for chrissakes! He clutched the bundle closer to

his body, put the paper down and leaned back in a state of epiphany.

Later, sitting alone on a seat near the rear of the bus to Memphis, Ramón Tofoya allowed himself to dream yet again of the rich and luxurious life of a multimillionaire in New Orleans. Nothing but the best. The absolute classiest, the finest of everything, diamonds and platinum, fox fur coats and Cuban cigars. No, he wouldn't have to consort with any bimbos from the bayous, brown people who waggled their Creole butts from Mardi Gras floats. He'd be grabbing off some high-class ass, now wouldn't he?

From the movie *The Big Easy*, he recalled the cool, beautiful district attorney—what was her name? Ellen Barkin, that was it—who'd gotten herself tangled up with the cop she was investigating. He remembered that she had been reluctant, something about not having much experience, but the cop had talked her into it, finally pushing her little skirt up amid the squeaks and bleats of passion. He remembered her long, long leg there. . . .

Oh, damn, he did like his women tall, now didn't he? Lithe and tall, sweet as gardenias in a big green Victorian garden on a humid night in the Big Fuckin' Easy.

He imagined himself smooth-talking Ellen Barkin, smoothly stroking Ellen Barkin's long, long leg—there now, don't worry none, honey, I got experience for both of us—smoothly letting her passion rise and overwhelm that charming, ladylike reluctance, oh *yes*, while somewhere outside on the street the old-timey jigs were strutting their stuff in the night, and through the window with its pretty French wrought-iron grillwork a warm wet wind blew in, carrying with it the happy strains of Dixieland. . . . Class, man, class.

Sergeant Anthony Ramirez hung up the phone, smiled, and stood up, tucking the tail of his crisp white shirt deeper into his trousers. He straightened his tie, slipped on his blue blazer, and with a small smile tugging at the corners of his mouth, shook his head and walked out of his office.

"Maria," he said. "You want to tell those people I'll see them in the briefing room?"

"They'll be real happy," Maria said. "They're hungry, like dogs. Watch out they don't eat you alive."

Ramirez picked his way through the maze of desks, cops, and computers and into a conference room that served as a press-briefing room as well, being big enough for about eight reporters and cameramen. He stood behind a lectern and waited for them. Presently, they bustled into the room, faces screwed up with eagerness, and sat down—among them the mousy little woman from the Santa Fe *New Mexican*, Samantha Burgess, who smiled pleasantly at him. He smiled back briefly, and stared idly at a tattered drug poster on the rear wall and waited while a TV cameraman in the back went through his nervous little routine, fussing with f-stops or whatever.

"Okay?" Ramirez said. "Okay. Just one announcement. Mr. Elijah Potts, a resident of Santa Fe, was arrested yesterday afternoon and is being held until his arraignment. He's been charged with homicide in the death of Anita Montague." He gave the date of the murder, the place, and the time. "Mr. Potts was arrested and taken into custody on the premises of Southwest Creations on Canyon Road. As you know, he is the majority owner of the gallery. The Montague woman was the gallery's manager. That is all the department will have to say about this until a later date. So," Ramirez grinned happily, "you can go ahead and ask your questions."

A man in a turtleneck sweater and an army jacket whom Ramirez didn't recognize stuck up his hand and asked: "Can you tell us a little bit about the evidence linking Potts to—"

"No, I can't," Ramirez said, still grinning. "Next?"

Several hands went up, and Ramirez nodded at one of them.

"Sergeant, what about a motive? Can you—"

"Our investigation revealed that Mr. Potts had a motive, yes. Any other questions?"

"Aw, come on, Sergeant," someone said.

Ramirez shrugged. "You guys know the drill."

"Hey, Sergeant, is this guy Potts the Trasher?"

"We have nothing that would link Mr. Potts to any other crimes. The other homicides remain under investigation, if that's what you're asking about. Carolyn Marcy and the other woman, who's still unidentified."

"But he still could be the Trasher, right?"

Ramirez sighed. "The Santa Fe Police Department has no evidence suggesting that there is any link between the three recent homicides in the city. This Trasher is just someone else's idea. Maybe a ghost haunting the media." Ramirez grinned again.

Samantha Burgess held her ballpoint pen up and waggled it at him.

"Miz Burgess?"

"Sergeant, yesterday afternoon there was crime-scene tape around the gallery. Do you usually put tape up just for an arrest? I mean—"

"What are you getting at?" Ramirez asked.

"The paintings."

"The O'Keeffe paintings? What about them?"

"That's what I'm asking. They've been saying they were tampered with. Maybe stolen. Is that why you put up the tape?"

Ramirez cleared his throat. Samantha Burgess looked up at him expectantly, her pen poised over her little notebook and her smile a bit of a smirk.

"As I understand it, a call was placed from the gallery, a 911 call, shortly before Officer Jameson and I arrived to arrest Mr. Potts. There had evidently been a burglary. Some paintings were in fact missing."

"The O'Keeffes?"

"Some other paintings are evidently missing."

"*What* paintings, Sergeant?"

"As best we can tell, they were copies."

"Copies? Copies of what?"

"Copies of the O'Keeffes."

The room erupted in shouts. Ramirez raised his hands for silence.

"Why there were copies of the O'Keeffe paintings, I have no idea," Ramirez said. "No idea. But the department is looking into it. It is still under investigation. But we have nothing further on that for you now. Okay, that's it, guys."

"How many paintings are missing?"

Ramirez raised a hand, part salute, part dismissal, and left the room, leaving Samantha Burgess with a frown of confusion on her face.

On his way through the desks back to his office, he felt a tug at his elbow. Irritated, he turned and found the reporter standing nearly in his face.

"You get it, don't you?" she said.

"Get what?"

"Can I talk to you, Sergeant? Privately?"

Ramirez looked around the room. The little cop, Maria, was looking at him with a smirk. Everybody's smirking today, he thought. He shrugged. "Okay. In my office."

Samantha leaned over his desk as Ramirez sat down, her eyes shining with excitement.

"It's like the thing at the Louvre," she said.

"What thing at the Louvre?"

"Sergeant . . ."

"I'm not being obtuse, Samantha. I don't know what you're talking about."

"Okay, okay. A few years ago some guys stole the Mona Lisa from the Louvre. You must've read about that. An inside job. The *Mona Lisa*!"

"Actually, no."

"It was a scam. These guys stole the Mona Lisa, and then they made a bunch of really expert copies of it. Or maybe they already had the copies. You know how art students are always sitting in those museums making copies of the masterpieces for art school. Anyway, the real one is stolen, and the thieves sell their copies to a bunch of different individuals. See, each buyer thinks he's getting the real stolen Mona Lisa. Pays a fortune to these guys to own the real Mona Lisa—imagine!—which of course they had to keep quiet, hide in some vault or some private gallery in their house. There are people like that. Then these guys, the thieves, once they've sold off a bunch of copies, they returned the real Mona Lisa to the Louvre. See, the suckers couldn't rat on them. They're stuck with fakes but they can't say anything. So that's what Potts was going to do. Arrange for the O'Keeffes to be missing—like stolen—and then sell off the copies. But instead someone stole the copies, not the real ones." Samantha Burgess beamed.

Ramirez leaned back in his chair and put his hands behind his neck. "That's a real interesting theory," he said.

"So what do you think?"

"What I said. That's a real interesting theory. If you don't mind, I'll pass it along to the guys in Fraud. And what are *you* gonna do with it?"

"I got some checking to do," Samantha said, flushed with the smell of prey. "I don't suppose you could—"

"No," Ramirez said. "I can't."

"That's okay, Sergeant. I'll see you around." She took two steps to the door, turned to smile triumphantly at him, and left.

Ramirez stared at the empty doorway for a moment, drumming his fingers on the desk in a quiet Latin beat. Something like bossa nova. The news that some copies of the O'Keeffe paintings had been stolen would be on the five o'clock news broadcasts. And Samantha Burgess would find some way to get her Louvre theory into tomorrow's newspaper. Something like: "Sources close to the department confirm that the police are looking into the possibility of a fraud similar to the one . . ."

Ramirez stood up and stretched, a luxurious stretch that pleasantly popped a few vertebrae. He looked into his in-box. The stuff from Kentucky had arrived. But first he had better talk to his boss, Lieutenant Ortiz, Ramirez thought. Bring him up-to-date. Lieutenant Ortiz liked to be up-to-date on things.

"The University of Illinois, huh? At Champaign. That's it," Mo said. He was standing in the doorway of Connie's office with his hands buried in his back pockets. It was quarter to five in the afternoon. "I got to hand it to you. This Internet stuff has its uses."

"Wasn't that where that waitress went? Carolyn Marcy?"

"That's right."

"So?"

"Coincidence," Mo said. "Just a coincidence, is my guess. My theory is that God likes to toss a few things like that into the real world—red herrings—just to confuse matters." He turned to the door. "They may have had the same professor there but at different times. Let's go. Manuel Trujillo should be here any minute."

"The low-rider guy? That little pirate?"

"Yeah. I figured a posse of two didn't amount to much. I guess that's him at the front door. I didn't tell him to come through the gate. I'll explain it all to you both on the way."

Connie shut down the computer, took a deep breath,

and put aside the first three thoughts that came to mind. A posse?

"Manuel," Mo boomed, opening the front door. "Good to see you. I'm real obliged. Come in."

Connie stepped into the living room and smiled. The top of Manuel Trujillo's head came up to Mo Bowdre's breastbone. They stood there like members of two different species, but both were dressed alike. Jeans, battered black cowboy hats, voluminous brown vests. Like that Schwarzenegger movie, *Twins.*

"Let's go," Mo said.

"Nice to see you again, Connie," Manuel said, an amused glitter in his eyes. He rocked back on his heels and squinted up at her. "You're lookin' 'specially—"

"Hello, Manuel."

"You're gonna love our ride tonight," Manuel said. "It's got everything."

"Not a low-rider," she said.

"Nah, that's for kids."

Connie sighed, closed the front door, jiggling the handle to make sure it was locked, and followed the two men out onto Canyon Road.

"Look, Luis, what I'm saying is I'm sick. Physically sick. I'm throwing up every ten minutes. So I won't be able to work tomorrow. What do you mean, irresponsible? I'm giving you time to find . . . Well, why don't you try Imogene? I know she's stupid, but it's not real demanding, you know, grinning at people and finding them a table. No, I don't want to quit. It's a fine job. I just can't . . . So, look, I've got to go."

Norah Vargas hung up the phone in her kitchen and stood for a moment, staring at it. Her world was rapidly falling apart. At least, if she had to go, the restaurant wouldn't miss her for a day or two. She tried to concentrate. But the voice kept ringing in her mind, the voice over the phone with the static behind it.

Bitch. Bitch.

What was happening? What had happened? Calm down. Calm down.

The paintings? That's just talk, for Christ . . .

Bitch.

I don't have the goddamned . . .

Standing in the kitchen, she heard herself moan, a high-pitched sound involuntarily escaping her chest. Calm down.

Okay. First, Potts is in jail. That worked. Good. But this stuff about the paintings. How had he done that? The son of a bitch. A double cross. So where were they? And now *I'm* the one that . . . Her mind began to spin again and she squeezed herself, hugged herself around the chest. There was still time. She went into her bedroom and sat on the bed. She'd better be ready, if things didn't . . . if there wasn't any way out of this. She looked at her watch. Five o'clock. She crossed the room to the chest of drawers, flicked on the little television that sat on it, and began throwing things from the drawers onto her bed. That blond guy was on the television, talking, the guy who covered Santa Fe.

". . . and, Jim, there is one new development, maybe a related one, in the Montague homicide. The Santa Fe Police Department has confirmed that some paintings were stolen from Southwest Creations. That's the gallery owned by Elijah Potts, who's been charged with homicide in the death of Anita Montague, the gallery manager. And Southwest Creations was where just last week Potts announced the existence of seven previously unknown paintings by Georgia O'Keeffe. But, get this, Jim, according to police, it is *copies* of the O'Keeffes that are missing. We're keeping on this . . ."

Copies! Mother of God. Holy Mother of God.

Norah watched the blond newscaster fade into the visage of the anchorman in Albuquerque and she shut off the TV.

Copies? What did that mean?

Breathing deeply—a calming ritual—she took a canvas suitcase down from the shelf in her closet and spent the next five minutes methodically packing it, thinking all the while that first she needed to get ready. Then she could think. In the full-length mirror attached to the inside of her closet door, she looked at the horizontal lines in her forehead and tried to relax them. Gently she massaged her forehead, let her jaw hang open, relaxed. Yes. Now then.

She smiled at herself in the mirror. A weak smile. Try harder. It would be all right. She lifted the loose white cotton shirt over her head and let it fall to the carpet, turned to stare at herself sideview, black lace bra, beautiful, and soft, nicely weathered jeans, deerskin boots. She selected from the closet a burnt-orange silk jacket with a sash, slipped into it, tied the sash tightly and, after a look of appraisal, crossed the room to the bed table. From its drawer she withdrew a chromium-plated .38 pistol with a short barrel and slipped it into the right-hand pocket of her jacket. She had never used it.

She looked around the room.

There.

Ready.

Nevertheless, she started when she heard the knocking on her front door, and resumed her deep breathing as she went into the little living room where a piñon fire had burned down to a few coals now giving off only a wavering orange glow in the fireplace under the painting of the kachina in the sky.

She leaned toward the door. "Yes?"

"Norah Vargas?" said a loud voice. An unfamiliar voice.

"Yes?" She held her breath.

"Police. Please open the door."

Police? She breathed out in relief. It wasn't the police that worried her. Not yet anyway.

She undid the lock and opened the door a few inches, seeing a large expanse of blue work shirt and brown vest only inches away. She looked up.

"You're not the police."

The door hit her shoulder, and she stumbled backward as it shot open and a huge man with dark glasses stepped into the room. It was as if a volcano had just taken all the air.

"What is this? You're—"

"Right, Mo Bowdre. We haven't officially been introduced." He closed the door behind him with a slam. "But we should know each other, at least in passing. Go sit down."

Norah stepped backward, staring at the man who stood as motionless as a wall.

"You're blind," she said. "What are you—"

"I said sit down."

Norah obeyed, taking a seat in the middle of her two-seater sofa, fleetingly touching her right-hand pocket.

"Your partner's told me the whole story about the paintings. That is to say, your *former* partner. You've been playing a pretty good game up until now, Norah. Okay if I call you Norah? Got ol' Elijah safely in the can. That was good. Got rid of Anita and got ol' Elijah arrested for it. Pretty damn good work. I guess Anita had figured it out, hadn't she? So she had to go. Poor dear, out for a ride and *whap*! With a damn bicycle chain. That's original. Real original."

"Look, I didn't kill anyone. What are you—"

"Me? I am the new partner. You've been, what do they say? Riffed. That's it. There's been a retirement in force around here and you are no longer part of the team. So you just tell me where you have those paintings and then you can trot off to Spain or wherever."

"Now *look*, you. I don't have any paintings. I didn't take any paintings. Anyway, the paintings weren't stolen. Copies were. Copies of the paintings."

"Norah, you got yourself a reputation as a world-class liar so I don't want to hear any of this. You just get me those paintings and I'll let you pack up your things and go."

"I don't *have* the paintings."

The big man, staring straight ahead and well over her

head, began to walk directly at her, stopping two paces away, looming huge.

“No more bullshit, Norah,” he said in an oddly quiet voice, almost sorrowful. “You’ve only got the one choice.”

“What’s to keep me from shooting you?”

Bowdre stood still. “Oh, that. Well, in the first place you’re just a little thing and you’d have a hell of a time gettin’ my carcass out of here all by yourself. The other thing is that my friend is standing outside. He’s a tiny little guy, name of Trujillo, but he’s got him a great big gun tucked in his belt, and just a terrible temper. Mean as a mongoose.” Bowdre took a pace backward. “You want to go over to the window and take a peek at him? He’s standin’ out on the grass there. Go ahead. You have a look.”

Norah stood up and stepped past the big man. She pushed aside the curtain that hung over the front window and saw the little man. He was standing on the grass, looking up at the sky. The last sun of the day glinted off his ear—a diamond earring. He had gray hair in a knot behind his neck. He turned his head toward the house, looking out of squinted eyes, and smiled broadly. Norah let the curtain drop.

“I don’t have the paintings. I don’t have the *copies* of the paintings. I don’t know what’s going on, but—”

“Well, then, you better just get them,” Bowdre said. “Never mind all this talk about copies. The real ones is what I want. The ones your dear old grandma gave you before she died with her silver cross clutched to her frail old bosom. Them.”

Norah turned away from him, heard the door open, the crunch of boots on the doorstep, and the door closing. She stood by the door, listening, and heard an engine start up, a car move down the street. She pulled the curtain aside and looked out. Bowdre, the giant, was gone. The little man with the horrid grin wasn't there. Old Mrs. Padilla was walking home on the other side of the street, holding a brown paper bag in one arm. Everything looked normal, familiar. The same old houses across the street, squat adobes with their little rectangular windows staring out. Three houses had lights turned on against the dying day. The Martinezes' Ford was parked in their driveway opposite.

Norah noticed that her hand, holding the curtain, was shaking. It was time to go.

Mo Bowdre had taken his hat off so his head would fit under the roof of Manuel Trujillo's 1959 Chevrolet. Even so, his thick blond hair brushed the ceiling. And, from the backseat, Manuel Trujillo's gray hair was all Connie could see, just the top of his head. They made a curious posse, Connie thought.

When the car turned the corner, Mo said: "Well, that sure as hell ought to stir things up."

"What are we doing now?" Connie asked.

"We're circling back to Norah Vargas's house, sit and wait for what happens next."

There was a sickening, bone-rattling thunk as the car hit a pothole, and Mo ducked his head away from the ceiling.

"Damn," Manuel said.

"Let me explain this to you," Mo said. "Potts says the paintings are gone, the real ones. The real fakes, that is. He says that Norah Vargas must've stolen them, set him up, framed him for the Montague murder. So he's out of the way and she's got the paintings. The real fakes. So I just suggested to Tony Ramirez that he announce it wasn't the real fakes—the ones everyone thinks are the real thing—it wasn't them that were stolen. Instead, he says what was stolen were some copies of the real fakes that Potts presumably got made. So now it looks like Norah Vargas stole the copies—the fake fakes—without knowing it. And now the word is out that the copies are gone. So her partner is gonna think that she's double-crossing *him.*"

"And her partner . . ."

"I figured she had to have some other partner besides Potts, one Potts didn't know about. Had to have. For one thing, she couldn't have killed Anita Montague because she was at the restaurant at the time. But she must've got wind that Anita knew too much, maybe found out about the whole scam, something. Anyway, Norah fingered her and got her killed. The killer has to have been her other partner. The one Elijah didn't know about. See, he just thinks he got screwed by Norah. All by herself."

"But," Connie said, recalling Mo's suspicions, "she was really working with that Lockman guy, the one from Chicago. Her other partner from the start."

"Him. Curator at that institute in Chicago and adjunct professor of art history at the University of Illinois, Champaign campus. Yes. That's him. Nelson Adams Lockman, the old Provincetown crony Elijah thought of when he needed an expert to confirm his fake paintings were the real thing."

Manuel Trujillo slowed down to a stop at an intersection.

"The real thing," he said. "The fakes. The real fakes. The fake fakes. The copies of the fakes. You know, this is pretty confusing for an old man, English is his second language."

Having delivered himself of this speech, Manuel stepped gently on the accelerator and made a right turn, and Mo resumed his explanation.

"The way I reconstruct it is this. A little over a year ago, Norah Vargas finds she's got these O'Keeffelike paintings. Probably she did get 'em from her grandmother, like she told Elijah. But she doesn't know what to do with them. She trots on up to Chicago to see her old art history professor—now, I'm guessing, but given what we know about her, I'd guess she had been a little bit more than just Lockman's student in art class up there. Anyway, she says what do I do with these things, and Lockman comes up with the plan.

"Get cozy with my old friend Potts, he tells her. He's got a gallery and that's helpful for legitimizing these things. He's got him a peculiar marriage and nine months a year he's free-roaming, and he's always been a womanizer. And there's always been a bit of larceny to his soul, ever since the old days when we were carrying on at Provincetown. Elijah'll go through the hoops and sure as hell he'll think of me, Lockman, when he needs to call in the experts.

"Then, when the time comes, when the paintings are all authenticated, announced to the public, and all the excitement calms down, we'll get rid of him and take the paintings and buy an island off the coast of Bali and eat chocolates or whatever.

"So Lockman and Norah teamed up to make a sucker out of Potts."

The car slowed down, and Manuel pulled into a space on the street about ten car lengths from Norah Vargas's house. Nothing was going on in the street.

"So off Norah goes," Mo continued, "back to Santa Fe, and twitches her aristocratic fanny at Elijah and the rest is history. Most of it. But my version of history says that Lockman was here in Santa Fe at the time Anita was killed. Checking on his nest egg, or whatever. So he and Norah find out Anita's on to something, or maybe they don't figure she's on to something. It doesn't make any difference if Anita was on to it.

"They just figure one way or another that if Potts is accused of killing Anita—there's motive there, her ten percent—he'll be stowed in the can. They figure, the two of 'em, that if Potts is out of the picture, they've got some time to grab off the paintings. So Lockman kills her that night.

"The records show that Lockman's a little guy, about five-five. I thought he was short, once I thought about him at all. Remember, Connie, at the gallery, he said he'd stand over beside the lectern? Probably it was too high for him, is what I thought, but not too high for Elijah. And that made him the right size for the way Anita got killed. The chain going up around her neck.

"See how that all hangs together? Anyway, now, see, the rumor is out first that the paintings are stolen, and then that it's copies that are stolen. Now *that's* a bit of a monkey wrench in the plan. Whatever really happened to the paintings, my guess is that Norah Vargas has probably got a lot of explaining to do to Lockman, or vice versa, so we'll just sit here and wait till she goes, or until Lockman shows up. Can you see her doorway, Manuel?"

"Sí."

Connie crossed her arms. "Why can't Tony, the police, take it from here?"

"Hah—hah. Tony's got all those constitutional amendments he's got to worry about. Unreasonable search, that sort of thing. Kind of hamstrings a man. But us criminal conspirators, we don't have to take them so seriously."

Whatever was going on with the damn paintings, Norah realized with icy clarity, her life was now in real danger. With Lockman calling her bitch, and wanting to talk, and with that big hulk Bowdre in on it somehow, it was time to run. To cut her losses and run. It wasn't the first time she'd had to cut her losses. She glanced at the wall behind the coatrack where the photograph of Vigil's Store hung—SANTOS, WOODCARVING, POPSICLES.

She had gone into her bedroom and looked around it once again as she picked up her canvas suitcase with only a few belongings in it—clothes enough for a day or two, some cash. She had found herself crying, tears turning cold as they slid down her cheeks. She hadn't been able to stop them. She wiped them away but they kept coming. It was all so crushingly sad. She knew where she could go.

She patted the revolver, still in the right-hand pocket of her jacket, and crossed the room to the narrow door, never used, that led out into the alley behind her house. She set her suitcase down, freeing both hands to turn the stiff old lock, and opened the door, then stooped down to pick up the suitcase. When she looked up she had time only to notice the black hole of a silencer pointed at her before the little orange fire—

fourteen

They waited wordlessly in Manuel Trujillo's perfectly appointed, lovingly restored car on the quiet street for five minutes that seemed to each of them a half hour. The residents of Lovatos Street had tucked themselves into their houses for the evening. Even here, in this relatively quiet neighborhood, there was a regrettable new world of nighttime danger these days. Lights had winked on inside most of the houses now, and Mo, sniffing the air through the vent window he had cracked open slightly, caught the faint aromas of beans and meat on the air. His stomach rumbled.

"Hey, amigos," Manuel said. "She hasn't turned on the lights in there. You want me to go have a look?"

"Good idea," Mo said.

Manuel opened the door slowly and slipped out soundlessly. He made his way to Norah's house, pausing on the sidewalk, and then ducked into the yard next door. Seconds later he emerged in the dirt alley that ran behind the houses, now fully enveloped in shadow. Outside Norah's house was the shape of a new Subaru which Manuel guessed was hers, parked up close to the house. As he got nearer, he made out a garbage can with a top next to a small, low stoop. A back door.

He took three steps closer and stopped again. The back door appeared to be open. Damn.

His breath rattled slightly in his throat. Too many fucking cigarettes, too much abuse, he thought. Why are people so stupid? Why am I so stupid?

He moved closer yet, holding his breath. The doorway was black in a black shadow, and he sensed more than saw something inside on the floor. He waited. Nothing moved. He took one pace nearer.

A boot. On the concrete stoop. Lying on its side.

He stepped closer and made out another boot, the legs, a hip . . . mierda!

Manuel leaned forward, took a cigarette lighter from his vest pocket and flicked it on. The little flame illuminated the body on the floor, arms flung crazily backward, long black hair in disarray across the face but not so much as to hide the blood and the garish hole where her eye had once been.

Mierda.

Manuel stepped over the corpse, made his way through the darkened house to the front door and went out on the path. The street was still as death. He walked quickly to his car, bent over slightly to talk through the vent window.

"Hey, amigo. Don't you gringos have some saying about the best-laid plans?"

Back in the driver's seat, Manuel explained what he had seen while Mo Bowdre sat still and erect in the seat next to him, arms folded massively across his chest. In the back, Connie too was silent.

For a long time no one spoke a word. Manuel wasn't sure what to make of these people, this blind gringo giant and this big half-breed Hopi woman. It was as though they were lost in some kind of silent mourning, some grief. So this vicious bitch, this crooked little *intriganta*, was dead. So what? Honor among thieves. Who gives a shit? Scum.

The big man was shaking his head. "Damn," he said. "Damn. That's one thing I didn't think would happen."

"What now, Mo?" Connie said from the back. She had a strong alto voice that Manuel liked. It made him think of rich cloth.

"Could you find Potts's house in Canones in the dark?"

"Yes, I think I can. Why there?"

"What other choice have we got? What other choice has Lockman got? Manuel, can this old classic do the speed limit? Or maybe a little more?"

"You watch, amigo. Oh." Manuel laughed, a phlegmy rattle. "You know what I mean, right?"

"Yeah. But let me off at a pay phone, huh? I got to call Tony Ramirez."

"Use this," Manuel said, holding up a cellular phone. "See, I got everything in here, man. Everything."

A little more than an hour later, Manuel Trujillo's 1959 Chevrolet with everything pulled up before a one-story stucco house with a sliver of yellow light escaping from the curtain that covered its small, square front window. A pair of ancient trees rose up in front of the house from a dusty front yard enclosed by a low, sagging fence of thin logs. A dog barked somewhere in the shadows. Manuel shut off the ignition, turned off the headlights, and stepped quietly out of the car.

"It's down there, Manuel," Connie said. "About a half mile more."

"Sí, I know," Manuel said. "I'll be just a minute."

The little man marched up to the door and tapped lightly. Presently the door opened and a shadowy figure, a woman bent over by age to a height even less than Manuel's, opened the door and was silhouetted in the light. He spoke to her in quiet Spanish, bobbing his head respectfully, and when she closed the door, he returned to the car.

"Okay," he said. "You can wait here in the car. I'll be back."

Mo and Connie sat in silence in the Chevrolet. Finally Connie spoke.

"I know why *we're* doing this. But why is he?"

Mo stirred in the passenger seat. The silence outside was broken by a distant scream. They both jumped.

"Burrowing owl," Mo said. "Probably thinks Manuel is a coyote, or some damn thing."

Connie broke another long silence. "Mo?"

"It's been a few years since Manuel has done much besides make those low-rider hydraulics for kids. Tame stuff for an old pirate, I guess. He told me he settled down after he got kidnapped once. It cost him a sixty-thousand-dollar low rider with everything and a lot of dignity to get away. Had to run buck naked from some old warehouse in Espanola in the middle of the damn day. Must've been a helluva sight. Anyway, he says that was the day he settled down."

"These are real monsters, these people," Connie said. "All of them. Elijah, too. I can hardly believe he'd do all this. Using me like that, that's just part of it."

"No redeeming features at all," Mo agreed.

"And the people who would buy these things. They're creeps."

"Agreed. Perps and victims. All lowlifes."

The owl cried out again. They waited in silence for another long interval.

"Okay," Manuel said, appearing like a ghost beside the car. "There's a vehicle outside, a rental Olds, and a light on inside. And someone's poking around in a shed out back, a little guy with white hair. Got a flashlight in there."

"Bingo," Mo said. "Lockman. The saints hear our prayers."

Manuel opened the door on the driver's side, and then the back door. "Okay, you're driving, right, Connie?"

The Chevrolet crept slowly down the dirt road, sinking and swaying in the ruts, until it came to a stop about a hundred yards from the house. Silently, the doors opened and the odd little posse stood under the sky. It had clouded over and the temperature was dropping rapidly. The little man disappeared into the dark, and Connie began their slow approach to the house.

"I think I'd best try this solo at first," Mo whispered.

"I know."

"You'll be . . . ?"

"Right there."

Connie watched Mo feel his way to the gate, open it, and walk down the path slowly, with small steps and one hand out in front of him, toward the house with a light showing dimly in the window. Off in the distance somewhere, a coyote yipped. Dinner, maybe. Or maybe, she thought, it was the trickster, showing the flag.

Mo knocked loudly on the front door. "Lockman!" he shouted. "You, Lockman. I'm here about the O'Keeffes." He stood on the front step, as still as the night.

"Come on, open the damn door."

Nothing.

He reached out and felt for the door handle. His fingers danced over the lock and withdrew.

The wood splintered with a loud crack when he kicked it, and he pushed the door open, stepping into the house.

"Put that down," Mo said. "You don't want to shoot me. I know where the real ones are. The real fakes, that is. You just got yourself a new partner. My name is Bowdre. T. Moore Bowdre, but my partners call me Mo. Now, sure as hell, they don't call you Nelson, do they?"

"You're blind," Lockman said.

"Blind as a mole on a bad day."

"That puts you at something of a disadvantage, doesn't it?" he said. "Mo," he added.

"It's damn rude, sneering at the visually challenged. Say, maybe they call you Whitey. They say you're just a pig's hair and a pink eye from being an albino. And, you know, there was an old ballplayer, played for the Giants, I think, when they was in New York, called Whitey

Lockman. Outfielder. Nobody remembers him these days because he wasn't all that good. My daddy told me about him. So, Whitey, tell me, are there any chairs in this place? I know there's a futon. Elijah and Norah used to celebrate on it, the way I heard it. Weekend recreation while they got your little scam all set up for you. Isn't that right? Not to change the subject, but did Elijah keep any beer here, Whitey? We need to talk. The three of us." He turned to his right and bowed slightly.

"Glad to meet you, Mrs. Potts. Claudia, isn't it?"

Mo heard a tiny hiss, an intake of breath.

"Magic," Mo said. "Pure damn magic. Sometimes I amaze even myself. That's nice perfume you got there, Claudia. What's it called? Eau de serpent? Say, I really could use a beer, if you got one."

"Get it for him," Claudia Potts said.

"Good boy, Whitey." When Lockman was out of the room, Mo whispered, "You don't need him anymore, Claudia. Just me."

"Fuck you," Claudia said.

"No, that won't be necessary. Here's Whitey." He held his left hand out as Lockman approached, and felt the cold bottle touch his palm. "Much obliged," Mo said cheerfully.

"Who are you?" This was Claudia, still to his right about ten feet away.

"Put it this way. I'm an artist, just like you, and once your husband found himself alone and in the can, he had no one else to turn to. Told me the whole thing. Or most of it. I was the one who figured out Whitey here did poor old Anita Montague. That was easy, actually. It took me a bit longer to get you into the picture."

"Go on. By the way, I've got the gun."

"Oh, Claudia, I know that. Little Whitey wasn't about to walk out of here without someone keeping an eye on me. Probably didn't realize it was him who's dispensable now. Right, Whitey?"

"Claudia," Lockman said. "Let's—"

"He's right, Nelson. Shut up."

"It was the jacket," Mo said. "The Norfolk jacket."

"What are you talking about?"

"I'm just showing off here, Claudia. See, the cops found some hairs off of your husband's jacket on the corpse. Very incriminating, like you planned it. You sent Elijah a present, a Norfolk coat made of special hand-woven Harris tweed only for the Peterman folks, a very distinctive garment, as we say, and he thanked you for it, said he loved it more than anything, wore it every day, or however you people talk to each other. And then you ordered up another one for Whitey here to use when you two framed the poor felonious bastard."

Silence.

"Isn't that about right, Claudia? Now, I can see why you'd hate him, open marriage or not. Women have a double standard about that sort of thing. Hate to think of their boy out floggin' the young nubiles. Or whatever. There's no explaining such things, is there, Claudia? But you and me, we can have a straight business relationship. Mutual greed, that's all. It's a kind of liberation, wouldn't you say?"

"You talk a lot."

"Like I said, just showing off. Now why don't you put Whitey out of his misery here and we can go."

"Claudia, for Christ's sake!"

"Go ahead, Claudia. You and me. We need each other. I know where the paintings are, see."

"Claudia, don't. Don't shoot me, for Christ's sake."

"And you need me?" Claudia said.

"Yeah. We're like the two keys the generals need to blow up the world."

"That was stupid of you," Claudia said. "That could mean only one thing, only one place. So I don't need either of you."

"Well, damn," Mo said.

"I'm free to shoot you both and go home and get the paintings, aren't I?"

"Well, damn," Mo said again. "I guess you are. Except that my friend Connie has been listening to all this from right outside the front door. And my friend Manuel is standing in the kitchen door, pointing that big old pistolero of his right at the back of your head. Right, Manuel?"

"Sí."

Mo heard the woman let her breath out.

"What was stupid, Claudia, was to forget that a blind man needed a ride out here. But I figured if I just kept talking fast enough about those paintings, you'd be blinded, too. Plain old off-the-shelf greed. Clouds a person's mind, doesn't it?" Mo cocked his head. "Hear that siren? I believe that's the state police."

Connie stepped through the front door and said, "Here they come, Mo."

"Connie, meet Mrs. Elijah Potts. You can relieve her of her weapon. And over there, you recognize Whitey Lockman, don't you?"

They stood in silence, listening to the sirens as the troopers made their way through the little town of Canones.

"I'd guess Tony's with them," Mo said. "He likes to be in on the kill. So things didn't work out, did they? I mean, when you were back cavortin' on the beach in Provincetown, I guess the world looked a little different, right?"

"Why don't you shut up," Claudia said.

"I mean, there you all were, the beautiful people, the sun shining, all that. Already had the sense that everyone else out there in the world was—well—just not so beautiful, not so smart. That about right? But I guess you know how it is. One thing leads to another."

Outside, the sirens faded into silence and doors slammed.

"You know what's funny, Claudia? After all that work, all that planning and scheming and of course killing you people did, you know what? Those paintings *are* really gone. Vanished."

"You mean real fakes or fake fakes?" Manuel said, a laugh rattling in his throat.

"Real fakes. Now there's a notion for you. Real fakes. Maybe they'll turn up someday." Mo yawned. "In some pawnshop somewhere. Or maybe a flea market. You find the damnedest things in flea markets. All kinds of flotsam and jetsam. Hey, is that you, Tony? Sure glad you're here. You know, we haven't had our dinner yet."

addendum

It had been an unusually clear day for summer in New Orleans, but now, seated on her rickety wooden front porch, Belinda Grace watched some gray clouds build up far beyond Lake Pontchartrain. They billowed up slowly, intent on taking command of the blue-gold sky, and Belinda watched the veins of lightning crackle silently in their bosom.

It was late, almost seven-thirty, and little Billie Grace was late getting home, late for his supper. Presently Belinda saw him, spindly little legs of anthracite black carrying him around the corner and up the sidewalk.

"Billie, you're late! It's almost seven-thirty!"

"I know, Mama. Me and Ollie, we was playin' down by the lake."

"I tole you not to go near that water, Billie, how many times do I—"

"You tole me not to lie, too, Mama, and I'm tellin' you the truth." He grinned up at her.

Belinda rose up from her chair, smiling back, and dusted off her dress. "What's that you got there, Billie?"

"It's somethin' we found down by the lake. In the

mud. They was a bunch of 'em, pretty much all the same, Mama, but this one is the best."

The boy held up a canvas to his mother. It was a painting of some big white bone, and what looked like a blue mountain with a flat top. Belinda stared at it, making out a pinkish thing in the blue hole made by the bone. It looked like a fetus.

"We can clean it off a little," Billie said. "Get a frame, maybe hang it in—"

"Billie, you put that down right there! You just leave that trash out on the street. We don't want nothin' like that in the house. You hear me?"

Don't miss the other
Mo Bowdre mysteries by Jake Page...

THE STOLEN GODS

A powerfully built wildlife sculptor, Mo Bowdre is also blind—but that doesn't stop him from pursuing the truth when a major dealer in Native American art is murdered.

THE DEADLY CANYON

Mo Bowdre's newest sculpture is commissioned for a remote desert research station rife with conspiracy and smuggling. When the corpse of a woman who was both a scientist *and* an FBI special agent is found, Bowdre goes into action.